Ashes of Time

The After Cilmeri Series:

Daughter of Time
Footsteps in Time
Winds of Time
Prince of Time
Crossroads in Time
Children of Time
Exiles in Time
Castaways in Time
Ashes of Time
Warden of Time

The Gareth and Gwen Medieval Mysteries

The Bard's Daughter
The Good Knight
The Uninvited Guest
The Fourth Horseman
The Fallen Princess
The Unlikely Spy
The Lost Brother

Other Books by Sarah Woodbury

The Last Pendragon
The Pendragon's Quest
Cold My Heart: A Novel of King Arthur

www.sarahwoodbury.com

A Novel from the *After Cilmeri* Series

ASHES OF TIME

by

SARAH WOODBURY

Ashes of Time
Copyright © 2014 by Sarah Woodbury

Cover image by Christine DeMaio-Rice at Flip City Books
http://flipcitybooks.com

To my readers
Thank you for traveling in time with me

Pronouncing Welsh Names and Places

Aberystwyth –Ah-bare-IH-stwith

Bwlch y Ddeufaen – Boolk ah THEY-vine (the 'th' is soft as in 'forth')

Cadfael – CAD-file

Cadwallon – Cad-WASH-lon

Caernarfon – ('ae' makes a long i sound like in 'kite') Kire-NAR-von

Dafydd – DAH-vith

Dolgellau – Doll-GESH-lay

Deheubarth – deh-HAY-barth

Dolwyddelan – dole-with-EH-lan (the 'th' is soft as in 'forth')

Gruffydd – GRIFF-ith

Gwalchmai – GWALK-my ('ai' makes a long i sound like in 'kite)

Gwenllian – Gwen-SHLEE-an

Gwladys – Goo-LAD-iss

Gwynedd – GWIN-eth

Hywel – H'wel

Ieuan – ieu sounds like the cheer, 'yay' so YAY-an

Llywelyn – shlew-ELL-in

Maentwrog – MIGHNT-wrog

Meilyr – MY-lir

Owain – OH-wine

Rhuddlan – RITH-lan

Rhun – Rin

Rhys – Reese

Sion – Shawn

Tudur – TIH-deer

Usk – Isk

Cast of Characters

David (Dafydd)—Time-traveler, King of England
Lili—Queen of England, Ieuan's sister
Callum—Time-traveler, Earl of Shrewsbury
Cassie—Time-traveler, Callum's wife
Llywelyn—King of Wales, David's father
Goronwy—Advisor to Llywelyn
Meg (Marged)— Time-traveler, mother to David and Anna
Anna—Time-traveler, David's half-sister
Math—Anna's husband, nephew to Llywelyn
Ieuan—Welsh knight, one of David's men
Bronwen—Time-traveler, married to Ieuan
Nicholas de Carew—Norman/Welsh lord
Evan—Castellan of Harlech
Cadwallon—Llywelyn's captain
William de Bohun—David's squire
Justin—David's captain

The Children

Arthur—son of David and Lili
Catrin—daughter of Ieuan and Bronwen
Cadell—son of Math and Anna
Bran—son of Math and Anna
Gwenllian—daughter of Llywelyn
Elisa—daughter of Llywelyn and Meg
Padrig—son of Llywelyn and Meg

Map of Wales

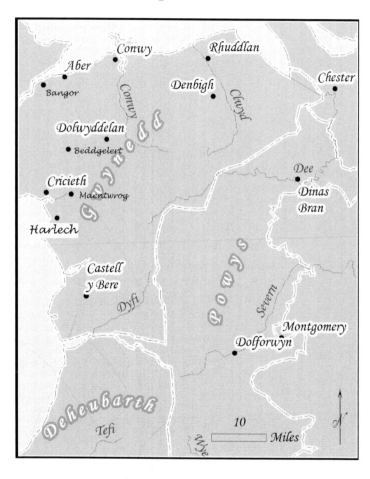

1

November 1291

Meg

Searching for the twins when they didn't want to be found was a thankless task and one Meg had been at for the last ten minutes. The inner ward of Rhuddlan castle was a maze of wooden buildings built three stories high along the inside of the stone curtain wall and included a chapel, two kitchens, sleeping rooms, and the great hall on the opposite side of the inner ward. The outer ward contained many buildings too, among them two stables and a forge.

In the inner ward, narrow passages ran between the rooms and the curtain wall, and circular staircases in the towers connected the levels to one another. Up ahead was the castellan's office, which doubled as a receiving room. Llywelyn had taken it over for himself while he was here. Meg thought she heard the giggle of young voices farther along the passage through which she was walking, but they faded before she could catch up to them.

If someone had told Meg ten years ago that she would give birth to twins at the age of forty-two, she would have laughed. If that person had prefaced the statement with the assertion that Llywelyn would be the father, Meg probably would have cried. By thirty-two, she'd already spent ten long years without him. It would have been a relief to know she had to spend only five more.

Meg walked into the receiving room just as Lili said, "Stewing again?" Meg's daughter-in-law perched on the table behind David, her hands going to the muscles in his broad shoulders and her thumbs pressing hard. Arthur, their son, played with a wooden horse at their feet, his blonde head bent as he focused on his toy.

"Did you sleep at all?" Meg said.

"A few hours," David said, which Meg thought might not be a complete untruth. She'd woken up in the night herself and passed him in the corridor.

David handed her a letter.

"What's this?" She took it, scanning it with a dubious expression on her face. It was from Tudur, Llywelyn's counselor at Chepstow Castle. After reading the first page, she passed the paper back to David. "Really? Madog and Rhys challenge us now?"

"They want more land—or in Madog's case, his father's land back," David said. "Rhys resents Dad's interference in Deheubarth and feels that he favors his cousin, Wynod."

"Of course Papa favors Wynod." Lili's blue eyes flashed. "Which one of them has stabbed him in the back a dozen times, and which one has always been loyal?"

"Tell that to Rhys," David said. "He wants Carreg Cennan."

"He can want it all he wants," Meg said. "He isn't going to get it. That he still retains Dryslwyn is bad enough."

"According to Tudur, Rhys is telling himself that Dad's hold on Deheubarth isn't as strong as it once was, especially with the new reforms he's introduced," David said.

"At your urging," Lili said.

"At my urging," David agreed. "This is my doing, more than Dad's."

"Nonsense." Llywelyn looked up from what he was writing, entering their conversation for the first time. He ran a hand through his still dark hair, which had less gray than Meg's own brown locks, and looked at his son with amusement and pity. "You have enough to trouble you without taking on the petty politics of Wales."

"It will be my problem if Rhys gets up to his old tricks," David said, "and brings Madog along for the ride."

"Your mother tells me that in your other world Rhys was sold to King Edward by his own men and then executed for treason."

"When was this?" David said, looking at Meg, who'd come around the table to hug her husband from behind as he studied the papers in front of him. The man was as ridiculously handsome as he'd been when she'd first met him.

"Rhys betrayed Edward—after betraying your father long before—in 1287." Meg straightened, her hands resting on

Llywelyn's shoulders. "Edward finally caught up with him in 1292."

"So you're saying that what Rhys is doing now is in his nature?" David said. "Since King Edward is dead, he naturally rebels against you instead?"

"I've been dealing with that old sot since I took my first steps to the throne of Wales." Llywelyn leaned back in his chair, twisting his torso and stretching his arms to get out the kinks after sitting too long. "To tell you the truth, I've been expecting something like this from him for years. Tudur knows that."

"So I guess you don't need my help after all," David said.

"Son—" Llywelyn dropped his arms.

David waved a hand. "I'm sorry. I'm feeling melancholy."

Lili pushed at David's shoulder. "It's the lack of sleep. Besides, your only job this afternoon is to sit at the head of the table and eat!"

Arthur looked up at the excitement in Lili's voice, abandoning his horse to tug on his mother's leg and ask to be picked up. Lili lifted him up and kissed his cheek. Then Arthur put out his hands to Meg, which was a rare gift since he didn't always condescend for her to hold him, and she took him in her arms.

"This democracy thing isn't easy," David said, taking Meg's place at his father's side and peering over Llywelyn's shoulder to look at the papers he'd spread before him. "We should alert your allies that we might have to act without Parliament."

"Already done," Llywelyn said.

"It would have been nice to enjoy our anniversary in peace without rumors of war—" Meg broke off as Cadell, Anna's eldest son, hurtled into the room, his small sword raised high.

"Arthur!" Then he caught sight of the adults arrayed in front of him and pulled up. Sheathing his sword in his belt, he sauntered towards them, an insouciant grin on his face and an irrepressible sparkle in his hazel eyes. "I have something to show you!"

Arthur instantly squirmed to get down, abandoning Meg for his six-year-old cousin.

Then a horde of small children—three-year-old Catrin, of the brown curls and green eyes; Bran, a black-haired, blue-eyed miniature of Math, even at only two; and the blonde-haired twins, Elisa and Padrig, who'd been born shortly after Bran—surged through the doorway behind Cadell. The decibel level in the room rose to that of an airplane engine. In other words—deafening.

"Dear God, Llywelyn," Meg said. "What have we done?"

Llywelyn laughed. "I prayed my whole life that such a fate would be mine." He stood to put his arm around Meg's shoulder, kissing her temple as they watched the children.

Last to enter was Gwenllian, Llywelyn's nine-year-old daughter by his wife, Elin, who'd died giving birth to her. Gwenllian shot Meg a rueful look as the children circled the room, shouting. Meg was glad to see that in preparation for the meal Gwenllian had already changed into her finery without being asked, pulling her blonde curls back from her face in a band. Gwenllian had spent far too much time with nannies as a small child, but in recent years she had grown into her own person, which sometimes meant not doing as she was told. She and David shooed the children out the door again.

"When's dinner?" Llywelyn said.

Even after all these years, Meg made a motion to check her wrist for a watch. Of course it wasn't there. "Soon. I'll see to it."

David's brow furrowed. "Marty hasn't arrived yet, has he?"

"No." Meg headed for the door, tipping her head to Gwenllian to indicate that she should come along.

"Aren't you looking forward to seeing him, Mom?" Gwenllian said in perfect American English.

Meg had been frowning, but she hastily cleared her expression. She hadn't been thinking about Marty at all, but about Rhys's and Madog's rebellion. Meg's son and husband were soldiers. More than that, they were leaders of men. If Meg allowed herself to think for too long about what could happen to either of them, the sick feeling that formed in her stomach took a sleepless night to conquer. They faced danger every day. Meg never got used to it.

"I don't know," Meg said to Gwenllian, forcing herself to answer the question as if nothing at all was the matter. That was another aspect of being the mother to one warrior and married to another: pretending that all was well when it wasn't. "The last time I saw Marty, he was flying his airplane out of sight while I cooled my heels beneath Hadrian's Wall."

"I can't believe he abandoned you," Gwenllian said, stoutly supportive. Marty had crashed the airplane in the Highlands of

Scotland, so he hadn't fared as well as Meg. She'd forgiven him, since it was years ago now. Cassie and Callum had reported that Marty had adjusted well to the thirteenth century, and the weapons he'd made from the remains of the airplane had saved them in Scotland, but Meg hadn't forgotten what he'd done. She didn't know if she could really call him a friend, or if she was truly looking forward to seeing him after all these years.

Part of Meg had hoped that Marty might have managed a visit sooner. But despite repeated invitations, not only from Callum but David and Meg too, he had declined up until now, citing the burdens of a wife and small child as his excuse. Meg secretly thought that he was afraid to face her. And for good reason. He'd abandoned her to her fate. It was hard to trust a man who could do that.

"It was a long time ago, sweetheart." Meg put her hand on Gwenllian's shoulder, banishing her unease as best she could.

Meg and Llywelyn had sat down with Gwenllian a year ago and told her as much of the truth about Meg, David, and Anna's origins as they thought she could bear and understand. They probably shouldn't have been surprised at how calmly Gwenllian had taken what they'd had to say. An eight-year-old child with an active imagination could accept ideas that adults fought. When they told her that David and Anna had been born in another world and that Meg and Llywelyn themselves had traveled to and from it, she'd been happy. The explanation had merely clarified what she'd eavesdropped to hear for years.

Gwenllian and Meg found Anna and Bronwen standing together in the castle's second, smaller hall near the southwestern tower, arranging the table for dinner. Known as the queen's hall, it had apartments above and below it and its own kitchen. It was accessed by four doors: one at the southwestern tower stairwell, two doors that entered through the west and south corridors that followed the curtain wall, and an exterior door that led down to the inner ward via external stairs.

The inhabitants of Rhuddlan would eat well tonight—as truly they always did—but the family's meal would be for them alone, more reminiscent of an eighteenth century dinner in a manor house than the typical raucous medieval meal in the hall. Here in the queen's hall, they would be isolated from the rest of the castle and win an hour's peace from the pressures of their positions. David had managed to leave the bulk of his court—counselors, ministers, and hangers-on—at Chester, though he'd still brought many of his men and attendants with him. As had Llywelyn.

They were celebrating a combined anniversary dinner for Meg and Llywelyn and a birthday party for David, though not on the right day for either. Whether or not the medieval people they lived with appreciated their need for privacy, Meg had made sure that today was just for the family.

Anna was counting chairs. "I'm going to separate the kids to try to cut down on the chaos."

Bronwen smirked. "Good luck with that. They'll sit quietly if Cadell or Gwenllian tell them to. I don't know what's come over Catrin. She listens to me at home but somehow not here."

"She's three," Anna said. "You have to expect a few tantrums. I'd like to keep Bran's to a minimum, but I make no promises."

It was odd being a grandmother to children older than Meg's own, but that was the Middle Ages for you. "Elisa and Padrig can sit with Arthur," Meg said. "He doesn't talk, and they talk only to each other, so they'll get along fine."

"That puts Cadell, Bran, and Catrin together," Bronwen said.

"Gwenllian, can I put you and Catrin between the boys?" Anna said. "That ought to cut down on the fighting. I swear, they pick at each other all day long—Cadell's fault, mostly."

"When you and David fought, I charged you a dollar for every incident," Meg said.

Anna's face lit. "I remember that! David and I would sometimes hit each other anyway and then swear to each other not to tell you."

Meg laughed. "I'm glad I didn't know, though I can't say I'm sorry to hear it. Better united in crime than not united at all." She pursed her lips. "Bran's a little young for that, though, and it isn't like you give your children gold for their allowance."

"Cadell and I need to have a sit-down," Anna said. "I'll have to think about what to threaten him with."

"Here they come," Bronwen said as the sound of children shouting echoed outside in the corridor. The troop stormed into the room.

Anna put up a hand to Cadell. "Stop!"

Cadell pulled up short and instantly all the other children stopped too.

Anna bent down, her hands on her knees, to look her son in the eye. "You will sit quietly for this meal, or I will take away that sword and you won't have it back until we leave Rhuddlan. Is that clear?"

Cadell nodded, for once subdued, maybe less by his mother's authority than by the decorated room. The girls had gone all out and the hall looked more like Christmas than a birthday party, with evergreen boughs and candles everywhere. But everyone would be together and that was the most important thing.

And within the hour, they were together, the table was laden with food, and the doors closed. Everyone sat quietly while Llywelyn said a prayer. Tears came to Meg's eyes before he was halfway through it as love for all of them filled her.

Bronwen, Ieuan, and Catrin; David, Lili, and Arthur; Anna, Math, Cadell, and Bran; Llywelyn, Gwenllian, Elisa, Padrig, and Meg. Only Cassie and Callum, who should have been with them, were absent. As Llywelyn's prayer finished, Meg looked at David, who'd been gazing around the table as she had. He leaned across the three little ones on the bench between them and said, "We'll get them back."

"I hardly knew them, and yet I miss them too," Meg said, not surprised that he'd read her mind. Meg knew that Callum, in particular, was often in David's thoughts. During Callum's absence David had personally overseen his earldom of Shrewsbury. "I can't believe it's already been two years since you had to leave them there. I hope we see them again one day, though I can't say I want to be the one who goes to get them."

"Cassie and Callum are both survivors," David said.

Then he paused. Everyone started spooning food onto trenchers, but David raised his cup and looked down the table to where his father sat. Llywelyn responded with a silent toast, and then David rose to his feet. "I have something to talk to you all about." He gestured with one hand. "Feel free to keep eating."

"We weren't going to stop," Ieuan said to general laughter around the table.

Meg looked up at David and realized that he'd grown serious. After a moment, the other adults realized it too. David glanced at Lili, who nodded her encouragement for whatever he was about to say.

David cleared his throat. "It's weird to say *I have a dream*, but I do. For a while now, I've been thinking about what we're here for and what we're doing all this for."

He paused again. He had everyone's full attention, even the children. Arthur, his little wooden horse clutched in his fat fist, crawled onto his mother's lap and stared up at his father.

"Please don't laugh, but I'd like to talk to you about—" David took in a deep breath, "—about working towards a United States of Britain."

"Thank God!" Bronwen set down her cup. "It's about time."

"I was wondering when you were going to get to that," Anna said.

Bronwen held up her hand, palm out, and Anna half-stood to reach across the table and slap it before dropping back into her seat.

David gaped at them both. "But—"

"I didn't say anything earlier because I knew you had enough on your plate," Anna said. "The whole women's rights thing has been difficult enough without me bugging you about a bill of rights for everyone."

"Well." David sank back into his chair. "I was afraid to talk about it because I thought it sounded romantic and foolish, even to me, but I guess not."

Bronwen leaned forward, her face intent. "It's off in the future, I get that, but just to say it and to have it as our ultimate goal is important."

Anna laughed. "I thought his ultimate goal was world domination?"

Bronwen grinned at Anna but then waved her hand, dismissing the joke and gesturing around the table. "None of us are in this just to survive. This isn't about us. Not anymore, if it ever was."

Anna nodded. "It's about changing the world."

"You've already started by creating the pillars that can support true democracy: universal education, economic independence—" Bronwen ticked off the items on her fingers, "and an impartial government, which includes a system of courts and laws. In England and Wales, all three are in place, if nascent."

Ieuan elbowed Math, who was sitting next to him, and said in an undertone, "That's my wife."

Llywelyn had been gazing at David as the women had been speaking, his expression disconcertingly noncommittal, but now he nodded. "You've talked of this before to me, son. A constitution and this—" he waved one hand as Bronwen had done, "*bill of rights*. We already have something like it in Wales and have had since the time of Rhodri Mawr."

"And in England too." David rose to his feet again, leaving the table to pace before the fire, as was his habit. Ever since he'd learned to walk at nine months old, his brain had worked in conjunction with his feet. "Though what England has is very rudimentary—and like the initial ideas produced by the American founding fathers—doesn't include women or men who don't own land."

Meg, of course, had been on board with his idea before he'd finished his first sentence but now said, "Before we get ahead of ourselves, what do you mean by a United States of Britain?"

David hesitated in his pacing. "A confederation of states, probably a loose one initially, founded on democratic principles. Probably more along the lines of a parliamentary democracy than the tripartite division of the United States government. I'm not even proposing the elimination of the kingship, though that should be on the table too."

"What's the biggest challenge we face in creating it?" Anna said, ever the practical one.

David mouthed the word 'we' and shook his head. "I was an idiot not to have talked to you all earlier."

"You're not in this alone," Anna said. "You never have been."

David cleared his throat. "I see that now."

"One of the barriers has to be the Church," Bronwen said, getting the discussion back on track. "David is fighting a rearguard action, trying not to undermine the Church's authority but not being much swayed by it either. As long as Peckham is the Archbishop of Canterbury, he's in good shape, but if David didn't have the personal authority he does, he'd have been excommunicated by now. You know he would have. Imagine if they knew he'd never been baptized in the Catholic Church? His only saving grace is that England is flourishing economically and that means income for taxes is higher, for him and for the pope."

"The Church wants David to let them prosecute heretics. But other than that, the separation of Church and State in England might be easier to accomplish now than after the Reformation," Meg said. "Peckham has stood by our acceptance of the Jews."

"That's only because we've become the banking capital of the world," Anna said. "It's hard to argue with success."

"That may be," David said, "but Aaron is keeping his ear to the ground nonetheless. He's heard frightening whispers among his kin in recent months."

Aaron, a Jewish physician, had befriended Meg when she'd come to the Middle Ages the second time and had helped her to return to Llywelyn. Through his contacts among his co-religionists, Wales—and now England—had become a haven for Jews wishing to practice their religion in peace.

"I would have said my biggest problems today—not necessarily in order," David said, "—are the ongoing unrest in Ireland, for which my Norman barons are much to blame; the barons themselves, who own the vast majority of land and resources in England; and the inquisition."

Anna nodded. "The Church, like I said. *Heretics and Jews aren't welcome here.*"

"Well," David said, coming to a halt and facing Anna, "both are welcome *here*."

"Which is going to cause you more problems than you already have if your enemies use prejudice to incite unrest," Meg said. "Look at Germany."

In 1287, a wave of anti-Semitism had swept across Germany, resulting in the murders of hundreds of Jews in a hundred and fifty different towns. In that other world where David wasn't the King of England, King Edward had expelled the Jews from England in the year 1290. David was hoping that because that expulsion hadn't happened, other European countries wouldn't expel their Jewish people either. David was particularly worried about France where the medieval inquisition had its strongest hold.

This inquisition, however, wasn't so much about Jews as about heretics—people who didn't abide by the doctrines of the Church. David and Llywelyn had welcomed people of all religions and beliefs into Wales and England, and it was driving the Pope crazy that David refused to allow his minions to arrest them.

"Give us your tired, your poor, your huddled masses yearning to breathe free," Bronwen said. The Americans around the table nodded. They lived and breathed that quote. Even if America had yet to be colonized, and somehow it might be their descendants rather than their ancestors who would do it, they could never allow themselves to forget where they'd come from.

Though not as economically and technologically advanced as nineteenth century America, England—with a population of only three million—had room to spare if people were willing to work. And people could work here as well as in France, Spain, or Germany. Recent immigration under David's benevolent eye had made London a sprawling capital of freewheeling mercantile expansionism.

Llywelyn lifted a hand. "It may be, then, that this rebellion we're facing is a blessing in disguise."

"How might that be?" Meg didn't see how war could ever be a blessing.

David answered for his father, "If my dream is to create a peaceful, united Britain, then fighting a little war now—putting down a small rebellion now, maybe even before it has a chance to gain a real foothold—could send a clear message to every other baron who might be entertaining the idea of fostering a similar revolt."

Llywelyn nodded. "You made an example of Valence. We may have to make one of Rhys and Madog too."

Before anyone could add to his comment—or in Meg's case, protest the very idea of a 'little war'—a knock came at the door to the inner ward. Since Anna was already standing, having risen to retrieve Bran and plop him back into his place on the bench, she went to open the door. Meg craned her neck to see who was asking to be admitted, but she couldn't see around Anna. Her daughter stood in the doorway for a second, one hand on the frame and the other on the edge of the door, not moving.

"Who-who are you?" The panic in Anna's voice had every adult at the table rising to his or her feet.

"An old friend." The voice came clearly from beyond Anna. She stepped back, holding out her hands in front of her, her posture stiff. Something wasn't right. Meg still couldn't see past Anna to whatever was the problem, but she moved with everyone else to find out.

As Anna took another step backwards, her hip hit the door, opening it wider and enabling Meg to see beyond her to Rhuddlan's steward, Alan, who had fallen to his knees on the landing. Meg's breath caught in her throat as a second man—the tardy Marty—grabbed Alan by the cloak, tugged him to his feet, and shoved him so that he stumbled through the doorway past

Anna and into the room. Alan collapsed against the wall a few feet from Meg, bleeding from a gash in his belly.

And then, the bloodstained blade flashing in his hand, Marty grabbed Anna, dragged her with him into the room, and kicked the door shut behind him.

2

November 1291

Anna

Anna's family stared at her, and she stared back at them, each individual a dark silhouette against a brilliant background because she was hyperventilating. Mom had been sitting at the near end of the table and was already on her feet by the time Marty—it had to be Marty because who else could be 'an old friend'?—had spun Anna around and put the knife to her throat. She was the only one who had been close enough to see him stab Alan. The poor steward—a thin, balding man in his mid-forties who hadn't been prepared to be assaulted with a knife—clutched his hand to his side, bleeding out while everyone stood frozen in shock at the scene and out of fear for Anna.

David had already been on his feet, since he'd been talking and walking, but he was yards away from where Anna now stood. Although six inches taller, twenty years younger, and far stronger than the somewhat tubby Marty, David couldn't subdue him from there. Ieuan, his jaw set, put his foot on his seat, prepared to climb over the table to get to Anna. Papa pushed back his chair and stood up, while Gwenllian slipped her hand into Lili's. Anna wished Lili had her bow because she would have trusted her to put an arrow through Marty's eye without blinking.

Anna's vision narrowed as she looked at each person, and then her gaze lingered on her husband. Math's face mirrored the horror Anna was feeling. He'd risen to his feet, but as Elisa had crawled into his lap earlier and was now clutching him around the neck, he was frozen too.

Then Bronwen hurried around the table to crouch in front of the steward. Marty didn't stop her, but he did edge Anna farther into the room, along the wall away from them. Anna couldn't move her head enough to see either of them clearly and hoped Alan wasn't already dead. In the Middle Ages, a knife wound to the gut was rarely anything less than a death sentence.

Marty looked at Meg and said in American English. "Hello Meg. Long time no see."

"Marty, don't do anything more stupid than you've already done." David advanced slowly, his hands out.

"Don't anybody move!" Marty squeezed Anna tighter against him.

David stopped. Anna's tongue had stuck to the roof of her mouth. She couldn't say anything and wouldn't have known what to say if she could speak. She ran through possible escape moves she could make. But as her sensei had told her so many years ago, when a knife was involved, somebody was going to get cut. And with the blade at her throat, that person was going to be Anna. In addition, after nine years and three pregnancies, she was really out of practice with karate.

She tried not to look anywhere but at Math. He'd schooled his expression after his initial reaction, and Anna felt her breathing slow to a manageable level in response to his calm face.

Marty took the knife away from Anna's throat for two seconds, pointing it at her family before putting it back to her neck. She was forced to raise her chin since the knife was now in a worse place than before, right at the bend where her jawline met her neck. Marty was only a few inches taller than Anna, which meant that if she could move her head forward without cutting her neck on the knife, she could bang the back of her head into his nose. Unfortunately, she hadn't been prepared when he'd moved the knife from her throat the first time and hadn't taken advantage of the opportunity he'd given her.

Mom put out a hand to David to stop him from coming any closer and took a step forward herself instead. She was less of a threat than David—physically, anyway. Otherwise, she was way tougher than she looked.

"What do you want Marty?" Mom said.

"What do I want?" Marty let out a laugh. It ended in a gasp that sounded like it had its source in pain—or grief. "I want to go home."

Nobody pretended to misunderstand.

"What about your wife?" Mom said.

"She's dead, along with our babe," Marty said.

He didn't have to elaborate. Everyone here, whether born medieval or modern, had lost someone important to them in the last nine years. Anna had lost a child. It seemed Marty had too and wanted no more of the grief that followed.

"Let Anna go, and we'll see about getting you home," David said.

"Just like that?" Marty laughed again, though his voice was strangely high and, again, the laughter showed more pain than amusement. "You'd take me back if I asked nicely?" Anna sensed him shake his head. "I don't think so."

"How is hurting Anna going to get you home?" Mom said.

"Oh, I'm not going to hurt Anna unless you make me," Marty said. "No, what the three of us are going to do is go to those stairs over there and take them up to the tower. You, me, and Anna. Everyone else will stay where they are, or this knife might slip."

The children had seen the steward's wound, so they'd figured out by now that something wasn't right, even if the rapid exchange of American English had passed the littlest ones by. Though his face was very white, Cadell stood on his bench beside Math and Elisa, his sword out as if he was going to launch himself across the table. Bran had started to cry, so Lili bent to put her arm around him. Anna ached to go to her boys and for this not to be happening.

"Come with me, Meg." Marty sidled along the wall towards the stairs.

Marty wanted the battlement, two stories above. If the family had dined in the great hall today, there would have been guards everywhere, but they'd deliberately sent everyone away so they could speak freely with one another for once without the possibility of being overheard. A terrible mistake.

"Mom, don't let him have what he wants." Anna felt the blade on her neck. She would have given anything for it not to be there. "Without me, he has no leverage. He knows if he kills me, he'll be dead a second later."

"What if I told you I didn't care?" Marty said.

The look on Mom's face told Anna that she believed Marty. Anna did too, and she really didn't want to die today.

"It's okay, Anna." Mom put out both hands. "Please don't hurt her, Marty." Mom was begging. Anna didn't know enough about the psychology of abduction to know if that was good or bad: if it would embolden him, calm him, make him angry, or make him feel more in control.

Regardless, Marty kept edging Anna towards the stairs, and Mom followed. Before she passed David, she put a hand on his shoulder and spoke to him in rapid Welsh, which Marty couldn't understand. Her voice was low enough that Anna couldn't hear what she was saying. David nodded.

Fifteen seconds later—far too soon—they reached the stairs. Marty turned Anna around so they both faced the room and Mom. Anna prayed for a stray soldier to come down from the tower, but she doubted any would. David had been very clear in his orders: short of a declaration of war, they weren't to be disturbed. Nobody disobeyed David.

Marty started backwards up the stairs. He was holding Anna with her arms wrenched behind her back. It was all she could do to fumble at the side of her dress with the fingers of both hands, trying to lift the hem of her long skirt so she wouldn't trip as Marty pulled her up the stairs with him. Anna was wearing her nicest dress, a dark red with embroidery at the bodice and on the sleeves, with a train that made her feel like a princess. Or it had until five minutes ago.

Anna managed not to step on the hem on the first step, but the second step had her coming to a complete stop with the fabric caught underneath her left shoe. She froze, suspended, unable to take a step forward because of Marty's grip and the knife, and unable to step back without ripping out the back of her dress, though Anna's seamstress was accomplished enough that it would take more than a few tugs to rip it.

More likely, it would hold, she would fall backwards into Marty, and find her neck sliced open. He would be dead or captured a few seconds later, but that wouldn't be of much comfort to Anna. She didn't want to die for her own sake, but more than that, she needed to live for her boys. Sadly, Marty was doing what he was doing because he felt absolutely the same: he had lost his wife and child and had nothing left to live for.

Fortunately, Marty had lived long enough in the Middle Ages to understand why Anna wasn't moving. He didn't tug at her but instead barked at Mom, "Gather it up for her."

Mom crouched at Anna's feet, and Anna shifted her foot from side to side so Mom could pull the hem out from under Anna's boot. Marty pressed his knife into Anna's skin the whole time, and she couldn't even look down as Mom swept up her train. Anna bent her left forearm enough so that she could hold the train and the tail of her cloak in her hand.

David had used the delay to move a few feet closer. "Marty—" His voice held a warning.

"Not you! I don't want you!" Marty squeezed Anna tighter and the knife scraped her skin.

David's face paled. Anna knew he was dying inside as much as Anna was, desperate to help, but helpless to do so.

Ieuan and Papa, meanwhile, had moved closer to the exterior door that Marty and Alan had come through and which led down to the inner ward. They were sidling slowly, waiting for their chance to move through it and summon help. Lili was bending over the steward, aiding Bronwen's attempt to stem the flow of blood.

From inside the stairwell, Anna couldn't see anything else of the room. Nor could she see where Math was standing, though by the quick glances that David kept sending to his right, he was close by. From where she stood on the first step, she could easily see through the doorways to the left and right, down the long corridors on either side. Unfortunately, Marty could see along them as well. If Math tried to leave the queen's hall through one of the side doors into a corridor, Marty would spot him. Again, Anna prayed for a maid or a servant—anyone—to come down one of the long hallways, but they were uncharacteristically deserted.

Marty took another step back. Now neither of them could see anything but the stone walls of the stairwell on either side. Anna leaned into Marty, trying to rest her full weight against him and drag her feet at the same time. She wanted to slow him down, to give the others time to get help. The wall-walk ran all the way around the top of the inner ward. If Math could reach the southwestern tower before they did, he could stop Marty at the top of the stairs.

But it seemed Marty had the same thought, fearing it as much as Anna was praying for it. In response to her stalling, he pressed harder with the knife. A trickle of blood ran down Anna's neck.

"Okay! Okay!" David's hands were up again. "See, I have no weapon. Nobody's going to do anything you don't want."

"Let's go." With Mom following, Marty began to climb quickly, circling around and around, moving up the stairwell so fast that Anna was practically running backwards to keep up. She fixed her eyes on Mom's, willing her to have a plan, willing her to get them out of this. But Marty kept his knife pressed to Anna's throat, and as long as that was the case, neither of them could act.

Anna lost sight of David almost immediately, though she could hear his footfalls on the stairs below them. He kept out of sight, presumably to put Marty at ease. Anna couldn't hear anything else but her heart pounding in her ears and her breath rushing in and out. She wanted to hear orders in Welsh. She wanted someone to save her—a thought which made her more mad than scared. There was a time when she might have been able to save herself.

Anna could feel Marty's manic determination in the way he held her and the knife. This wasn't a drunken man-at-arms who didn't know what he was doing, which had been the case with the last man who'd tried to hurt her. Marty had Anna pinned to him and wasn't about to let go. He wasn't at all the soft middle-aged village headman Callum and Cassie had described.

"I'm sorry about your wife, Marty." Mom kept her eyes fixed on Anna's. "But what you're doing now isn't the answer."

"Isn't it?" Marty said. "I know you can take me home, since you're the one that brought me here in the first place. I heard all about how you went back to the modern world when Llywelyn was sick. You jumped off the balcony at Chepstow. Well, we're just going to jump off the tower at Rhuddlan. Same difference."

He pronounced 'Rhuddlan' the English way—saying *Rudlan* instead of *Rithlan*—
but neither Mom nor Anna corrected him.

"Llywelyn and I jumped into a river, Marty," Mom said. "If it didn't work, if we hadn't travelled back to the modern world, we'd have just gotten wet. That's not what's going to happen here. What if it doesn't work?"

They had passed the next level and in only a few more circuits approached the top of the tower. Marty spoke around gritted teeth. "It's going to work."

They hit the top step and spilled out into the circular tower. Marty swung Anna around so that at last she was going forward. She had a brief image of Mom stabbing Marty in the back with her belt knife. He wasn't wearing armor, so a well-placed knife could go right through his clothing. But Mom wasn't a warrior. She didn't know how to kill with a blade. And even if she did, she couldn't risk stabbing Marty in the back on the chance that his arm would jerk and he'd slice Anna's throat.

Marty pushed Anna towards one of the crenels. Now that they were outside, Anna could hear men shouting in both the inner ward behind her and the outer ward directly below. Three men pounded along the battlement, coming from the northwestern tower.

Mom threw out a hand to them. "Stay back!"

In response to the threat, Marty brought Anna tight against him again and faced the soldiers. They slowed and pulled up, their faces drawn and white. Anna assumed that someone—Papa, Math or Ieuan—had told the soldiers what was happening, but hearing about the danger was very different from seeing it.

Or living it.

Anna was breathing too fast, and the world began to darken around the edges again.

Having neutralized the guards for now, Marty turned Anna so that his back was up against the battlement. With the guards to his left and Mom on his right, each at a forty-five degree angle to Anna, nobody could get to him without going through her. Mom's eyes were very wide, and her mouth worked as if she was trying to speak but was having a hard time figuring out what she could say to end this nightmare.

"It's okay, Mom," Anna said, though it really wasn't. The only part about this that was in any way 'okay' was that when Marty had grabbed her a moment ago, he had repositioned his left arm so it went across her chest rather than holding her arms wrenched behind her back. It meant Anna could move them. Which meant she might be able to fight him.

"Meg, get up into that gap." Marty was talking about the crenel. The classic gap-toothed appearance of a medieval battlement was composed of merlons—the higher bits—and the crenels—the gaps between them. When Mom didn't move right away, Marty clenched Anna tighter. "Now!"

"I'm doing it! I'm doing it!" Mom went to the closest crenel and put a hand on one of the merlons. She had to use the other hand to gather up her own skirt and cloak, and then she boosted herself up into the gap. Although Anna couldn't see what Mom could see, she'd been up here before, and she knew it was a *long* way down.

Anna wouldn't have been nearly so scared if Marty had taken them to the tower in the outer ward that overlooked the Conwy River. David was having problems with the river undercutting the bank and the curtain wall, and the water lapped right at the base of the tower. Jumping from there would have been much the same as when Mom and Papa had jumped from the balcony at Chepstow Castle. The three of them could have ended up in the river if the time travel part didn't work—instead of flat as a pancake at the base of this tower.

Out of the corners of each eye, Anna could see the men who had gathered along the wall-walk leading from the southwestern tower to the other two corners. Everyone was watching Marty. Nobody dared to move, not even the two men who stood with arrows nocked to their bows.

"Just shoot!" Anna said.

But because Marty was hiding behind her and Anna was the sister of the King of England and the daughter of the King of Wales, none of them would risk shooting her to get to him. Getting out of this in one piece was going to be up to her. She needed to *do* something. She just didn't know what that something should be, and she feared that whatever she might try would come too late to save any of them.

Then Math came through the stairwell doorway, his face white as a sheet. Anna wanted to say some word of comfort, but there was nothing to say that would make the fact that his wife was pressed to a stranger's chest with his knife to her throat any better. And that his mother-in-law stood in one of the crenels behind them. Anna didn't know how Marty had known about it, but the crenels in the southwestern tower were a foot lower, hitting slightly below her waist, than the crenels in all the other towers, where they rose to chest height.

"I don't mean to hurt you." Marty's words came low in Anna's ear.

"Don't you?"

Maybe it was the venom in Anna's voice, which surprised even her; maybe he'd expected to hear fear. Either way, it didn't matter. His knife dropped slightly, and Anna reacted, getting her arm between his arm and her neck, in order to shove the knife away, and slamming the heel of her right boot into his knee. Then Anna held onto his arm with all her strength and used his weight as leverage for her own.

"Damn you!" Instead of swinging forward away from the wall as Anna had intended, however, Marty used their combined weight to swing them around and pin Anna between him and the battlement. In doing so, Anna's forehead banged into Mom's legs. Instinctively, Anna's arms came up, releasing their hold on Marty's arm in favor of grabbing onto Mom.

Mom shrieked. "Anna!"

"I've got you!" Anna's arms clenched around Mom's knees.

But though Mom's hands scrabbled at the stones of the merlons on either side of her, the sudden weight of Anna falling against her and Marty pressing forward onto her lower half was too much. Her fingers couldn't maintain their grip. If this had been a movie, more often than not, Mom would have been saved from falling at the last second by heroics from Anna or David.

But Anna wasn't strong enough to stop Mom's fall, and since falling was what Marty wanted, he threw his weight forward against Anna's back. They toppled together through the crenel. As she fell, Anna made one last attempt to get free, twisting away from Marty. He screamed and released his tight hold around her waist.

But it was too late.

Anna squeezed her eyes shut. Black abyss or horrifying *thud*, she didn't want to know which it would be until she hit.

3

November 1291

David

"Mother of God!" Math was the first to reach the crenel, his hand clutching at empty air.

David was beside Math an instant later, and both men lunged over the parapet, their eyes staring and their hearts in their mouths. It was fifty feet to the ground, and David was sure he would see three bodies sprawled below the tower. But he didn't. Only one body lay in the grass of the outer ward: Marty's.

"They're gone." Math's voice was full of shock.

David had been sure as he'd come out of the stairwell, his eyes fixed on Anna and Mom, that there were a million things he should have done to stop Marty. But at the time, he couldn't think of anything other than what he did, which was to let Marty get this far and then try to do an end run around him. David put a hand on

Math's shoulder, trying to comfort him, though what comfort he could give at a time like this couldn't be much.

Dad appeared on David's right and looked over the wall too. "Dafydd—" He gripped David's shoulder hard, and David checked his father's face. In the fading light, David couldn't tell if his face was paler than usual, only that he'd gone white around the lips. David had a sudden vision of himself throwing his father over his shoulder and jumping too.

"Don't have a heart attack on me, Dad," he said.

"Your mother—"

"She'll be all right," David said. "They both will."

Math finally blinked and straightened, resting his hands on the stones of the crenel. "Where do you think they've gone? To Pennsylvania again? Or Cardiff?"

David shook his head. He hadn't a clue and didn't want to guess.

While David, Dad, and Math had chased after Marty, Ieuan had taken the opposite tack, maybe hoping to break their fall if they didn't time travel. He had arrived at the base of the tower within a few seconds of Math and David's arrival at the top. He looked down at Marty's body and then squinted upwards.

David leaned out to talk to him. "I assume he's dead?"

"Indeed." Ieuan toed the body. Marty's neck was set at a cruel angle, and two arrows stuck out of his back, arrows which had been released by the bowmen when Marty had turned his back on them. It was an ugly sight, even from here.

A man-at-arms ran to Ieuan with a torch. The way the soldier kept looking from the top of the tower to Marty had David's mind moving quickly to damage control. Ieuan was clearly thinking about it too because he spun on his heel and surveyed the crowd that had gathered in the aftermath of the fall. Though the sun had just set, it was only a little after four in the afternoon. So, while the craft stalls and smithy were closing up for the day, it wasn't as if everyone had gone to bed.

"How many people saw that, do you think?" Dad said in a low voice.

"Too many," David said.

And then David looked past him to see Gwenllian hovering in the doorway to the tower.

"Is she ... is she ...?" Gwenllian said.

"Honey, no." Dad was with her in two strides. "Mom's going to be just fine."

David followed, since there wasn't anything further to be done from up here, and tugged Math's elbow to make him come too.

"How do you know that?" Gwenllian regarded Dad with big eyes.

David had never spent much time with his little sister, and not for the first time, he felt bad about it. His half-sister Gwenllian was fourteen years younger than David, and he didn't know her well at all. But he didn't have to know her well to know that she loved Mom too. Mom was the only mother Gwenllian had ever known.

"Because she always is," David said. "She's done this twice before. I've done it. Anna did it to come here with me not long after you were born. It's terrifying when it happens, but they'll be back in a few days. You'll see." For maybe the first time in David's life, he took Gwenllian's hand, and they followed Dad downstairs.

The queen's hall was now full of people: kitchen staff packing up the uneaten food; a serving girl scrubbing at the blood on the floor, since Alan had been taken away and was no longer bleeding against the wall; counselors and advisors waiting for orders. One of David's most trusted counselors, Nicholas de Carew, stood next to Cadwallon, the young captain of Dad's *teulu*. Carew had come with David to Rhuddlan for the opportunity to confer at length with both him and Dad. The day hadn't turned out quite like anyone had expected.

Goronwy hustled through the exterior door, followed by Bronwen, who was drying her hands on the edge of her cloak. David caught her arm. "How's Alan?"

She shook her head and shrugged at the same time. "He's alive. That's about all that can be said." Bronwen picked up Catrin, who wrapped her arms around her mother's neck. "The wound is a nasty one to his gut, but it's pretty far to the left, and his bottom rib deflected the blade."

Lili had gathered all the children at one end of the table, out of the way of the activity in the room. Catrin, Bran, and Elisa sat on her lap, while Arthur's nanny clutched Arthur and Padrig to her. As David came over to them, Lili looked up, a terrible questioning expression her face.

"They're fine," David said. "Gone, but fine."

"What do we do?" Lili said.

"What we always do," Dad said. "We wait."

Feeling bereft, David sat down in the chair Mom had been sitting in. The party they'd planned for so long had barely started before Marty had arrived. When David had traveled to the modern world two years ago with Cassie and Callum, he'd seen the storm and guessed what was about to happen. His family—Mom, Anna, and himself—time traveled when their lives were in danger, and with the single exception of when Mom had returned to the modern world with Anna at David's birth, it always happened when they were in motion.

So far, by David's count, they'd survived three car accidents, a plane crash, a shipwreck, and three long falls from high places, with this latest incident making the fourth.

"Wherever they've gone, if they're going to get back, they're going to have to survive another brush with death." Math pulled out the chair next to David's.

"I know." David picked up Mom's uneaten roll and dropped it without tasting it. "I'll say the same to you as I said to Gwenllian. They're going to be fine. Maybe Anna will even remember to bring back lip balm for Bronwen."

Math didn't crack a smile, and David had to admit it was probably too soon for joking. Cadell came over and sat in his father's lap, his sword still in his hand. He didn't look at Math or David.

It was time to speak to everyone. David took in a breath and raised his voice to cut through the babble in the room. "Okay." The noise instantly ceased. Goronwy had his hand on Dad's shoulder; they'd been speaking quietly but now they both looked up. "Here's what happened and what we're going to do. Kids—" David gazed around the room at each of them and managed to gain their attention, however briefly, "Grandma and Aunt Anna have gone on a little trip. I know what happened in here was scary, but they are both completely fine."

"That man cut Mom," Cadell said. It might be a long time before he could see something other than that image whenever he closed his eyes.

"It was a surface wound, like a scrape," David said. "A couple of years ago, Grandma and Grandpa went away with Uncle Goronwy. Some of the littlest of you weren't born yet. They left because Grandpa was sick and the people there made him better." David rubbed Cadell's cheek with one finger. "Grandma is going to make sure that your mom stays safe."

Cadell put his arms around his father's neck and held on.

"Marty, however, is not fine." Dad scrubbed at his face with both hands, and then dropped them to take Elisa into his lap.

"I can't say I'm sorry about that," Math said into Cadell's hair.

Ieuan appeared in the doorway leading to the west corridor. David had been waiting for him to return before deciding what to do next. Bronwen went to her husband, and he put his arms around her. Catrin had gone back to her meal, which at the moment consisted of a well-buttered roll that dripped with honey.

After Bronwen released Ieuan, she glanced at Dad, who'd sunk into his chair and didn't look like he had the strength to leave it. Then she said to David, "You'd better go talk to everyone else, David."

He sighed. They had to come up with a story to explain the disappearance, and as usual, it would be that Mom and Anna had traveled to Avalon. "Dad?"

Dad grimaced with what David hoped was regret rather than pain. "I'm with you, son." He rose to his feet, Elisa still in his arms. David was glad to see that some of the color had returned to his face, though his skin was still grayer than David liked. Long and lean, with only a speckle of frost in his dark hair (though more in his beard), he didn't look that different from how he'd looked nine years ago when Anna and David had saved his life by driving their aunt's minivan into his attackers at Cilmeri. His twin two-year-old children may have worn him out at times, but they also kept him young, and most of the time David didn't notice the twenty-year age difference between him and Mom.

Today, however, was not one of those days. "Thanks, Dad."

Bronwen lifted a hand, almost as though she were in school. "I have an idea."

"I am open to any suggestion," David said.

"Then I need you to give me a second." She looked at Goronwy. "Will you come with me?"

"Of course."

With a last squeeze of Dad's shoulder, Goronwy followed Bronwen as she darted out of the room. Carew moved to Dad's side in Goronwy's place. Dad looked up at him but didn't nod or speak before looking away again. Everyone waited. David had no idea what Bronwen was up to or what to expect, but he trusted her, which was why he'd agreed to whatever she wanted without first asking what it was.

Five minutes later, she returned with a triumphant expression. "Goronwy has everyone gathering in the great hall. Come on."

Bunched into a group, kids and adults together, the family descended the stairs from the queen's hall directly into the inner ward. Lili held Arthur's hand and walked beside David. As they reached level ground, a bard's clear tenor soared from the open door to the great hall. *"Afalon peren a pren fion ..."*

David groaned. "Bronwen, what have you done?"

"If you're going to stand up there and talk about Meg and Anna traveling to Avalon, at the very least everyone can be in the right mood to hear it," she said. "Right now, we have a dead man at the base of the tower—"

"—I ordered his body moved to the chapel, actually," Ieuan said.

Bronwen shot her husband an impatient look. "You know what I mean. It's the only explanation that makes sense when so many people saw Anna and Meg vanish in midair."

David blew out his cheeks, knowing he was cornered and knowing she was right.

"You haven't fought this battle for years, Dafydd," Lili said. "Why fight it now?"

"I haven't fought it because you told me to do so would be a waste of effort," David said. "I prefer the story about the Land of Madoc, though."

"People from the Land of Madoc are solidly in this world. They don't have the ability to vanish," Dad said.

That was unfortunately true. "I don't like it. I'm not Arthur," David said.

"I'm Arthur!" David's two-year-old son gazed up at him with bright eyes.

David put a hand on his son's head and bent to kiss his nose, amazed that he'd spoken so clearly, but pleased too. "Yes, indeed you are."

Bronwen grinned and said with some of her old graduate school snark, "He speaks truth to power."

David scoffed, though not because she wasn't right. He and Lili had named Arthur with an utter cynicism about what they were doing and what it would mean to the people David ruled. Still, he didn't have to like it.

The group entered the hall as the bard was finishing his song. All conversation ceased as the entire royal family of England and Wales crowded through the doorway. Goronwy bowed from the dais. All of the inhabitants of the hall followed suit. Aaron stood to the right with his son, Samuel, and David caught his eye. He nodded gravely. Samuel was staring at his feet and didn't look up. They, along with a handful of other advisors, knew the truth about who David was, and that meant they also knew what had happened to Mom and Anna. Aaron, in particular, had seen it before. Goronwy had lived it.

There was no help for it, David opened his mouth and boldly lied to everyone else. About what had just happened, about Avalon, about who he was.

Avalon. Lili took its existence for granted—both what she knew of the reality and the myth. Although David used the myth to his own advantage, what he actually wanted was to make Avalon *real*, not just for himself and his family but for everyone. The poets had foretold it centuries ago, though David's vision wasn't anything like what the legends described. Avalon wasn't a fantasy world infused with magic. It was the place he'd been born.

And what made that place—America—special was what it brought to the table, namely an ideal of freedom and justice for everyone. The Avalon David wanted to build here was a mirror of that. More to the point, the reason David hadn't dared to speak about it out loud to anyone before, even to his family, was because he wanted to start the American Revolution five hundred years early. *Against himself.*

It was a big dream. A huge, impossible, ridiculous dream. But he'd been thinking about it for nine years, ever since he'd quoted Patrick Henry to his father before the defeat of King Edward at the Conwy River. At that time, David had thought it might be possible to achieve a united Wales, even if it took his lifetime and many generations of his descendants to accomplish it. Instead, it had taken three years. Now, as King of England, David had the power to make the much bigger dream a reality, and if any dream was worth chasing, it was this one.

He found it ironic, too, that many generations of kings of England had fought for this dream as well, though they'd pursued it at the point of a sword, which to David's mind would defeat the entire purpose. *The United States of Britain.* Even King Edward, God rest his soul, might have approved.

4

November 2019

Meg

Meg rolled down a slight incline, crunching through a bed of frozen leaves. After two revolutions, she came to a stop at the bottom. She breathed hard, the black abyss fading from her mind's eye, and sat up. Snowflakes fell steadily from the sky. The ground wasn't covered in white, however, so it seemed they'd started very recently.

Before she had a chance to panic, Meg spied Anna at the top of the bank she'd just come down. Anna pushed to a sitting position and looked down at her mother. "Are you okay?"

"I'm good." Meg got her feet under her and stood, shaking out her cloak and dress as she did so. "What about you?"

Anna rubbed at her forehead. "My head hurts." Then she swung her legs around and slid down the slope to arrive on a level with her mother.

"You've had quite a day," Meg said. "How's your neck?"

Anna put a hand to her throat and then removed it to look at her fingers. They came away bloody. She tilted up her chin so Meg could see her neck. "What do you think?"

Meg gently touched Anna's skin. "It isn't bleeding much." She pulled a handkerchief from the pocket of her dress and dabbed at the wound. "I think it'll be okay, though it would be better if we had a couple Band-Aids."

"Yeah, well." Anna took the handkerchief and continued dabbing. "Maybe in a bit we'll actually be able to get some." She looked around. "Where do you think we are?"

Anna was being really calm, and Meg didn't know if it was because coming to rest in a modern forest was less traumatic in comparison to being knifed by Marty, or if Anna really was this good in a crisis. Meg's initial panic was still subsiding, so she stalled for time before answering her daughter, chewing on her lower lip as she took in their surroundings more fully. They had fallen into a forest, in the snow, in the same murky heading-towards-nightfall that they'd left in Wales.

"Listen!" Anna held up a hand.

Meg didn't hear anything at first, and then her heart skipped a beat as a distant engine roared overhead.

"I don't believe it," Anna said.

"Given that the alternative would be lying at the base of the tower at Rhuddlan, this is much better," Meg said. "Did you think it wouldn't work?"

Anna shook her head. "I don't know. It's been so long since I did this. You and David have been back and forth a bunch of times, but I've only *traveled* with David in Aunt Elisa's minivan or with you. It has occurred to me more than once that I might not have what it takes to *travel* like you guys do. It would be logical if it were just you and David who have the genes—or whatever—for it."

"You almost came here when you went into labor with Cadell," Meg said.

Anna wrinkled her nose. "True. I'd forgotten about that." She shrugged. "I'm still not sure that really happened."

Meg hadn't seen it, but David had been sure. Meg didn't want to argue about it, since it didn't matter at the moment. She and Anna had *traveled*, whether because of Anna, Meg, or both.

Meg wiped her hands on the edge of her cloak. "I'm really cold. We should start walking."

"To where?" Anna said.

"Downhill," Meg said. "Isn't that what Math taught David? Follow the contours of the land downhill and then find a river to follow downstream."

If Meg had traveled back in time to Cilmeri with David and Anna, she would have had a lot to say about the sink-or-swim nature of that early training of David's. But she hadn't been there, and she could hardly complain about the man Llywelyn had turned David into, or the little bit of knowledge Meg herself could now relate because of what Math had taught him all those years ago.

"I have spent so little time in the woods over the last nine years it isn't even funny." Anna fastened three more of the wooden toggles that kept her cloak closed. The hall at Rhuddlan had been cold, and everyone in the Middle Ages wore their cloaks indoors as a matter of course, a fact for which Meg was intensely grateful now. "Could we be near Mt. Snowdon?"

"The trees look wrong to me for modern Wales," Meg said, "though what do I know? Maybe pine trees and Douglas firs predominate in one of those tree farms they've planted."

"If we can find some sign of civilization, we'll know." Anna gave a half-laugh as she pulled a leaf out of Meg's hair. "We'd better hurry before it turns completely dark."

Both women were wearing boots rather than slippers, which was another piece of good luck, but Meg missed her mittens. If they weren't close to a settlement, this was going to be a tough night. Walking would warm them, however, and the snow wasn't falling any more heavily than it had been when they'd arrived.

They started downhill, aiming for brighter patches between the trees. The woods didn't close in around them, and the trees were predominantly conifers. By November throughout most of the east coast of the United States, a thick blanket of deciduous leaves covered the ground, and most of the trees would have been bare, which ruled out all but a few locations in Pennsylvania as a possible landing site.

The snow provided some ambient light, particularly since, after falling fairly heavily for twenty minutes, it had slowed and then stopped. Within another twenty minutes, the clouds cleared enough to reveal stars. There'd been a new moon two days earlier in Wales. Meg didn't know whether 2019 wherever-they-were had a similar astronomical schedule to 1291 Rhuddlan, but for the moment, they were stuck with stars and not much else to see by.

Meg and Anna plodded along for at least another half hour, Meg worrying that she didn't know what she was doing, any more than she had when she'd come through three years ago with Llywelyn and Goronwy. They'd survived and escaped MI-5 during that trip, but it seemed due more to luck than any skill or intelligence on Meg's part. But she supposed that if luck was all they had, she would have to make it work for them.

But she wasn't feeling particularly lucky at the moment, and that made the edge-of-panic feeling that filled her hard to fight off. She continually scanned the terrain ahead—what she could see of it—for any sign of a man-made anything, all the while very aware that her heart was in her throat. It was a feeling she often got when she was waiting for something to happen—usually for Llywelyn or a child to return from whatever had taken them out of Meg's sight. She was growing to despise the vacillation between the sweet taste of anticipation and the sour one of crushed hope.

Given how she was feeling, she could understand why Anna didn't want to talk. Still, as her mother and being nosy by nature, Meg hated not knowing what her daughter was thinking, especially in a situation like this.

"The boys will be fine," Meg said after they'd walked another hundred yards, thinking of Elisa and Padrig and trying to tell herself the same thing. Whether Llywelyn and Math would be fine was something else entirely, but Meg didn't want to complicate matters by bringing them up.

"I'm trying to tell myself that a few days apart will be good for them," Anna said. "But it isn't like I can call Math and remind him to brush their teeth before bed. Even if I've lived in the Middle Ages for nine years, I'm not a medieval parent."

"Lili and Bronwen are there," Meg said. "Not to mention that Cadell has bewitched every woman in the castle with his smile. They have many adults to watch over them."

"But they're not me!"

It was a wail that Meg understood completely because she was feeling the same way. The invention of the cell phone had been a godsend to her as a parent. It meant that she could always reach her children no matter where they were, and they could reach her. Nine years ago when Meg's sister, Elisa, had called to say that David and Anna had disappeared, Meg's first impulse had been to call their cell phones. They hadn't answered them, of course, and the nightmare of their unexplained absence had begun.

Then Anna calmed a bit. "I think what I'm struggling with most is that I'm gone, and they don't know where to. Bran will be easily entertained away from thinking about my absence, but Cadell not so much."

"All the adults but Math and Lili have experienced exactly this before," Meg said. "They can explain to him what it's like, even if he can't really understand it. He knows that you're from this world, even if we call it Avalon."

Anna nodded. "That'll help. And I suppose you're right that it's a good thing we're here since otherwise we'd be dead."

Meg reached out to touch Anna's hand. "Do you want to talk about the fact that Marty didn't come with us?"

"Now that it's over, I feel bad for him. He just wanted to go home," Anna said.

"I get that," Meg said, "but I can't forgive him for threatening my daughter's life."

"He was holding on to me, pressing against me, while I was holding on to you. But then his grip loosened there at the end, which gave me a second chance to fight him off. He screamed and let go of me. I don't know why." Anna choked a bit over the words. "We were already falling."

"What's done is done," Meg said matter-of-factly. "The last thing you should feel is guilt about what might have happened to Marty. Now, we need to focus on getting back."

"I could do with a shower," Anna said. "Is that too much to ask before we return? One shower?"

Meg laughed. "I can't answer that. We have no money, no I.D., and we possess only what we stand up in. A lot is going to depend on where we are, and who we can call on for help."

"Cassie and Callum will help us," Anna said.

"We have to find them first," Meg said. "If we can find an internet café, we can look up MI-5 and send Callum an email."

Anna scoffed under her breath. "Do you think it will be that easy? MI-5 is a secret government agency."

"I imagine if I put *we're here* in the subject line, someone will pay attention," Meg said. "I don't want to end up in a cell like David, but it might be preferable to freezing to death out here."

"That isn't going to happen, not unless this place is really, really remote," Anna said.

"It looks pretty remote to me," Meg said.

"Yeah, but they know we're here, right? Callum keeps talking about a flash," Anna said. "They could be scrambling rescue helicopters even now."

Instinctively, both women looked up. Meg had a vision of men in Kevlar converging on their position, but the only sound was the rustle of the wind in the trees and the crunch of snow beneath their feet. The sky remained clear of rotor blades. "It's late afternoon. Maybe nobody's on duty."

"The world could have changed a lot in two years," Anna said, "Maybe nobody's on duty at all."

"That's a very nice thought, Anna," Meg said, "and I hope it's true, although it would be unfortunate if we've fallen into a world undergoing the zombie apocalypse."

"It's weird to think about, isn't it?" Anna said. "Anything could have happened here. Maybe MI-5 has taken over the world."

"We have too much to do to spend even an hour in a cell," Meg said.

"I don't suppose you have any modern money hidden in that dress you're wearing?" Anna said.

"No." Meg cursed to herself as she realized what an idiot she'd been. "In fact, I don't have anything good on me at all, not like last time."

Before Meg had taken Goronwy and Llywelyn to the modern world, she'd carefully sewn her passport, credit cards, and money into the hems of several dresses as a precaution against the day the opportunity to time travel arose or Llywelyn fell ill enough to make the need to come to the twenty-first century urgent. Which he had. Unfortunately, Meg was wearing a new dress today and hadn't bothered to transfer any of those papers into it. "What's really dumb is that I actively didn't do it. I told myself there was no need."

"Hindsight is 20-20," Anna said. "It's like when you're cutting a bagel with the blade towards you and you think—right before you slice through your finger—*this is really dumb.*"

"I had no business becoming complacent," Meg said, still kicking herself. "If we ever get home, I won't make that mistake again."

"I, however, have something." Anna loosened the strings on her purse, which was tied to the belt around her waist, and pulled out a piece of paper that had been folded into a small square. Unfolding it, she waved it at Meg, triumphant.

"Is that David's list?" Meg said, unable to keep the incredulity out of her voice.

"Yup," Anna said. "I started carrying it everywhere last year, just in case."

Meg's eyes had deteriorated since she'd turned forty. While many people her age couldn't see anything without reading glasses unless it was three feet or more away from their face, Meg had the opposite problem. She couldn't read (or see) anything clearly unless it was ten inches from her face. This low light didn't help at all, but half the time broad daylight wasn't much better. For the first time in her life, reading had become a chore. She never had enough light, and she ended up leaning closer and closer, trying to see what was on the paper.

She had acquired a pair of glasses for seeing distance, but they never felt comfortable to her eyes or on her face, and they couldn't correct the way she needed them to. She hadn't been wearing them to the dinner anyway.

"I'm glad one of us was smart enough to plan ahead," Meg said. "Or maybe you really do have the *sight,* like the legends say." In the Arthurian mythology that haunted David, Anna was Morgane to David's Arthur.

Anna shot her mother a disgusted look but didn't reply, turning the paper this way and that. She was trying to catch a bit of light so she could read it. "Some of what's on here isn't going to be easy to get."

"We'll do what we can, and David will forgive us if we fall short," Meg said.

After David had returned from modern Cardiff two years ago, he'd enumerated a list of items that he would have liked to procure if he'd had the chance and if he hadn't been incarcerated the whole time he was there. He'd come home with a stack of papers. The knowledge found there was useful, but it consisted only of what he could discover in an hour on the internet. He'd asked for two telephone calls: one to his Uncle Ted and one to an employee of the CDC (Centers for Disease Control)—and been denied even that.

Meg knew, even if she couldn't read it at the moment, that the list went far beyond the CDC and Bronwen's lip balm. It included heirloom seeds for foods like pumpkins, chocolate, and tomatoes; a couple different varieties of potatoes; vaccines for the children as well as other medicines, specifically more sophisticated antibiotics than the rudimentary penicillin Anna had developed; and maps of Great Britain.

David's most pressing request, odd as it sounded, was for a geological survey showing where minerals and resources were to be found throughout Britain and Ireland. He wanted a better map than what he'd downloaded off the internet when he was sixteen. Though David hadn't mentioned it today when he was talking about either the rebellion brewing in Wales or his grand plan for a United States of Britain, minerals meant wealth. No state—whether kingdom or republic—could succeed over the long haul without them. David had gone as far as he could with what he had. Unfortunately a map to the level of detail he wanted was classified.

Which meant they needed Callum—for that and for everything else.

"It feels like we've been walking for hours." Anna cinched her cloak tighter under her chin. "I was hoping I'd warm up, but I haven't."

She was right that they'd been walking downhill for a while now, and as they neared the bottom of the current slope, a prickling sensation started at the back of Meg's neck that she not only knew where she was, but that she'd been here before. Well, not here-here, but in the vicinity.

"What's up, Mom?" Anna said when Meg didn't respond to her complaint. "You've slowed down."

"One, I can't see a thing," Meg said.

"Maybe we can get you some glasses while we're here." Anna suddenly giggled. "When we do get back, we can say that we went to Avalon to do our Christmas shopping because we'd grown tired of the selection at the local mall."

Meg laughed too, though Anna was right about the glasses. Not being able to see properly was painful—like a sore toe that wouldn't heal. It nagged at Meg every moment of every day.

Lights flared ahead of them. After a few seconds, the single glare coalesced into two points of light, which meant they were headlights on a vehicle. The car was moving fast on a road that ran along the bottom of the slope. Within fifteen seconds it had passed them by, moving from left to right in front of them.

Anna broke into a run. "Thank God!"

The powerful smell of burning gasoline was overlaid by the scent of smoke. "Is that a woodstove?" Meg sniffed the air.

They were still fifty yards from where Meg thought the road should be, though they'd been plunged into darkness again, made worse by the flare of the headlights that had ruined what little night vision she'd had.

Anna spun around to look at her mother. "Even if all we run into is a log cabin next door to the middle of nowhere, we'll have heat."

"And the possibility of a phone," Meg said.

The two women went a little farther. One instant there was nothing, and then there was a road, a dark strip of black against the gray of the trees that lined it on either side. Meg wanted to hurry in case another car was coming along the road even now, but her vision hadn't improved in the last two minutes, and the ground was very slippery. She and Anna were wet and cold enough that they didn't want to add to their misery by having one of them step in a hole and go down with a sprained ankle. Given how remote this location appeared to be, it might be a while before they saw another car.

They stumbled into a ditch that was fortunately no wetter than the surrounding grass and leaves, and clambered up the other side onto the road, which had been cleared of trees for twenty feet on either side. The blacktop had been laid in a narrow strip, without the yellow line to delineate the two lanes of the road.

"Wow." Anna bent and touched the blacktop with one hand.

"Don't kiss it," Meg said. "It'll be dirty."

Anna laughed, bouncing up and down on her toes. "Who'd have thought a paved road could be such a beautiful thing."

"Not to rain on your parade, but we should start walking." Meg looked up at the sky, which was now clear of all but a few clouds. It was colder than before too, with a brisk wind blowing down the road towards them. "Can you see the north star? My eyes are so bad I can barely tell there are stars up there."

"I see the Little Dipper." Anna pointed.

"So we head this way." Meg turned into the wind and set off. If Anna had pointed to the correct star, it meant they'd come from the south, so now they were going west, which also happened to mean continuing downhill.

"Why west?" Anna hurried to catch up. "Do you know where we are?"

"If we're in Wales, west will eventually get us to the Irish Sea, right?" Meg said. "And if we're not in Wales ..."

"The whole United States is to the west of Pennsylvania," Anna said.

"I'm thinking the trees are wrong for Pennsylvania," Meg said. "These are evergreens."

Anna's step faltered. "Do you think we're in Oregon?" She looked stricken. In the years following Meg's and Anna's initial return to the modern world when Anna was three years old, Anna had forgotten her time in Wales, along with everything before David's birth. This included the existence of both her fathers, Trevor and Llywelyn. She'd blocked the memories so completely, she even told people that she'd been born in Oregon, as if her life had started the day they'd moved there. Eventually, Meg had stopped correcting her. Oregon had been home to Anna. Home to Meg too.

Meg cleared her throat. "We'll see. We could be in Colorado, though I can't imagine why we'd end up there."

"We end up where we're supposed to," Anna said. "That's what you and David always say."

"And we'll keep saying it until we don't," Meg said unhelpfully. She was getting that hysterical panicky feeling again and needed to keep moving to control it.

They walked for ten minutes, leaving the smell of smoke behind them. Meg had chosen to follow the road rather than find a house. She wasn't completely sure why. Maybe it was the awkwardness of appearing at someone's door in medieval garb and asking for help. If they flagged down a car, the driver would have already been moving, so picking them up would be less of an imposition.

The sound of an engine reverberated from behind them, saving Meg from having to analyze her own actions any further. The vehicle was coming from the east and heading in their direction. Anna and Meg stepped off the road so they wouldn't get hit if the driver decided not to slow down or couldn't see them in their dark dresses and cloaks. Committed at least to the attempt to find help, Meg stepped in front of Anna and waved both arms in a big sweeping motion to see if the driver would stop.

"What d'you think?" Anna said as she eyed the oncoming vehicle. The size of the headlights and their distance from the ground suggested they belonged to a truck. "Serial killer?"

"Let's hope not." But Meg didn't think so, and she was a lot less concerned about being in the middle of nowhere with Anna in the modern world than if they'd found themselves stranded somewhere remote in the Middle Ages. Rural areas in the United States were safer places for lost women than cities.

In the Middle Ages, the opposite was true. Rural areas were home to lawless men, who were *very* unsafe for women. Even though, relatively speaking, a village was a big place in the Middle Ages and a tiny place in the modern world, their characteristics were much the same. In both cases—rural America and urban Middle Ages—the key was the extent to which everybody knew everybody else and kept an eye on their neighbors.

Meg really did think she knew where they were too, a fact which was confirmed a moment later as the truck slowed down and the headlights revealed the license plate on the front of the truck. Oregon.

The truck had a king-cab, and was bright red, clean, and new. When the driver stopped and rolled down the automatic passenger side window, the seats inside proved to be leather. He could be a well-off serial killer, but somehow Meg doubted it, especially when a girl of nine or ten with a mane of black hair (the same color as her father's) peered at her from the back seat.

"Can I help you?" In his early forties, the man was clean-cut and handsome, with short hair and dark eyes. He was dressed well for any event on the west coast: dark khaki pants, a buttoned down shirt, and a black leather jacket. Meg couldn't see his feet, but he wouldn't be wearing tennis shoes.

"We were hoping for a ride," Meg said.

"Did your car break down?" the man said.

"Not exactly," Meg said, avoiding the question as best she could. "Are you headed into town?"

"I wasn't going all the way into Pendleton," he said. "We're having Thanksgiving near Helix."

"My grandmother lives there," the man's daughter put in.

Meg repeated the word 'Thanksgiving' to herself at the same moment that Anna breathed the name of the town. Pendleton was a small town in eastern Oregon. Meg didn't know it well, but she'd been here for the rodeo once and several times more for conferences. She'd visited the cultural center on the reservation where they now were, and knew something of the geography of the area.

Meg glanced at Anna again, seeing how she was taking this news. When Meg had gone into labor with David, she'd ended up outside her mother's house in Pennsylvania because clearly that was where she'd needed to be. But to return to Oregon where they'd lived for so many years caused an unexpected ache in her heart. Like Anna, Meg had real friends here and a life that had been totally, radically different from the one she now led in Wales with Llywelyn.

"We'd be happy if you can just get us closer than this," Meg said. "Could you drop us off at the convenience store in Mission?"

The driver looked the women up and down, concern in his eyes. In their medieval dresses and cloaks, damp and shivering, Meg had to admit that they must have looked a sight. "Are you sure?"

"Definitely." Meg pulled open the door. The man found the latch that would move the passenger seat forward, and Anna crawled into the back beside the man's daughter.

"I'm Meg, and this is my daughter, Anna."

"Nice to meet you," he said. "I'm Jim. This is my daughter, Star."

"Thanks for the ride," Anna put in.

Meg glanced into the back and saw Star scoot the blanket she'd been sitting under closer to Anna so they could share it. "Thank you too," Anna said.

Star smiled.

Jim started driving, and after yet another long look at Meg, he turned the heat to 'high'.

Meg put her hands right up to the vent and let the heat seep into her. She hadn't been back to the United States for seven years, and it was odd how natural it felt to be sitting in this truck. She had to acknowledge, for the first time in a while, how fundamentally *foreign* the Middle Ages still was to her.

Jim spoke American English and drove an American truck on an American road. Regardless of his ethnic background, Meg *knew* him in a way she could never know someone she had just met in medieval Wales. In the Middle Ages, even after all this time, Meg was still on the outside looking in.

"Do you have a phone?" Jim said.

"No." Meg shook her head.

"Not that it would do you any good out here. No service." He hesitated for a second and then seemed to decide something, because he added, "When we get there, you can use my phone to call who you need to. I can't just leave you in the parking lot." Then he glanced in the rearview mirror at Anna. "I don't mean to pry, but are you guys in trouble?"

Neither Anna nor Meg answered. Meg wanted to trust him, but after what happened the last time she'd come to the modern world—or when David had come the following year—Meg thought it might be better to involve as few people as possible in their problems. It was bad enough that her brother-in-law, Ted, had found himself mixed up with MI-5. Meg didn't want to inflict men in black SUVs and Kevlar on a total stranger.

Still, it was fortunate that Meg hadn't ended up in some place she knew better. She might have known Jim in that long ago life, and he would have been even more full of questions. He was her age, but since she hadn't grown up here, they hadn't known each other at school. And because he was her age, he was unlikely to have taken a class from her, if he'd even gone to college in Oregon. Nor was there any reason for him to recognize a random history professor who'd disappeared seven years ago.

"The reason I ask is that I noticed when you got in the truck that you have blood on your neck, Anna," Jim said. "Were you in a car accident or—?" He left his concern hanging, but Meg imagined he was thinking along the lines of domestic violence.

Meg glanced back at Anna, and they shared a long look. Meg still didn't want to tell Jim anything and wouldn't know what to say if she did, but Anna stuck her head between the seats. "Do you live around here, Jim?"

"Up Meacham Creek." Jim tipped his head to indicate back the way he'd come. "Why?"

"Actually ... um ... I was wondering if you knew Cassie McKay?" Anna said.

Jim jerked the wheel—just a quick back and forth—but it showed his surprise. Then he steadied the truck. "Are you friends of hers?"

"Yes," Meg said. "Have you seen her recently?"

"Not since last Thanksgiving," Jim said. "Do you know her grandfather, Art?"

"We've never met, but he should have heard of us," Anna said. "You wouldn't happen to have his phone number, would you?"

"Not on me or in my phone. I could take you to his house, but I don't think he's there." Jim checked his watch. "Another twenty minutes to Mission. Then I'll see what I can do."

Meg settled back in her seat, her head against the headrest, and closed her eyes. She could feel Jim's glances, and she knew that he wanted to ask more questions, but he didn't, for which she was grateful. She had declared to Anna what she believed to be a truth about the time traveling: that they ended up where they needed to be, even if it didn't seem like it at first. Last time Meg had come to the modern world, she'd landed in an indoor pool in Aberystwyth in a world-class health clinic whose doctors saved Llywelyn's life.

This time they'd found a friendly face already, and she was hoping that today wouldn't be the exception that proved the rule.

As Meg had said to Llywelyn only a few hours ago but in another world, and with humor then instead of trepidation, *Dear God, what have we done?*

5

November 2019

Callum

Callum's mobile buzzed, but since he was relaxing with his wife on a very squashy couch that would require considerable effort to rise from, or even to shift to reach his pocket, he ignored it.

In fact, he'd been ignoring unpleasant news from home all afternoon. Earlier, one of Cassie's relatives had turned on the television to the news—always a mistake—and it had been full of the riots in London, Manchester, and Liverpool, protesting the new austerity program the British government had instituted. The London office of MI-5 had averted a suspected terrorist attack at the Tower of London that morning. Callum's country was coming apart at the seams.

Then his mobile buzzed again.

"You'd better get that," Cassie said, pushing her black hair off her shoulder. "It isn't Thanksgiving in Cardiff. It's just a Thursday."

"It's half midnight on Friday now." But even so, Callum allowed two inches to come between Cassie and himself and felt for his mobile phone. A quick glance at the caller ID told him it was Agent Mark Jones, calling from Cardiff, as Cassie had guessed. Callum put the mobile to his ear. "What's up?"

There was a pause. "You've been spending far too much time with your American relatives," Jones said.

"Jones—"

"Someone's here."

Squashy couch or no squashy couch, Callum was on his feet in an instant. He and Cassie had been stranded in the modern world for two years. Having David or another family member arrive wasn't the same thing as going back, but it was a start. The rest of Cassie's family had been gathering over the last hour for a meal that would begin at six in the evening. Cassie and Callum had retreated to the living room with two aged aunts who couldn't hear a word Callum said—or possibly understand it if they did hear it— and about twenty kids.

Raucous or not, everyone looked at Callum as he stood up, the mobile fixed to his ear. He was taller than anyone in the room, with close-cropped dark hair and hazel eyes that snapped with concern.

That same concern was reflected in Cassie's nearly black eyes. "What is it, Callum?"

His adrenaline had already started pumping. "Where?" Callum moved towards the door, estimating how quickly he and Cassie could drive to the closest airport, which out here wasn't exactly close, and flight times to the UK.

Cassie grabbed both their coats and followed Callum onto the porch, allowing the screen door to close with a bang. Callum took his coat but didn't put it on. She shrugged into hers and tied the scarf. Compared to November in Wales, where the temperature hovered around seven degrees (Celsius, that is; forty-five degrees Fahrenheit to Cassie), eastern Oregon was experiencing lows below freezing. Callum's breath fogged as soon as it left his mouth.

"Well ... there, actually," said Jones. "I have your mobile location on GPS and the flash occurred twenty miles to the east from where you are standing."

Now Callum's heart really sped up. He wondered who had come and hoped also that what had brought him, her, or them wasn't the need for immediate medical attention. Twenty miles to the east of here was closer to the middle of nowhere than where he was currently standing, which was close enough for a man who'd spend most of his life in cities.

"Who else knows about this?" Callum held up one finger to Cassie, who'd moved right next to him, her hand clutching the back of his shirt. She stood on tiptoe, straining to hear what Jones was saying.

"Nobody," said Jones. "We're all but shut down, you know that."

Callum did know that. More than two years without a time travel incident coupled with a worldwide financial crisis had resulted in draconian budget cuts within an already discredited MI-5. Callum's new department, termed the Project, which he'd taken on with such guarded optimism two years ago, once had three divisions, each dedicated to one aspect of the time travel issue. The first section, in charge of identifying possible time travelers, had instead turned up and been responsible for the arrest of no fewer than eight terrorist cells in the last two years. That was a better record than the entirety of MI-5, and consequently it was the only section the government was continuing to fund. And the only reason Callum still had a job, at least until the year was out.

After that, Jones was to be shuttled from the Project back to MI-5 proper, Callum might find himself sent to Iceland, and the fact that the British government had ever funded a time travel initiative would be instantly—and conveniently—forgotten. Callum was contemplating asking for a pay rise so they could simply sack him for impertinence and be done with it.

"Send the coordinates to my mobile," Callum said, "and then monitor the traffic. Let me know if anyone—and I mean anyone—gets wind of this."

"Right," said Jones, not needing Callum to explain that just because the British government had been shortsighted enough to end the Project didn't mean that everyone else had given up on it. *Penny-wise and pound foolish,* Lady Jane might have said, had she still been alive. "And by the way—"

Callum could hear clicking in the background as Jones pounded away on his keyboard.

"—there's been another bombing. A bad one."

"What? Where?" Callum took the mobile away from his ear to check for other messages, but there were none. Two months ago, three bombs had gone off simultaneously in what otherwise had been nondescript government office buildings in London, York, and Bristol. Dozens of people had died and many more had been injured.

"The GCHQ in Cheltenham," said Jones, referring to the Government Communications Headquarters, known casually as 'Signals', an intelligence organization dedicated to providing communications intelligence and information to the British government. Since heading up the Project, Callum had worked closely with the director of Signals. The two agencies were dependent upon the same sources of information—satellites, mobile networks, internet communications—to do their work.

"Christ," Callum said. "When was this?"

"About twenty minutes ago," said Jones.

"Casualties?" Callum held his breath.

"It's too soon to know much. It'll be many, including, we think, the director."

Callum bent his head and put his mobile to his forehead for a moment, eyes closed, gathering his thoughts. He'd liked the director of Signals, as much as it was possible to like anyone who'd sacrificed as much as he had to reach the peak of his profession. "What was he doing at work at that hour?"

"How often have you worked that late talking to counterparts in Australia?" said Jones. "The only good news is that the flash may go unremarked, and nobody else will know about your friend's arrival."

"No one in our government, you mean," Callum said. "The Americans may have caught it."

Jones grunted his acknowledgment of that unpleasant fact.

"The Prime Minister might be regretting shutting us down about now," Callum said. "Without information from GCHQ's data streams, even MI-5 and 6 are blind."

"Should I call in whoever might be around?" said Jones. "Delany hasn't started work in London yet."

"Let me talk to Tate," Callum said, referring to the new director of MI-5. "We should be able to get some of our people back temporarily." The paperwork would be a nightmare, but it would be worth it. "Keep me posted. Given the bombing, I expect to be recalled at any minute."

"What are you going to do about whoever's come through?" said Jones.

"Go get them, of course." Callum pressed 'end' on Jones's bark of laughter and looked down at Cassie.

She was hopping up and down with curiosity, or maybe that was an attempt to stay warm. "What is it? I can tell it's bad."

"Someone's here, and there's been another bombing."

"What? Where?"

Her questions were the same as Callum's had been to Jones and were relevant to both halves of Callum's statement.

Callum chose to answer the first. "Right here ... well, to the east of where we are now." His mobile beeped, indicating that the map Jones had promised to send had come through.

Cassie and Callum put their heads together and studied the blinking dot. "That's way the heck out there," she said. "I don't think it's close to any road, not even a dirt one."

As the crow flies, the blinking dot was twenty miles from where they stood, but Callum knew from experience that if a road went there directly, it wasn't one he wanted to be on. This was rough country: grassland and wheat fields and long narrow draws turning to forested hills the farther into the mountains one went. The entire county, an area slightly less than half the size of Wales, had all of eighty thousand people in it.

The screen door screeched open, and Cassie's grandfather came onto the porch. He peered into the darkness and then flicked on the light. "Cassie?"

"We're here, Grandfather," she said.

"What's happened?" Art McKay thrust his hands deep into the pockets of his jeans. He had put on his Pendleton wool coat over a checked buttoned down shirt and a cowboy string tie. Shorter than Cassie, he nonetheless was a presence in any room he entered.

Callum had speculated more than once about those long dead Scots who'd emigrated to Oregon, resulting in Cassie's very Scottish last name. Many of her relatives had suggested that he return for the festival of Highland games that took place up the road every July. That Scottish connection was an odd coincidence among many odd coincidences in the series of events that had led in the end to Cassie's rescue of him after his company was ambushed by a host of angry Highlanders in Scotland in the Middle Ages.

"Some of our friends have arrived, Grandfather," Cassie said.

"You'll be missing dinner then," he said.

"I'm sorry." Callum turned the mobile so Art could see the map. "They're out there all alone."

Art pointed towards his truck with his lips. "Let me get my keys and tell the others. That's a lot of square miles to cover. You'll be needing help."

Gratefulness spread though Callum like a sip of warm mead. Cassie's family, led by her grandfather, had accepted him into her life from the moment he'd shown up on this very porch two years ago. And truthfully, while nobody else in the clan had married an Englishman—or a Scotsman rather—they were no strangers to welcoming newcomers into their midst. Callum hoped their openness wouldn't be tested too far when they found whoever had come through.

During that first trip two years ago (after Callum had recovered from the gunshot wound to his shoulder), he'd discovered how tightly knit this community was. Not only did everyone know his name and something of his history before he arrived, but while he struggled to put names to faces, they all referred to him as 'that guy Cassie married.' When he complained about it, she laughed and said that at least they were including him. If they didn't like him, they would have looked past him as if he didn't exist.

While Callum left a message for Tate about borrowing some of his former staff, Art organized four truckloads of men, many with rifles in case they encountered wild animals. Callum still hadn't heard from his employer, which was somewhat troubling. He'd known that he was being shunted to one side. He'd watched it happen. He wasn't sorry now, since it meant he could get on with what he viewed as his primary job, but it didn't bode well for his future employment. Callum didn't think he could go back to being a regular agent.

Or rather, he knew he couldn't.

As Callum got into Art's truck, he looked worriedly at Cassie. "For the first time it occurs to me that Jones could be wrong. What if we roused everyone and it's a mistake?"

"Has Mark ever been mistaken?" she said. "Have the flashes ever *not* been someone traveling forward or back?"

"No." Callum racked the seat all the way back, which put him halfway between Cassie in the back seat and her grandfather sitting in front of her. Art drove a big Dodge extended cab truck, beaten and battered but still running after twenty years.

"If Mark is wrong about this," Cassie said, "my family will blame you, and you'll be teased every Thanksgiving for the rest of your life for taking us on a snipe hunt."

"Oh, ta," Callum said, though on second thought, it might be good to give them something to tease him about besides his accent. As the truck hummed down the road, leading the other trucks, Callum sighed and stretched out his legs.

Thanksgiving dinner was taking place at the house of one of Cassie's aunts, somewhat south of Highway 84, which ran through the northern part of Oregon. The caravan of trucks crossed the motorway on a flyover, and then Art pulled into the truck stop next to the casino. Cassie stuck her head between the seats. "What are you doing, Tilla?" That was the Umatilla word for 'grandfather', which Callum knew from past visits.

"If we're driving up Meacham Creek, we need gas to make it there and back," Art said.

Callum exited the truck with Art. Courtesy said that he should be pumping—and paying—for the petrol, but Art brushed away his credit card. "It's on me. I know how worried Cassie is about your friends. I can see it in her eyes."

"Thank you," Callum said. "And thank you for helping us find them."

"We haven't found them yet."

Callum scanned the skyline to the east. "We will." The words came out a bit harsher and more guttural than he intended, and he returned his gaze to Art's face.

The two men studied each other for a second before Art said, "You should know by now there's nothing Cassie's family wouldn't do for her." And then he smirked. "And maybe for you."

Callum dared to ask, "Do you mean I've proved myself?"

"I see how you take care of her." Art slotted the nozzle into the petrol tank.

Callum laughed, genuinely relieved at his words. "Don't let Cassie hear you say that."

Art shot Callum an amused look. As an elder in an Indian tribe, Art was no stranger to strong women. He was also being far more talkative than usual, and in the last five minutes he was two for two in facial expressions Callum had never seen on him before.

Petrol acquired, Callum and Art returned to their seats in Art's truck. The other trucks circled around, each driven by an uncle or cousin, and fell into line as they headed north past the casino to the crossroads at Mission. The convenience store was still open, with a few customers pulling into the car park as Art turned the corner onto the road heading east.

Callum kept his eye on the map on his mobile phone. It was calculating and recalculating the miles they had to travel to reach the spot where the flash had occurred. The twenty miles would end up being more like thirty before they could pull off the road and continue towards the site on foot.

Then Cassie said, "Wait! Wait!" She shook Callum's shoulder to get his attention.

"What is it?" He turned to look at her.

Art had sped up after turning right, but now he glanced back at Cassie too. She peered through the rear window. The only thing moving within a mile were the people in the car park, which was lit by four streetlights. "Turn around, Grandfather. Please."

As usual, Art didn't expend words that he didn't have to use, just flipped on his turn signal and executed a five-point turn in the middle of the street. The other trucks behind him slowed and waited until they could turn around too. A few seconds later, Art turned into the convenience store car park, just as a woman in a long dress and a cloak pushed through the front door.

"It's them!" Cassie jiggled Callum's seat.

Callum had the door open before Art braked the truck, and his feet hit the ground a second later.

"Meg!" Cassie slammed the passenger seat forward and scrambled out behind Callum.

It had been Meg who'd pushed through the front door of the shop, and she stood on the sidewalk, a bag of crisps and a bottle of water in her hands. Callum had stopped too, one hand on the doorframe as he'd come around it, hardly daring to believe that Meg was really standing on the pavement in front of them. Cassie barreled past her husband and flung her arms around her friend. "I'm so glad to see you!"

Both women were laughing and crying at the same time. Anna had still been in the shop, and she tumbled out the door. Somehow, Callum crossed the distance from Art's truck to the pavement, and the four companions wrapped their arms around each other and held on.

Looking over the top of the women's heads, Callum saw Art and the man in whose truck Anna and Meg had arrived meet and shake hands. As was usually the case with tribal elders, Art's handshake was gentle, hardly a handshake at all by English standards, and then Art patted the man's upper arm as if they knew each other well.

Meanwhile, Cassie's other relatives had climbed out of their trucks and gathered around to be introduced to Meg and Anna. Two years ago when she'd returned to the modern world with Callum, Cassie had left it up to her grandfather to explain where she'd been for five years. Callum was pretty sure he hadn't told anybody anything but the vaguest truth. Certainly the time traveling to the Middle Ages part had been left out.

Callum released the women, who showed no signs of letting go of each other, and walked to where Art and his friend stood. "Thank you." Callum held out his hand to the stranger.

"No problem." As Art introduced Callum to Jim, they shook hands more like Callum was used to, with a firm grip that was almost a test of manhood. "I was happy to help."

"Where did you find them?" Callum said.

"On the road," Jim said. "Hitchhiking."

Callum grimaced. "I appreciate you picking them up. That would have been a long walk to Mission."

Jim nodded. "Good thing you showed up when you did. Meg wanted me to leave them here. I didn't want to do that, but I couldn't force them back into the truck if they didn't want to go."

Callum read curiosity in Jim's eyes, but after neither Callum nor Art explained what was going on, Jim nodded his head at Art. "I'll be off."

"Thanks again," Callum said.

"Glad it all worked out," Jim said.

Art watched Jim go and then turned to Callum. "Does this mean Cassie will be leaving again? With you? With them?"

"I think so," Callum said. "I go where she goes, so it's probably a better question to ask her."

Art looked at Callum for a long count of ten, his gaze back to impassive, and then he nodded. "I like who she became there. I like who she is when she's with you."

Callum blinked. That was as high a praise as he could ever imagine receiving from Art.

Then Art raised a hand, and somehow that small motion brought everyone's attention to him. "Dinner's waiting."

6

November 1291

David

Anna and Mom had been gone for two hours. The family's situation remained unchanged, but reality had set in, and the people at Rhuddlan had recovered from their initial shock. The family was eating the rest of their meal in the great hall, attempting to put a brave face on the disaster. Hopefully, David's calm response had helped to ease people's worries, but still, it was going to be the talk of Gwynedd for days, if not weeks, to come. Longer if Mom and Anna didn't return quickly.

David sat on the dais, watching his people and contemplating the great secret his family had been keeping these last nine years. All that time, David had walked a fine line between modern man and medieval lord, and with Mom and Anna's disappearance, reconciling the two wasn't getting any easier.

David glanced at his father, who was sitting back in his chair, eating no more than David. David caught his eye and then reached out a hand to his cup and lifted it to him in a silent toast, as he had before Marty had come. Dad drank as well, though like David, he wouldn't drink much tonight. David had learned—eventually, but he'd learned—that a king couldn't afford to allow wine to cloud his judgment. And especially not tonight, not with Mom gone and war on the horizon.

Arthur played at David's feet with a wooden horse that one of David's men-at-arms had whittled for him. Arthur knew horses and carts and carriages, but David couldn't help thinking that his birthright was equally cars and trains and spaceships. He spoke American to Arthur, while Lili spoke Welsh and his nanny spoke English. Until those words tonight, claiming his name, Arthur had barely spoken any of them beyond 'ma' and 'ta', which was an abbreviated Welsh word for father, 'tad'.

Mom insisted that Arthur would speak when he deemed it necessary, and David knew his son was perfectly bright in other ways. He just couldn't help wondering, if they'd lived in the modern world, if a doctor wouldn't have been able to explain what was wrong with him, if anything was wrong with him at all.

How would David know? And how would David know the right time tell Arthur that his father had been born in a distant world where there were planes, trains, and automobiles? Where men had landed on the moon? How did he tell him of a land where men didn't wear swords or ride horses into battle as he would be expected to? How was David to teach his son to be the King of England he needed to become, while making sure Arthur was a man whose mind could encompass far more than that?

The time traveling was a secret from the world at large lest one of them—more likely Anna, Bronwen, or Mom—be labeled a witch in this superstitious age. So David couldn't speak of it to Arthur, for fear that he would inadvertently betray the truth. Admittedly, Arthur wasn't talking now, but who was to say that his seven-year-old future self wouldn't want to talk to a friend about his father's hidden green minivan because he didn't understand why he shouldn't? When did keeping secrets from the rest of the world become keeping secrets from his son?

"Don't watch your people so closely," Lili said, leaning in to speak low in David's ear. "You're making them nervous."

"They are giving me more space than usual," he agreed.

She shook her head. "They were doing that already."

"Were they? I didn't notice."

"They remember the Prince of Wales you once were and wonder if the King of England they see before them is the same person or a different beast entirely. They're wary, especially now that you've sent your mother and sister to Afalon."

"I didn't send—"

Lili shot her husband a withering look. "You sent them to Afalon to save them from Marty."

"Okay, okay." David sat back in his seat. "It isn't what I told them, but it's what I mean them to think."

It was only then, as David watched Arthur put his head close to Cadell's, the two boys communicating in whatever fashion worked for them, that he recognized the evidence before him. What might be possible for Arthur stood right in front of him in the shape of his nephew. Cadell, like Arthur, was a child of two worlds and knew it because Anna had never tried to hide who she was from her children. And if Cadell had a certain swagger and confidence beyond his years, David could hardly begrudge the result.

Lili patted his arm. "Arthur is *fine*. We all are. You'll know the right time to tell him."

David's eyes widened in mock horror. "You've been reading my mind!"

She kissed his cheek. He had an urge to grab her and kiss her for a lot longer, but there were too many people in the room. Her eyes flashed as she read his thoughts again.

"Afalon is real, Dafydd," Dad said from the other side of Lili. "Don't run from it or yourself. This is who you are."

"Your people used to love you, Dafydd. They want to still," Lili added. "Let them. Show them you're the same boy who came to them when he was fourteen and won their hearts inside of a week."

"It wasn't exactly a week," David said, but at another one of her looks, he stopped arguing. Of course she was right. She always was. "Perhaps I should mingle." Standing, David bent to Arthur and swung him onto his hip. Arthur gave a squeal and put an arm around his father's neck, coming along willingly as David strolled from the dais. Small children were the perfect icebreaker. David made his way among the tables, greeting people as he should have greeted them earlier.

One man told a tale to his neighbors about that first battle David had fought against King Edward when he was fourteen; another lamented his gout; a third complained that his neighbor had moved a boundary stone. Everybody wanted to talk to him, and as the evening progressed and tongues loosened, David felt a real warmth directed at him.

Arthur listened while sucking on his finger, as he often did when he wasn't entirely sure of what was happening. When a woman introduced Arthur to her seventh son, who was the same age, David could tell that both he and Arthur were making real progress. The two boys eyed each other warily. But then Arthur took his forefinger from his mouth and squirmed to be put down, which meant that he'd decided the little boy might be a viable playmate.

An hour later, Ieuan, Carew, and Goronwy joined David by the fireside, and a small group gathered to discuss the state of politics in Wales. David found his breath easing out in relief. He made mistakes all the time, but some were correctable.

The door to the great hall swung open. "Sire!"

David turned to look. He didn't recognize the messenger, but Dad, who'd been sitting at the central seat on the dais, rose to his feet. The messenger strode down the hall towards him, and David drifted along in his wake. If Marty hadn't half killed the steward, the messenger would never have been allowed to get this far, and David had been remiss in not appointing a replacement immediately. News, whether good or bad, should have gone through Alan to David and should not be shouted to the whole castle without either Dad or David knowing the gist of it first.

"I will speak to the guards at the gate." Goronwy had come with David and spoke low in his ear. "Who should replace Alan?"

"I trust your judgment," David said. "You, certainly, for the time that we're here if it pleases you, but I'll need another soon. Better to choose him now."

"I'll see to it after we hear what the messenger has to say," Goronwy said.

David picked up the pace, striding towards Dad and the newcomer, who stopped a few feet from the dais and bowed.

"What is it?" Dad said.

"My lord! Sire!" The messenger looked from David to Dad and back again, and then went down on one knee, which was probably the best choice he could have made. "I bring news from the west. Harlech is under siege, and Carndochen and Cymer have fallen."

David cursed under his breath. Stunned whispers that rose to anxious chatter swept around the hall. David spun around and raised his hand, calling for his people's attention yet again. As everyone had their eyes riveted on what was happening at the front of the hall, it took only a few seconds before the crowd quieted enough for David to speak.

But then his father came around the table to stand beside him, and David bent his head, gesturing that he should take the floor. It was David's castle, but Dad was the King of Wales.

"We've had several shocks today, but this isn't one of them," Dad said. "Dafydd and I have been watching this situation closely and have already developed a plan to respond." Dad canted his head to David. "As of this moment, we are at war."

David nodded. "All men-at-arms should see their captains immediately. We will send out a general call for every man who can hold a spear or shoot an arrow, and for the rest—" He swept his gaze around the hall, looking at the old, the children, and the women, "—you should remain here where you will be safe."

As David had hoped, this little speech both settled the people down and brought those who should be moving to their feet. He placed a hand on the messenger's shoulder. "Come with me."

"Yes, my lord." The messenger swallowed hard. David hadn't meant anything by the words and hadn't thought his tone was particularly harsh, but perhaps the man was realizing for the first time that he'd done something wrong.

"Father?" David said.

"Indeed." Dad headed for the door.

David looked questioningly at Lili and Bronwen. If they were going to build this new world order, women needed to have a say in war as well as peace.

Lili and Bronwen looked at each other, however, and then Bronwen said, "We're good."

"We've got seven kids to care for between the two of us, and I trust you to do whatever needs doing." Lili waved a hand at her husband.

David eyed Lili carefully. Her bow was upstairs in their chamber, a stone's throw away. "Really?"

"You can always ask us if you need our help," Bronwen said. "And we'll be happy to second guess you later if you like."

David laughed, and Ieuan kissed the top of his wife's head. They departed, moving down the south corridor towards Dad's office with a phalanx of men. Samuel fell in beside Justin, and the two men nodded at each other. Samuel had been Callum's eyes and ears in Shrewsbury since before Callum's exile in the modern world. Like Carew, he'd come to Rhuddlan to consult with David— and instead found himself in the middle of a war.

David honestly was glad to think about something else besides the loss of Mom and Anna. Once in the receiving room, David, his father, and their advisors formed a half-circle around the messenger, who shifted from foot to foot, gazing from one lord to another. He hadn't often seen so much authority gathered in one place.

Dad said, "Speak."

The messenger cleared his throat and spoke as if reciting word for word what he'd been told. "I bring news from Harlech. Madog ap Llywelyn is attempting to reclaim Meirionnydd for himself, with the help of Rhys and Maredudd, sons of Lord Rhys ap Maredudd. Overnight, Madog took the castles at Cymer and Carndochen, and he besieges Harlech even now. I fled just ahead of them."

"Evan sent you?" Carew said.

The messenger bowed his head. "Yes, my lord."

The captains of David's *teulu* had a distressing habit of becoming so good at their jobs that David was forced to elevate them to ever higher positions of authority. Which then required David to find new captains. After becoming King of England, David had very reluctantly parted with Evan, who'd become his captain after David lost Ieuan to Bronwen. Evan's change of position wasn't because he had in any way failed in his post, but because he'd proved to be capable of far more. Dad and David needed men they could trust. Evan was one of them, and David's father had given him command of Harlech and its forces.

Since Evan's departure to Harlech, David had promoted a half-Norman/half-Saxon Englishman named Justin to be his new captain. Justin had distinguished himself during the battle of Windsor two years ago.

Dad's expression remained calm—unnaturally so. Underneath the façade, the fact that Madog had so easily taken Carndochen and Cymer had him in a rage.

"Harlech has never been tested," Goronwy said.

"But Evan has," David said.

After consultation with Mom, Dad had abandoned Castell y Bere after the English burned it in 1283 and built new castles to defend Gwynedd, one of them at Harlech, a stone castle built on a high bluff that made it possible to fortify it directly from the sea. King Edward, if he'd lived, would have built an iron ring of castles (as the history books said) all around Gwynedd to control the unrest he'd created in the populace by murdering Dad. With Edward dead instead, Dad had focused on defense against outside threats, rather than inside ones. Though, with David's ascension to the throne of England, even that had become far less of a concern.

Until now.

"How many men does Madog have?" Math said.

"Some two thousand," the messenger said.

"Where did he find two thousand men to betray Wales?" Cadwallon said. He'd been a boy when he'd ridden in Aunt Elisa's minivan outside Buellt six years ago. That he'd matured into a responsible young man was due in no small part to his near-death experience at the hand of Humphrey de Bohun, who'd left him for dead along with several others of David's guard. Cadwallon's recovery had been long, but he'd come through, eventually rejoining Dad's company and rising to captain. Still, Cadwallon retained a touch of innocence about him, and he was quick to show both enthusiasm and ire on Dad's behalf.

"Madog and Rhys have been sowing unrest among their men for forty years," Dad said. "Besides which, a good soldier goes where his lord points. Many men believe that it isn't their place to question their orders."

"We can't pity Madog or his men. This rebellion must be put down." Carew swept a hand through his blonde hair, which was receding from his temples now that he was approaching forty. "We can give no quarter."

Dad nodded at Carew, but then transferred his gaze to David, his eyes questioning.

"Do you think I might object?" David said. "Rule of law is all. Madog commits treason in marching on Meirionnydd, and his transgressions must be met with the strongest force possible. Afterwards, the moment the battle turns in our favor, I would hope that the killing could cease. I don't like seeing any man die after a cause is lost. Then will be the time for mercy. But that time is not now."

David hadn't always understood that. He hadn't been raised to be a soldier, and growing up in the modern world had not prepared him for the realities of ruling a medieval kingdom. But three years as the King of England had shown him the necessity of being selectively ruthless. William de Valence had swung at the end of a long rope because sometimes harsh measures had to be taken. Even so, Valence had been tried before a jury of his peers and found guilty of treason. His death was a consequence of the rule of law.

Democracy might be making inroads into this new medieval world they were trying to create, but Dad was still the King of Wales and held the reins of power. Someday, if David's vision of a united Britain came into being, he might not have the unilateral power to wage war. Perhaps it was hypocritical of David to be glad that change hadn't yet come. For now, men were dying and would continue to die until their king responded in force. Or gave in.

None of the men collected in the room saw that as an option.

While David wouldn't necessarily call himself a violent man, violence had become part of his life, and the potential for it was there always, latent and coiled inside him, waiting to be called forth as needed. David had killed men with his own hands. If Rhys and Madoc had their way, David would kill more. The taste of it was like ash in his mouth, dry and bitter.

Callum had told David of his Post-traumatic Stress Disorder. In hearing Callum describe it, David wasn't sure that his friend had anything on David himself or many of the men he knew. How could something be considered a disorder when more men had it than not?

"It's fifty miles as the crow flies from here to Harlech," Math said.

"Then we'd better get started," Dad said. "Send out a call. We must leave Rhuddlan before midnight to reach Aber before dawn."

With a nod from David, Ieuan left to take charge of the men who'd gathered here at Rhuddlan. He remained David's right hand man among the troops the way Goronwy had been Dad's before he'd become less able to ride. Dad filled the gap Goronwy had left with Cadwallon and others, like Carew and David, even if their counsel was available only occasionally. Dad had yet to find another companion as capable and trusted as Goronwy, and at this stage in his life, David didn't expect him ever to do so.

"Any who are able to ready themselves for battle within two hours should come with us. Those who come late can make their way to the muster at Maentwrog," Dad said.

"I'll send out riders." Cadwallon bowed and departed too, taking the wayward messenger with him.

Cadwallon meant that he would be sending word to all the commotes in Gwynedd and Anglesey; the messengers would be shouting something akin to 'the British are coming!' in order to roust the common men and send them marching to Maentwrog. This ancient village was located at a ford of a river, far enough from Harlech that the troops could marshal there without being detected by those besieging the castle, but close enough that the march to Harlech wouldn't exhaust them.

Then Dad looked hard at David. "You will come to Harlech by way of Criccieth." Criccieth was Dad's castle on the southern Lleyn Peninsula, situated on a promontory at the seaside. It also happened to be where Mom had come through from the modern world the first time, and where she and Dad had met.

Math rubbed at his chin. "You want him to arrive by sea?"

"That doesn't make sense." David shook his head. "You need me and my men at Maentwrog—"

Dad put up his hand. "Your safety is paramount, son. You are the King of England and upon you all our hopes rest. It is gratifying to know that were any danger to befall you on your journey across the sea, you would be kept safe."

Safe in the modern world, he meant. David ground his teeth and tried again. "I can bring the full force of England to bear against Madog. Surely—"

"I am not in my dotage yet!"

David put both hands up, palms out. "I didn't say it. I didn't even think it."

"Madog and Rhys challenge me now because they are thinking it," Dad said. "My son may be the King of England, but if I run to you whenever I am challenged, from where does my authority arise?"

David wasn't going there, not in a million years. "I don't see how sending me to Criccieth is going to help. It's farther away. It will take longer."

"You will relieve Harlech with men and supplies from the sea," Dad said.

David stared at him. "You want me to handle the baggage? Not even to fight?"

"There will be plenty of fighting to go around before the end, and you know it," Dad said.

Goronwy was glancing worriedly from David to his father. He cleared his throat and changed course. "We don't know the full extent of Madog's plan, sire. It might be to draw you from your seats of power, leaving Rhuddlan, Aber, and Dolwyddelan vulnerable."

"We will ride through Gwynedd, and anyone who opposes us will be swept away," Dad said. "I've done it before."

"I know," David said, and then shut his mouth on the rest of what he wanted to say before the conversation turned into a real argument. He would use the time between here and Caernarfon, where their forces would have to part, to dig a little deeper. David had fought in plenty of battles—with his father and without him.

David sensed there was more to this decision than his father's worry about his dotage or David's safety.

Dad nodded and turned to look at the map tacked to the wall. Math had opened his mouth to speak or argue, but David shook his head to stop him. "I'm just visiting, and for all that I am a prince of Wales, I know Gwynedd far less well than he. We'll let it go for now."

Math chewed on his lower lip, clearly wanting to continue the conversation, but then he nodded. He and Goronwy stepped to Dad's side to look at the map with him. Carew, Justin, and Samuel remained behind. Both Samuel and Justin spoke and understood Welsh, but David could hear them analyzing the plan in English.

Carew spoke low to David. "It isn't the best use of you. Anyone could sail from Criccieth to Harlech."

"I know that."

"For us to have just heard of Madog's coming today, he must have force-marched his men through night and day," Carew said. "With two castles already taken and Harlech under siege, Madog will have had to split his force. And his men will be tired."

David glanced to where his father was discussing the disposition of men with Math and Goronwy. "I won't say you're wrong."

Carew pressed his lips together as if he, too, wanted to discuss this more, but then he tipped his head towards the map, silently suggesting that they look at it with the others.

David decided to pretend that their disagreement hadn't happened. "Tudur, Clare, and Wynod should see about putting pressure on Rhys from the south." Tudur was all the way in the southeast corner of Wales at Chepstow, but if Rhys took a few more castles, Tudur might find his lands threatened too. "If Rhys thinks he can send his sons up here to help Madog take what isn't his, then he should face some of the consequences of his actions at Dryslwyn."

"I should have deprived Rhys of all his lands long ago," Dad said.

"You were making peace out of war at a time when you could afford to be magnanimous," Goronwy said. "You gave Dinefwr and Carreg Cennan to Wynod, a gift for which Rhys has never forgiven you. That, however, is his problem, not yours."

Dad growled, "It's my problem now."

Math, meanwhile, traced the road leading to Harlech with one finger. "If I ride south from here, through the standing stones at Bwlch y Ddeufaen, and swing west to Dolwyddelan, gathering men to me as I come, I can meet you at Maentwrog in two days' time."

"I will count on your coming." Dad waved a dismissive hand, which all of the others took to indicate that they should depart, leaving David alone with his father. Dad moved to sit behind the table. Maybe he had meant to dismiss David too, but David didn't go.

And then David laughed inwardly. Nobody dismissed him anymore. He left only when he wanted to. He didn't share the thought with his father, who was in a foul mood.

David pulled one of the chairs beside Dad's desk closer and sat in it, his elbows on his thighs and his head down. He was suddenly exhausted, which wouldn't do at all. They had a long way still to go tonight.

"Son."

The word was heavy with meaning. Maybe even with a bit of an apology on Dad's part. David sat back in the chair with his elbows on the arms and his hands folded in front of his lips, looking at his father over them.

"You look just like me when you sit like that," Dad said.

David didn't move, glad to hear the affection in his father's voice. "I'm concerned that Madog's plan is about more than the taking of a few castles. You are concerned about it too."

"Valence haunts you still, two years on. Not everybody is as intelligent as he was." Dad tucked his cloak closer around himself. The fire was dying, but no servant would dare to enter to stoke it if it meant interrupting this meeting.

"I don't deny it." David rose to his feet and tossed a few more logs on the fire.

"Valence was in a class above Madog, who is ten years older than you and still untested." Dad looked David up and down. "Scrawny too, in comparison."

"It is my experience that intelligence and size can be inversely proportional."

Dad chuckled. "I have no idea what you just said. I can tell you that Madog has had to borrow men from Rhys. He's a tool, nothing more, getting his hands dirty so Rhys doesn't have to."

"What about Rhys?" David said.

Dad made a face that said *maybe*. "We can guess what else might happen tomorrow or next week, but we must address what faces us today. Quickly. I told the hall that we were prepared for this war and had a plan, but the truth is that Madog has caught us on the hop."

"You only half lied," David said. "We do have a plan. We just hadn't come up with it yet."

Dad tipped back his head and laughed. "Oh, how I've missed you, son." Then he sobered. "I still think what I said earlier today is true: this war could be a blessing in disguise."

"You mean my plan to create a united Britain?" David said.

"It begins here," Dad said. "When we crush Madog and Rhys, we show every lord in England and Wales that what happened to Valence was not a one-time thing—that you and I are willing to do whatever it takes to keep the peace and maintain the unity of our country." He gaze gazed at David through a count of ten. "And then, if all goes well, we give our power away."

7

November 2019

Anna

While Mom seemed so calm and matter-of-fact about the time traveling thing and Anna was trying to follow her lead, it wasn't really working. Her initial adrenaline had carried her through their arrival and down the hill to the road. It had been cold outside, but Anna hadn't realized that she was frozen all the way through until Star handed her a blanket and Jim turned the heater on high.

She'd sat in the back of the truck and shivered—with fear and anticipation and the shock at having survived the bout with time travel at all. The whole day kept playing like a movie reel in her mind. She still hadn't come to terms with Marty's betrayal, much less their arrival in Oregon, followed by the sudden appearance of Cassie and Callum.

Anna wanted Math. She wanted her boys. For the first time, Anna truly understood what it must have been like for Mom when Aunt Elisa called to tell her that Anna and David were missing. It was as if fate had ripped out Mom's heart, thrown it onto the floor, and stomped on it. Mom had been forced to live alone for a year and a half. It must have been unbearable. And yet, she'd had to bear it. Anna wanted to be as strong as her mother, but she didn't know that she could be.

Anna looked to the front of the truck where Mom had found a seat between Art and Callum. Anna was in the back with Cassie, who'd given Anna her gloves, but Anna's hands still weren't warm, and she tucked them between her thighs. Art started the truck and drove away from the store—in total silence. After the initial rush of joy at being reunited, none of them knew what to say to each other. Anna certainly didn't.

Cassie and Anna hadn't spent as much time together as Anna would have liked. Callum was the Earl of Shrewsbury and David's advisor, which meant that he traveled a lot. Because Cassie was married to Callum, she traveled with him. It had been more than two years since David had returned to the Middle Ages without them, and Anna was a little worried that Cassie might have become a different person.

But then Cassie glanced at Anna, her eyes bright, and Anna knew it was going to be okay. "How have you been?" the two women said together.

Everyone laughed, and the tension evaporated. Anna rested her head back against the seat.

"Tell us how you got here," Cassie said.

Art drove down a long, straight road while Mom related the events of the afternoon so far.

Cassie squeezed Anna's hand. "You must have been terrified!"

"I was," Anna said. "Even so, I'm sorry Marty died. If he'd been able to hold on to me, he would have come with us."

"You're a very nice person, Anna," Mom said. "I would never have wished him dead, but I'm still too angry at him to mourn him."

"From your description of what he did to you, Meg," Callum said, "he'd become a better man in Scotland than he'd ever been before."

"Maybe he's not dead," Cassie said.

"He fell from the top of a tower at Rhuddlan," Mom said. "I can't see anyone surviving the fall."

"And then there was that scream he let out," Anna said. "Do you think one of the archers got him, Mom?"

Mom shrugged, but she turned in her seat and caught Anna's eye. Yeah, she thought so too.

"Happy Thanksgiving," Cassie said, deadpan.

Mom turned back to face the front. "Is that what brought you two to Oregon?"

"We've come every year since we came back to this world," Cassie said. "Given what's going on with our jobs, it seemed especially important to be here this year."

"Your jobs?" Mom said. "David is going to want to know all about what happened after he left."

"Good things happened at first," Callum said. "If you'd arrived a year ago, you would have found a very different situation from what faced you and Llywelyn—and David too. Unfortunately, with recent budget cuts—

"—my job ends December 1st," Cassie put in.

"—we've been trying to come up with a way to still be here for you when you needed us even if we've been sacked," Callum finished.

Anna leaned forward. "What exactly are you talking about? What do budget cuts have to do with our *traveling*?"

Callum shifted in his seat so he could look at Mom and Anna at the same time and gave a two minute summary of what had happened to him and Cassie after David returned to the medieval world.

"You wouldn't believe what it took to bring me to life again, legally speaking. It was only all resolved—" Cassie glanced at Callum, "—what, nine months ago?"

Callum nodded.

Art hadn't said a word the whole drive, but he spoke now. "Now that your friends are here, if you disappear again, I won't let anyone declare you dead."

Cassie froze, and Anna took a moment to absorb that comment. It meant that Callum and Cassie might want to return to the Middle Ages with them when they went.

"Thank you, Grandfather," Cassie said softly. Callum's arm had been lying along the top edge of the front seat behind Mom's head, and he moved his hand so he could grasp Cassie's hand.

"I'm sorry your jobs haven't worked out," Mom said.

Cassie shrugged. "Your appearance today may change everything."

Mom frowned. "Are we going to find MI-5 agents beating down the door?"

"At the moment, Mark Jones is the only agent who knows you're here," Callum said.

"We're hoping it stays that way," Cassie said.

"But how long we can keep it a secret, I don't know," Callum said. "Our colleagues in the CIA pulled out a year ago. They may have their own people on this, but if they continued the Project, they did it without telling us."

"The CIA can't work inside the United States," Anna said.

Callum gave her a completely blank look.

"That's—that's the law, right?" Anna said.

Cassie gave a brief laugh that was more of a scoff. "I'm not sure we can count on strict adherence to the law. Your arrival here would be counted as one of those 'drop everything' events if Callum's office had anything to drop."

"But you're right," Callum said. "Neither the CIA, MI-5, nor my office have jurisdiction inside the United States. I have no authority to act, either to take you in or to let you go."

"That's convenient," said Mom.

"It is, isn't it?" Cassie grinned. "It means we are currently acting as concerned citizens only, helping friends in need. Whether Callum would be remiss in not reporting your presence is something that he can debate with his boss when we get back to Wales."

"Who's your boss?" Anna said to Callum.

"It was the Prime Minister himself," he said. "Unfortunately, the man now in office is not the same one who was in power two years ago, which is largely the reason for our budget cuts. He has different priorities. That and the worldwide economic downturn."

In medieval Wales, Anna gave zero thought to how this world was turning out, beyond hoping Cassie and Callum were okay. A 'worldwide economic downturn' and its consequences just wasn't something she had ever felt the need to think about.

"But he's not your boss now?" Mom said.

"We are being reincorporated back into MI-5," Callum said. "A man named Tate is the new director."

"So you're not going to tell either of them that we're here?" Mom said.

"Not yet," Callum said. "For two reasons, and the first has nothing to do with you at all. The British government has been facing a series of internal crises since Cassie and I returned. Over the last six months, the problems have escalated. There have been bombings, protests, and general unrest, culminating in the destruction of the GCHQ about an hour ago. It's—" He broke off and shook his head.

"It's a mess, is what it is," Cassie said. "This may be only the beginning too."

Anna looked from Cassie to Callum. "Did people die?"

Callum nodded, his face drawn. "I don't know what we're going to find when we get back."

"I'm sorry," Anna said.

Mom made a sympathetic noise too. "And the second reason?"

Callum took in a deep breath. "Well, it's past one in the morning in England, and since we're all here in Oregon, it isn't as if I can bring you into the Prime Minister's office as proof that time travel really exists."

"Oh, I get it now," Anna said. "He doesn't believe what we can do is real."

"He does not," Cassie said.

"Well, good for us," Mom said. "That leaves only our own government to worry about."

"And it just so happens that it's Thanksgiving," Cassie said, beaming. "Nobody's watching."

That made Anna feel a little bit better about being here. Mom and Dad's journey across Wales and David's imprisonment the following year had been haunting Anna from the moment she opened her eyes to find she and Mom were in the modern world. Anna had grown up in Portland, but even at the oblivious age of seventeen, she'd known how neglected these small communities were, with little in the way of infrastructure, including poor to nonexistent cell phone coverage or internet. While a big city might provide anonymity, a small, friendly town might close ranks around them. Plus, it had less surveillance.

"It's a huge relief to think that it might take some time for the government to find us," Mom said. "I feel sorry for the poor schmuck on duty if he realizes that something has happened and has to call his superior away from his Thanksgiving dinner."

Callum let out a mocking snort. "I was that schmuck once. It isn't fun. Maybe he'll take a few minutes to work up his courage."

"It's been a few minutes," Mom said. "We've talked about best case scenarios. What's the worst?"

Everyone looked at Callum, who chewed on his lower lip. But it was Art who answered, "They see you're here, a call is made, then more calls. The closest FBI field office is in Portland. Three hours away."

"It wouldn't be the FBI," Callum said. "Homeland Security, maybe."

"Salem, then," Art said. "A little farther."

Nobody asked him how he knew that, and Art didn't say. Cassie seemed to take it for granted that he'd have that knowledge at his fingertips.

"What about local cops?" Mom said.

Art pursed his lips. "Pendleton police, tribal police, county sheriff, and state patrol."

"Without knowing who of you has come through, they would have no alert to send out," Callum said. "They'd have to send someone to the site, and then track you back."

"I don't see that happening tonight," Cassie said.

Art pulled into a driveway and stopped the truck. Anna hadn't been paying attention to where they were going, but everyone got out of the truck, so she did too. They followed Art across the porch to the front door of the house. It was a small two-story. Their arrival included the return of Cassie's uncles and cousins, who'd intended to search for Mom and Anna and had followed them back, so now the house was full to bursting.

"What if it did?" Anna whispered the words to Cassie.

She bit her lip. "I hope I didn't speak too soon."

The turkey had come out of the oven only three minutes before, and the house was full of delicious smells. Anna was curious to taste modern food again, with all its chemicals and additives. Would it taste bad to her? As it turned out, however, Cassie's family did things the old fashioned way, and the table in the kitchen was loaded with unprocessed food not that different from what they'd been serving at Rhuddlan earlier that day, except that instead of roast pork and chicken, they were eating turkey and a bunch of other New World foods not available in Wales in the Middle Ages.

Five minutes later, Anna found herself with a loaded plate, sitting on a couch in the living room between Cassie and one of her eighteen-year-old male cousins. "So," the boy said through enormous bites of food he wasn't bothering to chew before swallowing, "how do you know Cassie?"

Anna glanced at Cassie. From their conversation in the truck, Anna had understood that Cassie had told something of her story to her relations, but obviously not to this one or not the whole story. Admittedly, the whole story was pretty far-fetched.

"I met Anna and Meg while I was away," Cassie said between her own bites of food.

"In Scotland?" he said.

"Right," Cassie said.

Fortunately, before he could ask any more questions, Cassie's grandfather approached, and the boy stood up so Art could sit down. Art began to eat with utter focus, chewing each bite thoroughly. Nobody said anything. Anna thought about repeating a phrase her mother would sometimes say when David brought his friends home: *all's quiet while the beasts feed*, but she didn't know that everyone would get it and didn't want anyone—especially Art—to take offense.

Fortunately, before Anna could put her foot in her mouth, Art said, "You'll be leaving us, then, Granddaughter?"

Cassie looked over at her grandfather across Anna, who shrank back on the couch, wishing she wasn't between them. She felt like she was eavesdropping on a conversation that should be private.

"Callum and I haven't talked about it yet, but he's worried about someone finding Anna and Meg. It'll be tonight or first thing in the morning that we'll go."

"When you do go, you can take my truck, but I didn't mean that," Art said. "I meant *leaving*."

Cassie didn't answer for a second, and then she ducked her head in a nod. "I have to. I think we have to."

Art nodded. "I will miss you."

A buzz from Callum's phone interrupted whatever else Art might have been going to say. Anna was glad, because she had been feeling more than a little uncomfortable witnessing that exchange. Clearly Cassie loved her grandfather, and in a way it was Anna's fault—and Mom's fault—that they would be separated again. Because if Cassie and Callum were returning to the Middle Ages, the only way they were getting there was to hitch a ride with Mom and Anna.

It wasn't Anna's fault, however, that they wanted to go.

Callum had just sat down in a straight-back chair set kitty corner to the couch, but he stood without having taken a bite, his plate in his hand. He checked the screen and then put the phone to his ear. "Callum."

Cassie and Anna kept their eyes fixed on his face. As Callum listened without speaking, the muscles around his eyes and mouth tightened. The phone call wasn't going well. In anticipation of immediate action, Anna split a roll in half and filled it with some of the turkey and cranberry sauce from her plate. As she was working, Mom entered the room. Seeing Callum on his phone, and Anna making a sandwich, she set her plate down on the coffee table and stood looking at him, her hands on her hips.

Callum said, "Do we have any leads?"

Anna glanced at Cassie, who leaned in to her. "This must be about the explosion, not you."

Callum hung up. Cassie's whisper had caused Anna to miss the rest of Callum's conversation.

"We should go." Callum looked at Art. "Any chance of finding Meg and Anna a change of clothes before we leave?"

Art stood and disappeared through the door that led to the kitchen, which Anna took to be a 'yes' or at the very least a 'maybe'. Callum tipped his head towards the hallway that led to the bathroom and bedrooms. If nothing else, Anna was determined to use the toilet before they left.

"Who was that?" Cassie said as the four companions formed a huddle, their heads together.

"*That* was Dave Smith," Callum said, and then added for Mom's and Anna's benefit, "Smith works for the Permanent Secretary of the Home Office, who has overseen MI-5 for many years. Since September, I have reported to him. Before that, as I said earlier, the Project was independent, subject to the oversight of the Prime Minister himself."

"September was when they started reeling us in," Cassie said.

Callum held up his phone. "First things first: the Home Office wants us to go dark until they can confirm what might have been stolen from GCHQ before the bombing and how catastrophic the loss of intelligence is." Callum turned to Anna and Mom. "GCHQ was an information gathering agency like your NSA. All of our assets and resources may have been compromised, including our mobile numbers, IDs, and personal information." He swiftly dismantled his phone by removing the back cover, the SIM card, and the battery. He nodded at Cassie. "You need to take yours apart too."

Cassie pulled her phone from her pocket. She hesitated for a second and then took the plunge, taking off the back as Callum had. "I feel naked without it."

Callum smirked.

"What about us? Does MI-5 know we're here?" Mom said.

"Not that Smith said to me, and you would think he would have done if he had known the flash had taken place twenty miles from here," Callum said.

"You are trusted," Cassie said. "Smith would have said something."

Callum glanced at her and then continued, "I'm sure of nothing at this point."

"So the call was only about the bombing?" Anna said.

Callum nodded. "It was a call I've been waiting for since I spoke with Jones earlier about your arrival. MI-5 is recalling me to help manage the aftermath. I am to make my way as soon as possible to the consulate in San Francisco, which will arrange for a plane to take us home."

"Take you home, you mean," Mom said.

"How bad is it?" Cassie said. "Did Dave give you the number of casualties?"

"Not precisely." Callum checked his watch. "It's been only two hours since it happened, if that. It's still burning. At least a hundred were known to be in the building."

"Even this late at night?" Mom said.

"These are technical people mostly," Callum said. "They don't sleep at night, and even if they did, GCHQ was manned around the clock."

"What about getting in touch with Mark?" Cassie said.

"He texted me right before the call from Smith came in. He's picked up some chatter," Callum said.

"What kind of chatter?" Mom said.

"I assume David told you about his abduction from MI-5 two years ago?" Callum said.

"As much as he knew, which wasn't much," Mom said.

"It was accomplished by a private security company—the Dunland Group," Callum said. "Since the start of the Iraq war back in '03, it was the top bidder on dozens of military contracts all over the world, particularly for the British government."

Cassie nodded. "The company was discredited in the UK because of the fallout from what happened with David, but they've rebranded and continued to win contracts in other countries, including the United States. The CIA promised us a different outcome, but it didn't happen. The company is now called CMI—Conflict Management Industries—and it's like they hardly skipped a beat. They're bigger than ever."

"So ... they might be after us?" Mom said, looking from Cassie to Callum and asking the question in a more calm way than Anna would have. What MI-5 had done in the last two instances of time travel was bad enough, but the Dunland Group hadn't had MI-5's restraint. Which was saying something.

"We have a source inside CMI, and he reports that the head office lit up like a beacon starting at 4:30 this afternoon, moments after you arrived," Callum said. "Admittedly, it could have something to do with the bombing. The two events happened very close together."

"Why do we have to do this over and over again?" Mom said. "It's the same every time."

"Maybe it doesn't have to be," Anna said.

"What do you mean?" Mom said.

"I know that two years ago MI-5 agents sold David to the Dunland Group, but most of the time the people chasing him or you—the vast majority, in fact—were just doing their jobs. Like Callum was doing his when he organized the hunt for you and Papa. These aren't bad people. There's no good guys and bad guys here. Just guys."

Callum rubbed his chin. "It is kind of you to suggest that MI-5 would do the right thing if it had the whole picture."

"It did have the whole picture," Anna said. "Your office is proof of that, even if the new Prime Minister has lost his nerve."

Mom nodded. "Callum was in charge of all of this, and even if it's fallen apart now, it indicates that some of these people want to do the right thing."

"It's a nice thought, but we can't take the time to explain it to Director Tate," Callum said. "If he refused to listen to reason, the consequences would be too severe."

Anna let out a breath, trying to put aside her disappointment. She'd had a hope there for a second that reasonable people could find reasonable solutions, but maybe she was too used to dealing with David and Papa.

"Why would CMI still be pursuing us if your government isn't?" Mom said to Callum.

"Their priorities and pressures are not the same," he said.

"You may be right about individual choices," Cassie said, "but everything else has become about money. The Middle Ages has plenty of corruption, I know, but in this century it has only gotten worse."

"We could go home," Mom said. "Stop this before it starts."

Anna started to say, "We can't—" but Cassie looked at Callum and said, "The whole crash-the-car thing could work just as well in my grandfather's truck as in any other vehicle."

"And if it doesn't?" Callum said.

"We won't know until we try," she said.

"We need to think hard about the how and the why before we throw ourselves over a cliff," Callum said. "We have to be sure."

"We can't ever be sure," Cassie said. "You know that."

"But we can minimize the risk," Callum said.

"Like Meg did at Chepstow when she jumped with Goronwy and Llywelyn?" Cassie said.

"Exactly," Callum said.

Cassie rubbed the back of her neck, and Callum tapped on his lip with one finger. He knew more than Anna did about the danger they were in, and if they needed to go back to medieval Wales now, she would go. But she had David's vision in her head too. It wasn't just his. It belonged to all of them. Anna decided to say it:

"I know you want to get home, Mom, and you want me safe. I want to be safe. We've all had enough danger for one day, and it would be great to make it home almost in time to finish that meal and to put my boys in bed. But we can't. David's agenda is too important."

"Agenda?" Callum said.

Anna pulled out the list and handed it to him. "We don't want to waste this trip if we can possibly help it."

Callum unfolded the paper. While he read it, Mom said, "If we don't try to return right away, where should we go and what should we do? I don't think it's safe to stay here."

"It isn't." Callum spoke absently, still studying the list. "We have to assume the worst, not the best." He looked up. "We shouldn't put Cassie's family in the crosshairs of either the government or its subsidiaries more than they are right now by association with us."

"Are they in real danger?" Anna said.

Cassie's brow furrowed. "Not for their lives." She shot a quick glance at Callum. "Not that, but they might find themselves answering uncomfortable questions—and with the anti-terrorism statutes, those questions could get quite uncomfortable indeed."

"So we go." Anna didn't feel up to asking about anti-terrorism statutes.

"I don't disagree. But I repeat: go where?" Mom said.

"You need glasses, Mom," Anna said.

She rolled her eyes. "That's the least of our worries."

Cassie looked at Mom. "How bad are your eyes, Meg?"

"It's nothing—"

"She can't see anything anymore unless it's five feet in front of her," Anna said. "Or maybe three. She needs those progressive things, which we don't have the technology to make back at home."

Callum looked up from the list. "Strangely, I'm thinking that this time around you'd be safer in the UK than here. If we can get you there, we can find ourselves a nice castle with a moat to fall into."

Anna laughed.

"Anna and I don't have passports," Mom said, ever practical.

"We can get them out on a diplomatic visa, can't we?" Cassie said to Callum.

He rubbed his chin.

"You've had an idea, I can see it," Cassie said.

"There's no reason not to bring the rest of you on the plane to Cardiff too. Until then, we'll stay out of contact with anyone from our government or yours," Callum said.

"Not even Mark?" Cassie said.

Callum held up one finger. "With the exception of Jones."

"How are you going to work that?" Anna said.

"He and I have a backup plan," Callum said, "saved for just this type of occasion."

Cassie made a 'hm' sound and fluttered her eyelashes for a second. She looked pleased. "As do we."

Callum nodded. "We may get to that."

Anna didn't know what they were talking about and guessed that she wasn't meant to. And least not yet.

"I'm impressed. You're going to pull us in under the radar," Mom said. "The bombing is the perfect excuse. Nobody is going to question you as long as you look serious and make noise about national security."

Callum canted his head. "Exactly." And then he added, "It helps that I am serious about national security."

Then his attention was caught by something behind Anna. She turned to see Art coming down the hall, followed by one of Cassie's aunts, who held a stack of clothing in her arms.

"We guessed your sizes as best we could." She held the pile out to Anna, who took it.

"Thank you."

Cassie's aunt turned away without another word. Art made a small movement with his mouth that might have been an apologetic smile. "She's worried that you have brought down trouble on the family."

"I don't think we have," Callum said, "especially if we leave within the hour. Only Jones knows we're here, and he's scrubbing any trace of our conversation as we speak."

"Good." Art gestured to the bathroom. "Use whatever you need."

"Thank you," Anna said again.

But Mom stepped forward and dipped her head. Anna had honestly never seen her do that, since nobody in the Middle Ages held a rank higher than hers except possibly her son, and he didn't count.

"We really appreciate your help," Mom said to Art. "I'm sorry for whatever inconvenience we've caused you or your family."

Art looked back at her, his face impassive. And then he said. "You are family to Cassie." As if that made all the difference. To him, it seemed it did.

Mom and Anna crowded into the bathroom, which was long and narrow, wallpapered in shades of brown and yellow, a fashion that predated Anna's birth. Art and his sister weren't wealthy by any means, which only made it more generous of them that they were sharing what they had.

"Do I have time for a two-minute shower?" Anna said.

Mom nodded, and Anna turned on the water, stripping down while she waited for it to warm up. The sight of water pouring from the showerhead had tears pricking at the corners of Anna's eyes. It was silly of her to have missed showers enough to cry over them. Though, after a moment's contemplation, Anna could see that she wasn't crying about the shower as much as feeling overwhelmed by their circumstances.

She didn't make the mistake of washing her hair, because that would ruin the balance of natural oils that had taken years to achieve, but she scrubbed at her scalp with her nails and soaped up the rest of her. The two minutes went by far too quickly, and then she was out, and Mom was in.

Anna stood with the towel wrapped around her body and stared at the long mirror above the sink. She hadn't seen herself properly in nine years. Most mirrors in the Middle Ages were simply highly polished circles of bronze, tin, or silver. Mirrors made of thin sheets of glass backed by metal had been invented, but they were expensive. Anna had a small one at Dinas Bran, but she'd grown used to not seeing what she really looked like.

The woman who stared back at her was hardly recognizable as the seventeen-year-old girl she'd last seen. Leaning forward, Anna inspected her face. It was thinner than she remembered, and when she smiled, tiny crow's feet appeared at the corners of her brown eyes. She hadn't cut her hair in nine years either, and even with the curls, it fell past her hips, dark on her white skin.

"It's weird to see yourself, isn't it?" Mom stepped out of the shower. "I thought so too when I came back the first time."

"I'm not even the same person," Anna said.

"I would hope not," Mom said.

Anna turned to look at Mom, thinking about the girl her mother had been—and she herself had been—the first time they'd time traveled to the Middle Ages. "I'll just ask this once because it needs to be asked: are you sure you want to go back?"

"Do you?"

"Yes."

"Showers, sugar, antibiotics—they don't draw you?" Mom said.

"Of course they draw me." Anna snorted laughter. "But hot showers are hardly what living is about."

"It may take some effort to return," Mom said. "And it will be dangerous."

"I know. And you didn't answer my question."

Mom blinked. "I didn't think I had to. But I'll say it out loud if you want: yes. My life is there, not here. I spent every moment since your brother was born trying to get back to Llywelyn. I'm not leaving him now."

"It would be easier."

"Would it?" And then Mom nodded. "It's hard work caring for other people. Being a mom. Sometimes you just want to go to bed and sleep for a week."

"But you never can," Anna said.

Mom smiled. "Living isn't for the faint of heart, is it?"

8

November 2019

Meg

A nna had taken a shower first, but Meg was ready before she was. While Meg was waiting for her daughter to come out of the bathroom, Callum pulled her aside. "Do you trust me?"

"Of course," Meg said. "Why do you ask?"

"There may come a moment when I will need you to do what I say, when I say it, without asking questions," he said.

Meg raised her eyebrows. "You forget who you're talking to. Llywelyn has asked that of me more than once." She looked down at herself, arms spread. "The modern clothes are just a cover for the medieval me."

He coughed and laughed at the same time. "Are you saying you're a submissive medieval woman now?"

"It hasn't been my experience that medieval women are all that submissive," Meg said dryly. "Uneducated and without rights, yes." She paused. "What I meant was that taking orders won't offend me—you know more about what's going on than I do. I don't have a problem with that."

He nodded.

Meg looked at him carefully. "Don't think for a second that Anna and I aren't aware what you're risking for us."

Callum didn't try to deny it. "It's my job."

"Your job is not to smuggle us out of the United States. You could lose everything if you do."

"Not everything," he said. "I went down on one knee before your son and swore my allegiance to him. If smuggling you out of the United States is the best way to serve him and keep you safe, then that's what I'm going to do."

He was sincere and serious, and Meg fumbled for a reply. David was her son, and she adored him, but because he was her son, the fact that he was the King of England too usually passed her by. "I've watched him grow into the leader he's become, but it's so strange to me how he manages to turn everyone around him into loyal followers."

Callum's brow furrowed. "Is that what you think I am? Some sycophant?"

"No-no!" Meg put out a hand. "I didn't mean to insult you at all. We all follow him."

But Callum was still shaking his head. "You really don't understand, do you?"

Meg eyed him. "Understand what?"

"Who David is." When Meg didn't answer, he added, "His rule isn't about accruing followers."

Meg looked away, a little ashamed. "I know." She lifted one shoulder, trying to explain. "I look at him sometimes, and I don't even know him anymore. He makes a decision and it affects three million people. How can such a person be my son?"

"I'm sorry I haven't been there to help him carry the burden for the last two years," Callum said.

Meg let out a dry laugh. "I remember when he was in middle school—those boys with their machismo and their fears— they mocked him for all those qualities that have turned him into a king—honesty, integrity, and righteousness. How David hated it."

"And now we rise—or we fall—on his decisions. It's his shoulders that carry us. His qualities that determine our future."

"Anna isn't ready to return home because she's figured that out about him too," Meg said. "She sees him the same way you do."

"You're his mother," Callum said. "You see his flaws. The rest of us can't afford to."

Meg bit her lip and looked away. Callum wasn't entirely right. She adored her son. She'd known how special he was before he was two years old. She'd forced herself to see his flaws because if she didn't, who would?

"By the way," Callum said when she didn't answer him, "I've spoken with your brother-in-law several times over the last two years and hopefully patched things up a bit between you."

Meg was glad for the change of subject. "I have worried about what happened to him after Llywelyn and I left, but since I had no way to find out, I tried to put it out of my mind."

"Aye," Callum said, reverting to his Scottish roots. "I worried about him too." He gave a rueful smile. "I didn't fear for his life, but Lady Jane could be a bit merciless when she chose. She could have thrown him into a cell, whether or not he was an American citizen. But after Chepstow, Lady Jane let him go. Cassie and I stopped in to see them on our way home from Oregon two years ago, and I gave him and your sister your best wishes."

"Thank you," Meg said, and then her breath caught in her throat. "If Homeland Security or this military contractor know that we've arrived, even if way out here in Oregon, is Elisa going to find men in black beating down her door at 3 am?"

Callum made an 'ach' sound at the back of his throat. "To say, 'I hope not' isn't adequate, I know. If someone from your government discovers you're here and cares that you're here, he might contact them. It is something to be concerned about."

"I should warn them," Meg said.

Callum shook his head. "You can't. Not yet. It could be the red flag that starts the ball rolling. Besides, Elisa and Ted know what to do."

"What do you mean?"

Callum let out a *whuf* of air. "This was all theoretical before two hours ago." He looked up at the ceiling for a second, marshalling his thoughts. "Cassie and I have been working on this problem—your problem—nonstop for two years. We knew one of you could come through at any time, and we wanted to be ready. It was an impossible task, I know, but we tried to think of every contingency, every possibility. It meant that Cassie and I spoke at length with Ted and Elisa, trying to impress upon them the extent of the threat against you if the government came knocking. We concluded, with their consent, that it was better for them not to know anything. That way, they wouldn't have to lie."

"That means I can't talk to my sister." Meg looked down at her shoes.

"That's what it means."

Meg brought up her head to find him looking at her thoughtfully.

"I admit I didn't expect you to arrive on Thanksgiving night in the wilds of Oregon." Callum gave a bark of laughter. "When the best-laid plan comes face to face with reality, guess which loses every time."

Twenty minutes later, the four of them piled into Art's truck, Cassie at the wheel. Callum was an equal-opportunity kind of guy, but still, having her drive didn't strike Meg as his natural tendency any more than it had been Llywelyn's when she had driven across Wales in the dead of night, pregnant with twins. But driving on the right side of the road would have been even less natural for Callum. Also, it had started snowing again, and Meg was willing to bet he hadn't had a ton of experience driving in snow either.

"Back way or highway?" Cassie said to Callum, starting the truck and shifting into drive.

"I'd like to avoid metropolitan areas if possible." Callum glanced at Anna and Meg sitting in the back seat. The space between Meg's knees and his seat wasn't a lot, but the seat was comfortable and the heater blasted warm air into her face. "At least nobody is following us out of this driveway, and with no mobile phones and an ancient truck—" He put out a hand to Cassie, "—no offense to your grandfather, Cassie."

"None taken," she said.

"—nobody, whether MI-5, Homeland Security, or anybody else, can track us."

"I looked up the Oregon DMV online before we got in the truck," Cassie said. "There's a pair of highway cameras at Arlington and another at Biggs, before the turnoff south to Bend. Then it gets worse. Highway 97 through Bend has a ton of cameras."

"That's not ideal," Callum said. "And those are only the ones we know about. What are our other choices?"

"We could head south out of Pendleton on 395. There are only three traffic cameras between here and the California border," Cassie said. "There's a lot less traffic, too, and it'll take longer, so those are two drawbacks."

"Less traffic is bad?" Anna said.

"You can't get lost in the crowd if you're the only car on the road," Cassie said.

"It's still Thanksgiving night," Meg said. "If we can get farther faster, would that be better?"

Callum spread a map across his lap. He nodded as he looked at it.

Meg sat back in her seat. "I can drive too, Cassie."

Anna poked her mother in the arm. "You haven't driven a car in three years."

"It's like riding a bike," Meg said. "You never forget."

"I thought you needed glasses?" Anna said.

Meg grimaced. She'd forgotten that her night vision was particularly awful.

"We can get you glasses at Wal-Mart," Cassie said. "Maybe in Klamath Falls."

"How are we going to do that?" Meg swallowed down an accompanying snort of disbelief.

"You wouldn't believe what they've got kiosks for these days," Cassie said. "They craft the lenses right then and there. You stick your head in this machine, it evaluates your eyes, and once you choose the frames, it makes the lenses to fit." She glanced up to the mirror again to look at Meg. "You probably ought to choose simple metal frames so they don't cause comment at home."

"I'd like that." Meg swallowed back the emotion that had formed in her throat, not only over the idea of being able to see again, but at Cassie's use of the word *home*. Meg had been inadvertently responsible for Cassie spending five years alone in the Middle Ages. Cassie had never faulted Meg for it or complained about it when she thought Meg wasn't listening. And now it seemed that Cassie was taking for granted not only that it was home for Meg but that it was home for her too.

Nobody else seemed to have noticed Cassie's use of the word, or at least they didn't comment on it.

Because of that, Meg decided she'd better bring it up. She wasn't a big fan of elephants in the living room, even if they were of her own making. "Are we all on the same page here about going back? Anna and I have already talked, and I've gathered from brief conversations with both of you that you're on board, but maybe we should all just say it. Or say we don't want to."

Cassie and Callum exchanged a quick glance and neither answered, prompting Anna to lean forward. "Mom and I have husbands and children there—a whole family, in fact. You two are part of our family, but you have each other and are under no obligation to return to the Middle Ages with us. David would understand, Callum."

Something was going on, because still neither answered. Then Callum said, "Say what you're thinking, Cass." They were on the highway now, heading west.

Cassie took in a breath. "Okay. Here's the truth, which is what we all need to put out there: I've thought about it a lot. So much that sometimes I think I'm going crazy thinking about it." She glanced in the rearview mirror and caught Meg's eye. "Two A.M. is not my friend."

"I hear you," Meg said.

"I've known for a while, though, that I don't belong here as much as I belong there. Those five years in Scotland changed me. It isn't just that I found Callum, but that I found myself."

"Your grandfather told me that he liked who you became there," Callum said.

Cassie smiled, but her eyes were very bright, and when she spoke next Meg could hear the tears in the back of her throat. "The last thing my grandfather said to me when he hugged me goodbye just now was that we needed to go if we could. He believes that everything happens for a reason, and I would be wrong to turn off the path laid before my feet."

Meg gave that admission the moment of silent respect it deserved. It was exactly what she herself thought. Then she looked at Callum. "What about you?"

Callum turned in his seat so he could see Meg and Anna better. "Does David want me back?"

Meg choked on a laugh. "Want you back? Are you kidding me?"

"That's a 'yes', then?" Callum said.

"Definitely a 'yes'," Anna said. "He trusts you and sometimes feels like he's ruling Britain by the seat of his pants. He has plans, but a lot of the time I don't think he trusts himself completely."

"What do you mean?" Cassie said. "Is this a power corrupts thing?"

"Power, adulation," Anna said, making Meg think about the conversation she'd just had with Callum. "But more than those two, David worries that he'll take short-cuts and compromise his beliefs. That he'll come to think that the end justifies the means. He knows he needs all of us to keep him sane and on the right track. It would be easy to get off it."

"I've tried to put all my responsibilities back there out of my mind since I couldn't do anything about them," Callum said. "But I have to ask: am I still the Earl of Shrewsbury?"

"You are," Anna said. "David has taken personal responsibility for your people while you've been absent, Samuel continues to oversee the day-to-day stuff, and Math has been checking in from time to time too. You have a very capable sheriff, which is good, and everyone knows that you are in Avalon and will return when you can."

Cassie laughed. "Did you say 'Avalon'?"

"She did," Meg said, "and you might want to laugh, but it's the only explanation that anyone can accept. If David has to put up with it, we all do. And honestly, thank God for it because otherwise we'd all be branded as witches."

"Which we want to avoid," Cassie said. "I'm good with that."

"What happened when David returned to you?" Callum said. "We haven't even asked."

Now it was Meg's turn to laugh. "A war, that's what!" And between her and Anna, they spent the next hour as Cassie drove west down I-84, telling them about William de Valence's rise and fall, along with the continued development of reforms David and

Llywelyn were working on in England and Wales. They concluded with David's vision for the future he'd just told them about.

When they'd finished, Callum folded his hands at the back of his head and stared up at the ceiling of the truck. "I wish Lady Jane could have been here to hear this."

"It's just as well she isn't," Cassie said. "The time travel initiative can die an unmourned death, and we won't be here to answer anyone's questions. If we can get out of our current situation in one piece, that is."

"I hope we don't have a military contractor on our tail." Meg patted Callum's arm. "I thought MI-5 was bad, but they sound much worse."

"I'm about to be sacked," he said, "so I can hardly complain if you point out how poorly you were treated."

"David was treated worse," Cassie said, "and it was the military contractor that drugged him. I'd take Homeland Security any day over them."

Callum glanced at his wife. "They aren't the buffoons the media makes them out to be. They have resources and the full power of the American government should they choose to wield it."

The windshield wipers started sweeping faster, and Meg put up a hand to wipe away the steam on her window. The snow was falling harder. "We probably should go all the way to I-5 in Portland," she said. "The road to Bend is often closed with blowing snow in winter."

"I know." Cassie ground her teeth. "It isn't even December! Why is it snowing?"

"You've lived in Britain for too long," Meg said.

"We'll all be back in Britain a bit sooner than we intended if the snow keeps up," Anna said, looking out her window. "We won't have to worry about finding a tower to jump off."

In theory, that would have been just fine with Meg, but David would be disappointed that they hadn't managed to gather anything on his list except for Cassie and Callum. Though even he would have to admit that finding them was a pretty amazing thing for Meg and Anna to have accomplished within two hours of their arrival.

But for better or for worse, they didn't crash. Cassie safely navigated the highway interchanges in Portland. As they passed the city, Meg thought about her life and friends there and then put them from her mind. They couldn't help her.

As the hour approached midnight, they passed the sign marking the city limits of Eugene, Oregon. Cassie pulled off the highway to get gas for the second time, and after Callum paid the attendant, drove to the twenty-four hour Wal-Mart.

Never mind that it was midnight on Thanksgiving when all sane people should be sleeping off their turkey and pumpkin pie, the parking lot was packed with Black Friday shoppers. It seemed they'd just missed the midnight crush to get inside the doors. Last Meg had heard, 'Black Friday' had been pushed to as early as four A.M. That appeared to have changed since she lived here. Pretty soon the stores would open on Thanksgiving Day, and everyone could skip the turkey entirely.

Callum slung his backpack over his shoulder and handed a second backpack to Cassie. He saw Meg looking at him and said, "I know it's paranoid of me, but I don't want to leave anything in the truck that will identify us. What's in here—" He raised the backpack, "—is too precious to lose to a sneak thief."

"Or Homeland Security," Cassie said, shrugging her pack onto her shoulders.

"Is that all you brought?" Meg said. She and Anna owned only what they stood up in, but Meg had thought she'd seen a suitcase in the hallway before they left. Cassie had taken their medieval clothes, and Meg's stomach sank to think they'd left them behind.

"We left our bigger bag at Cassie's aunt's house, so we wouldn't be burdened with it," Callum said. "It just contained clothes, and we can buy new if we need them."

Cassie saw Meg's crestfallen face and made a sad face of her own, "I'm sorry, Meg."

"They're just things," Meg said. "They aren't worth our lives. I suppose if we had them with us and were caught, they would be a huge giveaway."

"Which we wouldn't want. We want to keep you under wraps." Cassie touched Meg's shoulder sympathetically.

But Anna leaned close to her mother. "My belt knife is in my boot. How about yours?"

Meg had left that behind too. She shook her head.

"I should have said something." Anna frowned. "Does Wal-Mart have metal detectors?"

"I guess we'll find out," Meg said.

"Are these people mad?" Callum said as he bulldozed his way through the crowded entryway, the three women in his wake.

The companions popped out to the left of the entrance, in front of the endless row of cash registers. A wave of heat blew over Meg, so she pulled off her hat and unbuttoned the black wool coat she'd borrowed from Cassie's aunt's house. Anna shrugged out of her bright purple parka and hung it over her arm. The store was lit up as if it were already Christmas—which Wal-Mart clearly hoped it was—and Meg averted her eyes from the blinding fluorescent lights.

The colors and variety of items for sale were almost too much to take in. People like to have choices, but they were actually happier with fewer choices than more, which might explain the intent and grim expressions on everybody's faces. Shopping was definitely a serious business in Eugene, Oregon on Black Friday. Meg had been hoping it would be merrier—like a party.

"Over here, Mom." Anna hauled her mother to where Cassie was standing in front of the eyeglasses machine.

"It says it takes forty minutes, all told. Thirty if you choose one of the eight standard frames," Cassie said.

"That I can do." Without hesitating, Meg put her face up to a rubber sleeve, which strongly resembled a diving mask, and did everything the machine told her to do. Beside her, Cassie punched numbers into a keypad, and then Meg heard the distinct sound of a card being inserted. The lights that flashed in Meg's eyes had momentarily ceased, so she pulled out her head. "I can't let you pay for this."

"You can, and you will," Cassie said. "That's what we're here for. Besides, Callum left a wad of cash with my grandfather. If we return to the Middle Ages, my grandfather will pay the bill. You're not to worry about it."

The machine was beeping at Meg, ready to start again. She didn't feel so guilty that she didn't put her face back into the headrest and let the machine continue its calculations. She needed glasses.

Anna said, "Are you using a fake ID?"

Cassie laughed. "Of course. Credit cards are the worst for sending up red flags. Nobody can buy anything without the government knowing because both the store you bought it from *and* the credit card company know. This machine won't take cash, of course, so we have no choice but to use a card. Callum will use a different card to pay for what he's getting."

Callum had wandered off and came back just as the machine was finishing with Meg's eyes. He'd lined his cart with an open duffle bag. "Let's see the list again, Anna," he said.

Meg pulled out her head. "You're thinking we should get started?"

"We have half an hour until your glasses are done. We might as well use the time," Cassie said.

Callum nodded. "Best to be prepared for every contingency."

They left the glasses machine to do its thing and wandered the aisles of Wal-Mart with what seemed like half the population of Eugene. Meg kept getting distracted by the colors and the plastic, but Anna and Callum took to the project with a will. Within fifteen minutes, they had worked their way through the basics of David's list, including the coveted potatoes (three different kinds) and tomato seeds. It was too bad that neither chocolate nor coffee beans (these were from originally from Africa, but they hadn't been 'discovered' and cultivated by 1290) would grow in the British climate.

Meg knew, and had to restrain herself from explaining in a David-esque manner, that some historians had even suggested that the introduction of the potato as a staple of food production in Europe after 1492 was enough to account for the rise of Western Europe as a superpower. Meg wasn't big on increasing the population too fast, but greater population meant more minds at work and could lead to more scientific advances and more hands to do the work that needed doing. So, potatoes it was.

Cassie took it upon herself to organize the items they were buying into categories. With a smile at Meg, she took an entire box of SPF 15 lip balm and tucked it into the duffel bag. "Bronwen specifically mentioned the blue kind."

"I believe you," Meg said.

"Anything you want, Mom?" Anna flourished the list in one hand.

Meg gazed around at the choices and—quite frankly—the excess, and shook her head. "I'm sure I'll want to bring some things back, but I keep thinking about what it looks like for us to have modern luxuries—plastic in particular—and so I decide to do without. What I want most are the things that I really can't have: a cell phone, a ball point pen, a car, and—" she picked up a novel with a picture of Stonehenge on the cover, "—something to read." Then she smiled. "I could do with some thick cotton socks."

Anna smiled back. "We'll swing by and pick up a couple pairs on the way to see if your glasses are done."

While Callum paid for the pile of goodies, Anna, Cassie, and Meg trooped back to the vision center where a very helpful—and very tired—employee presented Meg with glasses in a bright red case. Meg had chosen simple pewter frames, more angular than round, which appeared to be the current style. She put them on and about fell over. Meg had forgotten what it was like to *see*. She spent a few minutes alternating between looking through the glasses and lowering them to look over the top of the frames.

"What do you think?" This time it was Cassie bouncing up and down, clearly pleased with the gift.

"I don't know what to say," Meg said. "Thank you just isn't enough."

"My pleasure," Cassie said. "Truly."

Callum had also bought four cell phones, and once he joined the women, they all stood in an out-of-the-way spot near the bathrooms and customer service, and he opened one of the packages. It was so loud in the store that nobody was going to overhear what they were discussing.

"You got four phones?" Cassie accepted hers. "Why?"

"One, the Black Friday sale had these marked two for the price of one, so why not get four?" Callum said. "And two, these mobiles work internationally. The odds of anyone tracing them before we get out of the country later today are very slim, and I want to be able to keep in contact in case we get separated."

"They're nice." Anna turned hers over in her hands. "Last I saw, touchscreens were expensive."

Meg squeezed her shoulder. "It's the little things that trip you up."

Callum looked up from his phone. "Can you keep driving, Cassie? I have work to do."

"Get me some coffee, and I'll be good to go," she said.

Meg didn't offer to drive again, even with her new glasses. When she looked over Callum's shoulder at his phone, amazingly, she could read the small print on the screen, even though it wasn't two inches from her nose. Twenty minutes earlier, she wouldn't have been able even to see it. "What do you mean, 'work'?"

"We're on a blackout with MI-5 due to the bombing, so I'm not expected to make contact with anyone until I return to Cardiff. I need to talk to Jones, however. He and I established a procedure—not just for me but for any agent in distress or who's been compromised—to fall back on pre-arranged email accounts and new mobiles. Give me a second."

Callum worked furiously on his phone for five minutes while the three women unpacked their phones and turned them on. Then Callum looked up at Anna and Meg. "Jones sent a message to my account, giving me his new number. Before I ring him, I need your photos."

"Our photos?" Anna said.

"ID, Anna," Meg said. "I think we're about to see what technology can do again."

Callum lined up Anna and then Meg against a square of white wall in the lobby of Wal-Mart, taking photos of each of them in turn. He texted them to Mark and then switched to telephone mode and dialed Mark's number that, as far as Meg could tell, he'd memorized in the two seconds he'd been looking at his email.

Mark picked up. Meg could hear his tinny voice, even from a few feet away. "I received the photos. Where are you?"

Callum brought the phone down, put it on speaker set to a low volume, and the four friends huddled around it. "About to start driving again. This is a big country and it's going to take a while. Where are you?"

"Hang on." There was a pause, a flurry of conversation in the background, and then the slamming of a door. "Good job I had a spare mobile ready to go because I wouldn't have had a chance to slip away. I'm in the maintenance closet."

Cassie and Callum exchanged a bemused look, which Meg didn't understand, and then Callum said, "What's the situation?"

"It's chaos in here right now. We've been taken over by Signals."

"What's 'Signals' again?" Meg said.

"It's the nickname for the agency that got bombed," Cassie said.

"Has there been any mention of the Project?" Callum said.

"Not so far," Mark said. "Earlier, I spent two hours orienting the techs who arrived. They're rebuilding the system from the ground up. They assume Signals was compromised before it was bombed."

"That's what Smith said when he recalled me," Callum said.

"You're still seen as lily white, by the way. Incorruptible. Wish you were here to glare at these people, because they don't trust me," Mark said. "I've been twiddling my thumbs for the last half hour. They took over my whole system."

"I can't be sorry about that," Callum said, "because I need you." He gave Mark a brief rundown of the last few hours since he'd gone dark, and his concerns regarding his ability to arrive safely in San Francisco.

Meg looked sideways at the Black Friday shoppers around them. No one even seemed to notice them.

Mark said that he couldn't use the usual channels because of the blackout on communication, but he could still monitor the situation and see what the chatter was like at other agencies. "My coffee shop has been open for two hours. I'll go there with my own laptop. And I'll see what I can do about getting Meg and Anna ID."

"We'll call you when we get closer to the airport in San Francisco," Callum said.

"I should have a better grasp of the situation by then," Mark said.

Callum ended the connection.

"I thought we were going to the consulate?" Anna said.

"Did I say that? I didn't mean it. With communications down, neither MI-5 nor we can risk it," Callum said, "though they don't know why I agreed so readily since they don't know about you two." He smirked.

"Callum waves that badge around, and everybody obeys," Cassie said. "It isn't far off from being the Earl of Shrewsbury, come to think about it."

Meg gazed out the store window at the parking lot, lit up with a million fluorescent lights. They were there to make the parking lot safer, but the harsh bright white was anything but comforting.

Anna reached out and took her hand. "I feel like this ought to be different, somehow. Like I ought to be feeling something more momentous, or doing something more momentous, than shopping at a Wal-Mart."

Meg squeezed Anna's hand. "I don't know about that. Shopping is the worst and the best of American living. Twenty-four kinds of toothbrushes and a pair of glasses that lets me see your face clearly from across the room for the first time in two years. I'll take it."

9

November 1291

David

"My lord ... may I ask you something?" William de Bohun said.

At sixteen years old, William had become a full-fledged member of the Order of the Pendragon. Although no longer a child, he still looked at David through the same calm brown eyes he'd shown in the church outside Llangollen. David had taken him on as his squire not merely as a way to control his father, which was a good reason in and of itself, but because he was a member of the up-and-coming generation of Anglo-Normans. If David was to rule England, he needed to win the hearts and minds of William and his peers.

Besides, David liked him.

"Of course," David said.

"About what happened this evening ..." William paused again, and David could practically see the gears turning in that blonde head as he tried to think of the best way to phrase what he wanted to ask.

David waited while William stalled by tightening down the buckle on David's left bracer a little too tightly. David put his free hand on William's arm and looked at him. "Just ask."

"I was standing on the battlement with a sentry when your sister and mother arrived at the top of the southwest tower. I had no other duties at the time." He hastened to add these last words with a worried glance at his lord's face.

"It is fine, William," David said. "I was with my family and had given you leave to go. There was no reason for you not to be on the battlement."

From David's perspective, it was better for William to be there than in the storage closet with the latest girl he'd taken a fancy to. David needed to have a conversation with William about his responsibilities in that regard. If the girl became pregnant, William's father would never in a million years allow him to marry her, and it would open the whole can of worms about what it meant to be illegitimate. It was okay in Wales as long as the father acknowledged the child. Not so okay in England. And the Church wouldn't like it, of course.

William swallowed. "Yes, my lord."

"So you saw them fall." David wasn't asking a question.

"And disappear," William said. "I don't understand how such a thing could happen."

David laughed under his breath. "Neither do I, William. I only know that it did, and we must continue to act as if such a thing was meant to happen."

"Oh, I know that." William gazed at David intently. "Such was not my concern."

David narrowed his eyes at his squire. "Then what?"

"It's about the man who fell with them and died," William said. "Who was he?"

"A mistake, clearly," David said.

William's lower lip jutted out a bit because he thought David was either dismissing him or not being truthful.

So David added, "Martin knew my mother from years ago. I was raised in Avalon. You know that, right?"

William nodded. "Your father sent your mother there before she gave birth to protect you."

"Right." David didn't even grind his teeth at the lie he was telling. Though he'd fought it that very afternoon, he had to admit its necessity now more than ever. "When Anna and I returned here to save my father's life, my mother was left behind. A few months before I turned sixteen, she too returned, inadvertently bringing Martin with her. He had to leave Avalon because of her."

"Is that why you invited him to Rhuddlan? Because she felt guilty?"

It was both insightful and brave of him to ask that, and David decided not to slap him down for his impudence. The boy's intensity was making David cautious, and he chose his words carefully. "Not guilt so much as an apology. I sought to mend the rift that event caused in our lives and in his. I had hoped Martin would visit me in London two years ago, after he aided Lord Callum in his moment of need. I wanted to thank him. As King of England, I could have granted him whatever he wished."

"Except to return to Avalon," William said.

Again, William's response was more perceptive than David might have liked. He lifted one shoulder, wishing the conversation would end. But William had asked permission to speak, and David had agreed to answer his questions. He could hardly complain if they were more to the point than he expected.

"You're right. I wasn't going to offer him the chance to return to Avalon. Not because I didn't think he had earned it or because I didn't wish to, but because it isn't in my power to grant or deny. Two years have passed since I myself left Lord Callum there, against my will and his. I would have returned if I could have, but even I do not choose the moment when I am allowed entry."

"Only those of pure heart can enter Avalon," William said knowingly. "That's why Martin died. When your mother left Avalon with him, it was because she was needed here, but it seems to me that he must have been cast out at the same time."

David gave William a sharp look, which his squire didn't see since he had moved on to buckling David's right bracer. "Who told you that?"

William looked up. "No one. But it seems obvious, doesn't it?"

William had surprised David again. His thinking was clear, even if he was wrong. And it was a wrongness that David would be a fool not to exploit. "Perhaps it is I who have been cast out. That is why I have not been able to retrieve Lord Callum."

"Oh no!" William's face held an eager look. "It is not yet your time. Your sister and mother went to Avalon to save their lives. Isn't that what happened to you two years ago with the storm in the Irish Sea? You would have drowned if God hadn't held you in the palm of his hand."

At some point, William was going to realize that David was as human as he. But the boy had been a witness to much of what had happened to David and what he'd done over the past three years, ever since William's father had surprised David by putting William in his care to protect him. William still thought David infallible. "Thank you, William, for your faith in me. I pray I will continue to deserve it."

"Do you think I might be worthy to travel with you to Avalon one day?"

Ieuan had asked David that once, approximately five minutes before the English had shot him and David had taken him to the modern world. David sincerely hoped William's asking wasn't an omen of things to come.

Before David decided how to answer him, Lili stepped through the open doorway. "Only God knows the answer to that question, William. Every day you should bring yourself to account, to ensure that if the opportunity arrives, you won't be found wanting."

"I will do that, my queen." William bowed. "Thank you."

Lili made a dismissive motion with her hand.

"I will meet you in the outer ward, William," David said.

William shot David a bright-eyed look and bowed. "My lord." He departed.

David shook his head at his wife. "You are incorrigible."

"It's a good thing I am," she said. "Otherwise, you would have tried to rid yourself of this story a long time ago."

"You are right. I would have." David stepped past her to look down the corridor. Men guarded both ends, but they were too far away to overhear.

His men were wary now, and more on their guard. They—like David—had thought everyone safe at Rhuddlan. It was a bit like closing the barn door after the horse had escaped, but security had been beefed up at all the entrances and exits, and nobody came or left without being searched. That said, even the lowliest villager carried a knife at his waist and wouldn't be asked to give it up. Marty had been where he was supposed to be, with a weapon he was supposed to have. David's men couldn't have been expected to read his mind.

Lili tugged David's cloak straight around his neck and smoothed the fabric across his shoulders. "I've become spoiled."

"In what way?" David was beginning to lose feeling in the fingers of his left hand because of William's over-enthusiastic tightening of his bracer. He began to work at the buckles to loosen them.

Lili saw David trying to deal with the armor one-handed and brushed away his hand in order to do it herself. "I have grown used to you not going to war." She tapped his chest, which was hard due to the steel-reinforced layer of Kevlar that lay underneath his armor.

"I hate to repeat what men have told their wives for thousands of years, but I will be fine," David said.

"You don't know that."

David stopped her fussing by taking both her hands in his and bringing them to his chest. "If I know anything, I know that. I have increasingly come to understand that I am here for a reason. I don't believe that reason has yet been accomplished."

"As long as it doesn't make you reckless," she said.

"When have I ever been reckless?" Though perhaps David should have crossed his fingers behind his back as he said this.

She dropped his hands and gave him a quelling look. "Shall I list the times?"

David held up a hand. "Scout's honor. I will behave. It would be stupid to die in such a little war."

"You'd better not." Lili went up on her toes and put her arms around his neck.

Since she was there, David kissed her. And then again. He didn't want to leave. By rights, it was bedtime, not the moment to be riding away from Rhuddlan in pursuit of a traitor and his army.

It was Lili who pulled away. "You'd better go. Arthur is not yet ready to be king, and you don't want me to change my mind about not coming with you to protect you."

"You're staying here to protect Arthur, Rhuddlan, and all the rest," David said. "I have already promised to celebrate Christmas at Westminster Palace and I intend to keep that promise."

Arthur had been put to bed, but David looked in on him and kissed him too. He didn't wake, even when David stroked a lock of his blonde hair out of his face. He'd already asked—in his little Arthurian sign language—to cut his hair so he could look like Cadell. David was resisting the loss of his babyhood, but it was a battle he was going to lose, if only because time was against him.

Ieuan met David as he descended the stairs into the inner ward. "Lili is well?"

"I didn't even have to ask her to stay behind. She won't leave Arthur, and she will help Goronwy defend Rhuddlan if need be."

Ieuan shot David a wry look. "Let's hope it doesn't come to that. Bronwen is the same, not that she has the training for war."

They reached the outer gatehouse where the men were gathering. It wasn't quite midnight. Math had already left, riding east by torchlight. Even now, scouts were scouring the countryside on all sides, calling to service men in outlying areas and making sure Madog was as far away as they thought he was. Those few common folk who owned horses would join the cavalry, and those who didn't would walk through the night and day tomorrow to arrive at Maentwrog when they could. Welsh armies, like all armies in this time, were composed primarily of citizen soldiery.

"You didn't send to Chester for reinforcements," Ieuan said.

"You noticed that?" David said.

"We have good men there," Ieuan said.

"Do you know why I didn't?"

"Oh, I know why, I just wanted to make sure you did."

David raised his eyebrows. "I am Welsh first, Ieuan, and I know my history. I know the poor precedent it would set if my father welcomed English troops, even his son's, into Wales. I ride today not as the King of England, but as a prince of Wales only."

Ieuan nodded, and his expression told David he was not only satisfied with the answer, but he agreed with it.

"If Madog and Rhys want to start a war with everyone, then England will come to the aid of Wales as an ally," David said. "But I'm hoping it won't come to that."

It was odd to see Dad mount his horse without Mom at his stirrup to bid him goodbye. David took his place beside him. They would lead a contingent of one hundred cavalry out of Rhuddlan, a combined force of David's mostly English *teulu* (the word meant 'family' in Welsh, a word heavy with meaning), which the English referred to merely as the king's guard, and Dad's entirely Welsh one.

Since David had arrived at Rhuddlan with his *teulu*, relations between the two sets of soldiers had been good. Better, in fact, than they historically would have. Prejudice against the Welsh hadn't exactly disappeared in the few years since David had become the King of England, but victory and prosperity had gone a long way towards fostering peaceful relations between the two countries. It wasn't only American presidents whose popularity ratings plummeted when the economy went bad.

David didn't know how many of his men trusted Dad; he hoped the majority of Dad's trusted him. But they all trusted Ieuan, which was the most important thing. Ieuan mounted just behind David, flanked by the captains of the two companies.

"Where do you think they are now?" Dad said by way of a greeting.

David knew without his father saying their names that he was referring to Mom and Anna, not Madog's army.

"You were there almost as recently as I," David said. "I don't know where they ended up. If they're in modern Wales, it's a small country, and I assume their first step would be to come to Cardiff to find Callum and Cassie. If they ended up in the United States ..." He shook his head. The soldiers were forming up behind them, and the shouted orders and stamping hooves were loud enough to prevent anyone else from overhearing.

"I wish I could have visited it," Dad said.

"It's a big country," David said. "From Pennsylvania to Oregon where I grew up is the same distance as from here past the Caspian Sea. Of course, if they have far to travel, they'll be able to fly the distance."

Dad made a rueful face. "Your mother, Goronwy, and I drove in a vehicle from Aberystwyth to Chepstow overnight. That's eighty miles as the crow flies, almost double the distance to

Harlech. How much easier it would be to put down this rebellion if we could travel more quickly."

"I would take communicating more quickly first," David said. "I want to talk to Evan. I want to know what is happening at Harlech."

"At least our enemies can't communicate any better than we can," Dad said.

"I've sent the pigeons to Tudur and Clare, and the rider should have reached Bevyn by now," David said. "At the very least, the castles we hold should be prepared for attack or treachery."

Bevyn, who'd been posted to Anglesey since David became King of England, was the castellan of Llanfaes Castle, one of the new fortresses Dad had built in Gwynedd. In David's old world, after Dad's death, King Edward had destroyed the village to build his castle of Beaumaris. He had been intent on squashing the fiery independence of Anglesey and the rest of Gwynedd after Dad was killed.

In this world, rather than a means to control the populace, Llanfaes and the rebuilt Aberffraw had become centers of power and havens in times of attack on Anglesey. That had been the purpose of Harlech too. Obviously, Madog and Rhys, Dad's wayward Welsh lords, wanted Harlech for that very reason. They couldn't be allowed to take it, or Dad might end up burning down his own castle to get it back.

Dad's estimation of the distance to Harlech was as the crow flies. By road, it was a bit longer: fifteen miles from Rhuddlan to Caerhun, another ten to Aber, fifteen more to Caernarfon, and then roughly thirty south to Harlech. Even pressing hard, that would be a lot of miles in a day, but that wasn't the plan. Five miles an hour was a perfectly comfortable speed to ride and would allow the company to reach Aber well before morning. Everyone would sleep through the dawn and then leave again by noon.

If Father continued to follow his overall plan, he could reach Maentwrog, ten miles short of Harlech, and David could reach Criccieth, by early tomorrow evening. From there, each would have to decide whether to set out for Harlech immediately, or wait until another night had passed. This time of year, the sun went down around four in the afternoon, so they had only eight hours of daylight. If a man needed to see well to do his work, he needed to work fast.

The road from Aber was well-maintained, and the men around David carried torches, so nobody had to pay much attention to where they were going. Besides, horses saw better in the dark than humans. Ieuan and Carew were speculating about what the army might face when it reached Harlech. Dad didn't join in and remained deep in thought. David kept looking at him carefully. Finally, after they'd passed Caerhun, he interrupted Dad's reverie.

"If you're having second thoughts about any of this, now would be a good time to speak."

Dad blinked and looked over at David. "I'm not having second thoughts."

"Then what is it?"

He didn't answer for a few seconds, and then he moved his horse closer to David's so the words he spoke would be for his ears alone. David sensed the others fall back slightly to give them space. "What if they don't come back?"

He meant Anna and Mom. "Dad," David said. "They'll come back."

"How can you be certain?" he said. "Anna hasn't been to your world since she came to this one nine years ago. And your mother had a life there. She may not have one much longer with me ..." His voice trailed off.

David's father had outlived the average medieval man by fifteen years. It shouldn't have been surprising to learn that he was feeling his age and his own mortality, but David didn't want to hear it or think about it.

David tried to figure out how to say what he believed to be true in a way that would make his father believe it too. "Anna's children—and Math—are her life. Mom feels the same about her children and you. She spent fifteen years trying to get back to you. Of all the things you might be worried about right now, that should not be one of them."

Dad was silent.

"What's this really about?"

"I have been thinking of late how much living in this world has cost your mother, your sister, and you." He reached out and grabbed David's shoulder. "If something should happen to you, if you should fall in battle, it would be my fault. You could have stayed in your world and lived until you were eighty."

David stared at him, not actually saying, *what the hell?* though he was thinking it. "Dad, you are not responsible for my decisions. We're long past the point where anything I do is or is not your fault. Yes, you and Mom are my parents, but I am a twenty-three-year-old man. I make my own choices, and while they may be rooted in decisions you or Mom made, they are my own. Don't deny me the right to own them."

"My brother, Dafydd—" Dad paused. He really was feeling his regrets.

David picked up the thread. "Uncle Dafydd made his own choices—bad ones, mostly. I don't believe there is anything you could have done that would have kept him at your side. You didn't give him the land he demanded. Too bad. He tried to murder you, he betrayed you three times—"

"Four."

"Okay, four. Whatever. *He* did that. He would be loving it right now if he knew you blamed yourself for his actions. Even in death, don't give him that satisfaction." David was pretty worked up by now, but Dad was still looking downcast. David leaned closer. "Are you ill?"

He sat straighter in his seat. "No. Of course not. Just tired."

"We'll be at Aber within the hour." David clicked his tongue at his horse and picked up the pace slightly. He didn't want to wear his horse out, but it was better to wear him out than Dad. David was worried now. For all Dad's optimism earlier about how this war could be the first shot across the bow, telling the world that they were serious about forming a united Britain, it was already looking like a lot more trouble than it was worth.

10

November 2019

Callum

Callum didn't like their situation one bit. Cassie, Meg, and Anna had an affinity for Oregon, but he felt stranded here, bereft of the resources he'd grown used to having at his command. Worse, the women were counting on him to get them home safely, and he was worried about what it might take to accomplish that.

Then Meg put a hand on Callum's arm and spoke to him like nobody had since his mother died. "This isn't *your* problem, Callum. It's our problem. You have capabilities we might not have, but this isn't all on your shoulders. We're in this together."

Callum glared down at her. "Do you read minds?"

"I have spent years watching my son doing exactly what you're doing," she said. "I know the look."

Cassie felt for Callum's hand. "He can't help it."

"I know," Meg said, "and I appreciate everything he has done and will do for us. I'm not asking for him not to do it. But the situation is difficult enough without him feeling like he's responsible for all of us."

"She isn't saying that we can take care of ourselves," Anna said, glancing at Meg. "We all need to take care of each other."

Callum rolled his shoulders to ease the tension in them and to clear his thoughts. The Wal-Mart was crowded and inherently insecure, but there was safety in numbers. Even with the snow and rain, the darkness, the ridiculous amount of traffic on the road for a Thanksgiving night, and everybody going the same direction, sometimes for hours at a time, Callum had kept track of individual vehicles on the dual carriageway. He was very confident that they hadn't been followed to Portland from Art's house.

Once past Portland and as the hours of driving to Eugene had worn on, however, he'd had to acknowledge his growing feeling of insecurity. It hadn't dissipated in the three quarters of an hour they'd been in Wal-Mart and, in fact, had turned into a rock of tension in his stomach. If they'd picked up a tail once Cassie turned south, following them wouldn't have been as difficult, and it wasn't like they'd done anything to make tailing them hard. They'd forsaken subterfuge for speed. Now that it was nearly two in the morning, there should be fewer cars on the road. The rain that had started to fall wasn't going to make driving any easier either.

"We should get going." Callum tipped his head towards the door. They'd been standing off to the side, just inside the front lobby of the Wal-Mart. The rush of people that had come in at midnight had dwindled to a handful every few minutes. Callum was strangely pleased with the bargain on mobile phones the shop had given him. That feeling must be why so many people had charged into the shop at this hour in the first place.

They left the lobby, pulling up their hoods against the rain. Before they'd stepped off the pavement, however, Callum put out a hand to the women. "Bloody hell."

"What is it—" Cassie didn't continue. She too saw the panda car pulled up right behind Art's truck, it's blue and red lights whirling. The officer had left it running and was standing at the back of the truck, entering something into his tablet.

Anna tapped Callum on the arm to draw his attention towards another row of parked cars. "There's a second cop."

"They got to my grandfather," Cassie said. "It's the only way they would be chasing his truck."

"They could have gotten the description and license from the DMV," Meg said.

But her words were of little comfort, and a quick glance at Meg showed Callum that she knew it too.

He put an arm around Cassie's shoulders and turned her back towards the entrance to the shop. Wal-Mart was one of half a dozen large stores in the outdoor shopping center. They started walking, just a little bit quickly, which Callum thought would appear normal given the weather. "He'll be okay."

"It depends on who's doing the questioning," Cassie said. "He wouldn't have given us up, not for anything."

"They could have talked to him and noted that his truck was missing," Callum said. "That's all. They wouldn't have had to do anything more than start looking at the camera feeds along the motorway."

"Were there cameras at Mission Market?" Meg tucked her arm through Anna's, and the pair hurried after Cassie and Callum.

Cassie looked back at Meg. "Of course." She laughed in relief. "That's it. Whoever is tracking us, if they noted the flash of your entry into this world, they would have accessed whatever cameras were in the area."

Meg gave a snort of laughter. "You mean the one camera within fifty miles?"

"You can be sure there aren't a lot of cameras on the rez," Cassie said, "but with the casino, we do have them."

"And we'd be on the ones both at the travel plaza and the market," Callum said. "Your grandfather was there too, and we were in his truck. One plus one equals two."

Cassie nodded, and Callum could tell she felt a bit better.

"By the way, who's *they*?" Anna said.

"That was a real copper by the truck." A vision of an army of panda cars blanketing Eugene rose before Callum's eyes. "That means official channels, so either your government, or an entity with a hand in the government, is behind this."

Meg pulled out her mobile. "If Cassie wants to talk to her grandfather, she could do it through the back door. I could call Jim, and he could call Art."

Callum picked up the pace, heading for the last shop in the row, wanting to put as much distance as possible between them and the police vehicles as quickly as he could. "You can't ring Jim."

"Why not? You know him, right, Cassie?" Meg said. "He gave me his phone number as we pulled into the parking lot, and I memorized it. We could have him check on your grandfather."

Callum turned to look at Meg. "You memorized his number?"

"I've always been good with numbers, and it was the first phone number I'd seen in seven years. I thought it might come in handy if Anna and I got stuck somewhere."

They ducked around the last building and turned into the rear car park. Many of the cars had been parked here since before the rain began, which meant they belonged to employees or very serious shoppers. If Callum chose correctly, it might be a while before one was missed.

"You can't ring Jim," he repeated.

Meg hesitated, the mobile in her hand, and Callum reached out and took it from her. Despite their earlier discussion, she was hesitating. He hoped it wasn't because she didn't trust him, but because she wasn't thinking like an agent.

"What I'm about to do is bad enough," he said.

"What are you about to do?" Anna said.

Callum pulled out his mobile and redialed Jones. "I need the entry code for a Toyota Highlander." He walked around the vehicle he'd chosen to commandeer. "Last year's model."

"You are not going to steal a vehicle," said Jones.

Callum was glad he had the mobile pressed to his ear so neither Meg nor Anna could hear what Jones had said. Callum was fairly certain Cassie already knew what he was going to do. She was standing by the corner of the building, keeping an eye out for any pursuit.

"We have no choice. The police are circling Art's truck. We have no other avenue out of here." He glanced at Cassie. "And while you're at it, see if you can find out if Art McKay has been arrested."

"I'm not giving you that code, Callum. So far, you've done nothing wrong," said Jones. "Stealing a vehicle is a felony."

"If we get arrested, the charge may well be terrorism. That'll be it for us until they decide to let us out," Callum said. "You know that."

Then Anna tugged his sleeve. "Wait. Maybe there's another way."

Callum turned to look where she was pointing. A bus depot lay fifty yards from the rear car park with four buses waiting at it. As Callum watched, another bus pulled up and people surged off it, all heading to the shopping center.

"Eugene sure is a happening place the day after Thanksgiving," Meg said. "Who knew?"

Without waiting for Callum to agree to the revised plan, Meg and Anna legged it across the car park toward the depot. Cassie and Callum followed, not even very reluctantly. Callum liked the freedom of having his own vehicle, but he could see Jones's point too. As they approached the buses, Callum said to

Jones, who'd remained patiently on the line, "Okay, we have a new plan. We're getting on a bus, hopefully one that will take us south."

Jones grunted, which Callum took to be assent but that he was too busy to actually speak. As always, Callum could hear keys clicking furiously in the background. "A bus traveling south from Eugene is leaving in five minutes, with stops in Roseburg, Grants Pass, and Medford. I've purchased four tickets. They should be coming through on your mobile right now."

"I owe you."

"You surely do."

Callum looked at the screen and, five seconds later, an email popped up. "Got it."

They reached the depot, and after a minute of loping from bus to bus, they found the one they wanted. Callum herded the women on board and held out his mobile to the scanner. It beeped four times as it accepted the evidence that he'd paid for four tickets to Medford. He didn't know that they were going that far, but that's what Jones had bought. Callum would have kissed him if he were here.

He settled next to Cassie in a row near the rear exit. The seat was surprisingly comfortable.

"How bad is it?" Jones was still on the line.

Callum put the mobile back up to his ear. "The bus is fine." He peered out the window towards the Wal-Mart. "We've seen only local police. Can you tell us what they've been told? We need to know if this is lucky accident, or if it's the spearhead of a wide-scale search."

"Give me a second to get into the system." Jones might be a valued member of Callum's team and an employee of the British government, but he remained a hacker and a rebel at heart.

"It would be nice to know who's looking for us." Cassie had put her head next to Callum's so she could hear what Jones was saying.

"Lucky for you, Wal-Mart is one of the least hackable corporations in the world. They don't play well with others," said Jones. "Their surveillance system is on a closed circuit. Whoever is hunting you will need a court order to gain access."

That was the first good news Callum had heard in a while.

"It's Thanksgiving here." Cassie's head now rested on Callum's shoulder. "No judge is going to appreciate being woken at two in the morning on the second day of his four-day weekend to authorize a hunt for time travelers."

"I doubt that's what he would be told." Callum automatically checked around the bus to see if anyone else was listening in and lowered his voice. "It's always a matter of national security, you know that."

The bus had started moving now. The bus depot was a stone's throw from the motorway, and Callum let out a sigh of relief as the bus turned onto the entrance ramp that would take them south.

"I didn't use my own credit card for any of our purchases," Callum said.

"If you had done that, it would be time to hang up your hat," Jones said.

"What's happening where you are?" Callum said.

Meg shot Callum an irritated look from across the aisle, undoubtedly wanting to hear the conversation too. But this was a public bus. Six other passengers had joined it before the driver closed the doors and eased away from the curb. Callum couldn't put Jones on speakerphone.

"I am being recalled to the office," Jones said with a touch of humor in his voice.

"They shouldn't have kept you on the sidelines in the first place," Callum said.

"Nobody likes hearing, *I told you so.*"

"I'm not following you," Callum said.

Jones was like this sometimes. It took effort to get him to articulate complete thoughts.

"A month ago, we red-flagged the group that has since taken responsibility for the bombing at GCHQ. We even gave the anti-terrorism division of MI-5 the name of their possible leader and his address."

Callum frowned, remembering the meeting. The Project had access to a special police unit—like the American S.W.A.T. team—but didn't sustain one in-house, so Callum had passed on the information to MI-5. "Didn't the organization have an oddly inappropriate name?"

"E.L.F.," said Jones. "Economic Liberation Front."

"I remember them too," Cassie said. "Someone's been reading too much Harry Potter."

"Are you going to the Office or our office?" Callum said.

"Our office. And I'm taking my own sweet time," said Jones. "They won't notice anyway. It's bedlam there."

Meg waved a hand to get Callum's attention. "I have an idea."

Callum moved the mobile phone a few inches from his ear. "I'm open to ideas."

"Could Mark reserve a rental car for us? Untraceably?" she said.

"It's two in the morning," Cassie said. "We can't get a rental car at this hour."

"Airports tend to be open twenty-four hours," Meg said. "Try Medford. It's a bigger and busier airport than you might think."

Callum returned his attention to his mobile phone and relayed Meg's question to Jones.

"What else do you have with you for ID, Callum?" said Jones. "Any United States document would be easiest, but not the same card you used at the shop."

"John MacDonald." Callum reached into his backpack and pulled out a blue passport.

Cassie glanced at it, her mouth twisting into a sardonic smile. "Who needs citizenship when you have MI-5?"

"How far to Medford?" Anna said.

Cassie and Meg exchanged a look. "Three hours?" Meg said.

"We're in a bus," Cassie said. "It might take longer."

"Oh dear. Look at that," said Jones, deadpan. "The traffic cameras along Interstate 5 just went out." Now there was no mistaking the glee in his voice. "I am good."

"Are you hacking into the Oregon Department of Transportation?" Callum said.

"Hacking has such unfortunate connotations," said Jones. "I prefer a more circumspect vocabulary."

Callum snorted laughter, but Cassie said, "Any luck with identifying who's chasing us?"

"A nameless, faceless bureaucracy," said Jones, unironically. "It's out of D.C., but I don't have more information than that and—" He cleared his throat; Callum could hear him speaking to someone in the background before he came back on the line. "I have to go. They sent a car for me. I'll keep on this, and you should have a vehicle waiting for you at the Rogue Valley airport in Medford."

"What car hire company?" Callum said.

"Hertz. I told them you'd pick it up sometime after 4 A.M."

"Thanks," Callum said. "We'd be lost without you."

"Yes, you would." Jones closed the connection.

Callum leaned back in the seat and shut his eyes for a second.

Then he remembered how abrupt he'd been with Meg back when she'd wanted to ring Jim and turned to her. "I'm sorry about closing you down." He took her mobile out of his jacket pocket and handed it to her. He'd had bigger problems ten minutes ago than he had now. "I know that Cassie is worried about her family, but we can't call Art."

"Why not?" Meg said.

Callum grimaced. This kind of thinking had become second nature for him again since his return to the modern world, but even though the laws passed since 9/11 had received a lot of publicity, civilians still underestimated the scope and power of security agencies. "It's two in the morning, and if someone is sitting with Art, any call to him would immediately put us on the radar."

"Especially at two in the morning," Cassie said.

"Maybe it's unlikely they've connected Jim to Cassie, but it's a risk," Callum said. "If the authorities are tapping Art's phone, or Cassie's aunt's phone, they would have Jim's number, and that could lead them to yours."

Cassie sighed and took out her mobile. "To all of our phones." She removed the battery.

"I didn't call him, Cassie. We're okay," Meg said.

Cassie shook her head. "How may calls to the UK went through the closest cell tower to Art's truck in the last hour?"

Callum groaned. "One." Perhaps he wasn't as used to this as he'd supposed.

Cassie motioned that Meg and Anna should take apart their mobiles. "If we get separated, you can put them back together, but until then, we should keep them all off."

Meg's face held a wary look. "How exposed do you think we are now?"

"It depends on how quickly whoever is hunting us can move," Callum said. "They have Art's truck. The next thing would be to look for us individually. Phone traffic in and out of the United States is monitored. I just spoke with Jones, and my mobile number is now on the grid. If they get a warrant, they'll learn that a mobile with that number was bought with three other mobiles an hour ago in the Wal-Mart in Eugene where they found Art's truck. Whether or not they discover we're on this bus, they'll put a trace on the mobiles and find us."

"You make them sound like they're omnipotent," Anna said.

"Nobody is off the grid anymore," Callum said. "Given how quickly they found Art's truck, I am inclined to believe that with enough manpower and computers, they can find anything. The question is just how much time it's going to take them."

"Text Mark quickly one more time and tell him what we're thinking," Cassie said. "We can catch up with him after we leave the bus for the rental and get new phones again with a different ID."

Callum wished they were in Medford right now and cursed the long distances between cities in Oregon. "When we get there, I'll drop you off at a hotel and then take an airport shuttle to the car hire agency. There's probably nothing we can do about the authorities guessing we're headed to Medford, since we've clearly bypassed Portland and driven south, but they won't know more than that." He gazed around at the three women. "We should sleep if we can."

They all nodded as if they agreed with him, but Meg looked wary, and Callum wondered if the way he'd taken the mobile from her was going to color their relationship for a while. Cassie immediately leaned back her seat and closed her eyes, though she slipped her hand into Callum's and left it there. If he'd had his mobile to work on, he would have had to release her hand. But he didn't. Callum was staring at three hours of tense waiting.

Anna curled up in her seat, but Meg, who was sitting across the aisle from Callum, looked out the back window of the bus. "I keep expecting to hear a siren."

"Me too." Callum leaned across the aisle. "I am sorry for taking the mobile from you."

"Thank you, but you don't have to apologize. You were busy, and you didn't want to take the time to explain." She shot him a calculating look. "I'm a big girl. I can take it."

Callum sat back. "Aren't you going to sleep?"

"No. You should."

Callum grunted. "I don't know if I can." Sometimes it took more discipline to sleep than to stay awake.

"When we talked earlier at the Wal-Mart about you not being responsible for us, I meant what I said. But we still need you alert. Let me do this, because it's something I can do. I'll wake you if I'm at all worried."

Callum thought about that for a few seconds and then said, "Okay." He closed his eyes.

11

November 2019

Meg

Meg was way too old to stay up all night any more. Since having the twins, she'd been up in the night plenty, but not recently, not unless one of them was ill. Being the Queen of Wales had its perks, and one of them was having nannies both children adored, and whose attendance meant the possibility of sleeping through the night long before Meg ever would have with Anna or David.

That her children would be asleep at this very moment made not being with them easier to bear. Someone else had dressed them for bed; someone else had told them a story or read from the stack of children's stories she'd written down so she wouldn't forget them. Meg had memorized dozens of stories out of sheer repetition when David and Anna were little, and she figured Dr. Seuss would forgive her for pirating his books seven hundred years before he wrote them.

Even without her promise to keep watch, even without children, husband, or nannies, Meg wouldn't have been able to sleep on this bus. She'd never been able to sleep while traveling. She had no reason to think she might start now. Callum had laid his seat back and seemed to be genuinely sleeping. Meg had been afraid he'd be too hyped up.

In her case, whether it was the image of Marty with his knife to Anna's throat, the raw taste of fear in her mouth when they fell from the tower, or the sight of the policeman standing by Art's truck, Meg couldn't settle her mind. Too much had happened, and it was all jumbled up in her head.

Seeing Cassie and Callum hold hands as they slept warmed Meg's heart, but it also made her feel the absence of her own husband more strongly. She missed Llywelyn. He had David to console him and had been to the modern world himself. At least he knew something of what she'd faced over the last few hours. She told herself she would get back to him. She knew how.

Because the bus driver had dimmed the lights, Meg could see outside the windows, and she watched the mile markers pass by, her heart pounding unnaturally fast, as it had in the woods as she and Anna had searched for a road. It was a fight or flight response, but her adrenaline had nowhere to go because nothing happened. The bus kept rolling down the highway, and the endless unsettled anticipation and fear kept circling through Meg's system. At any moment, she feared to see blue and red swirling lights on the road behind them.

But they didn't come.

Three hours of exhausting but uneventful travel later, the first sign for Medford appeared on the side of the road, telling Meg they had six miles to go. She reached out a hand to Callum to wake him.

He sat up, shaking his head to clear it. "Are we there?"

"Yes," Meg said. "How worried are we that men in black are going to greet this bus?"

Cassie stretched and yawned. "Nobody was at the stop at Grants Pass."

Meg had woken Callum there, just as an extra pair of eyes. At that time, he'd spoken to the bus driver, feeling him out as to whether any alerts had come through about his passengers, but none had.

"That was an hour ago," Callum said.

"A lot can happen in an hour," Meg said.

"This is a ridiculously large country." Callum stood and made his way to the front of the bus. When he'd chatted with the driver earlier, they seemed to have come to some kind of accord, augmented by the three twenty dollar bills Meg was pretty sure she'd seen pass from Callum's hand to the driver's front shirt pocket. This time, the driver nodded his head, and Callum returned to his seat.

"He's going to drop us at a group of hotels to the west of the highway one exit before the bus depot," he said. "I assured him that he'd barely have to stop since we brought our luggage on the bus."

"How far will we be from the airport?"

"Easy walking distance," he said, "and all the hotels have shuttles. We're slipping by under the radar at the moment, and we have to pray that we can continue to do so."

"While you get the rental car," Cassie said, "I can email Mark from the hotel if it has a public computer. Lots of them do."

"I hate not being able to use my mobile," Callum said, "but there's no help for it. I still can't believe they found Art's truck as quickly as they did."

The muscles around Cassie's eyes tightened. Callum put a hand on her shoulder. "Only a few more hours. We can't help your grandfather from here anyway, and you can call him from the plane."

"I have another idea." Meg sat straighter in her seat.

Callum looked over at her, interested.

"What if we turn on our phones and leave them on the bus?" she said. "Or, if we want to get really crazy, we could give them away. They have a certain number of prepaid minutes, right? It might be a real gift to someone without much money."

"That's good." Callum's eyes lit. "That's very good."

"You're a genius, Mom." Anna started putting her phone back together. She looked up at the rest of them. "I'll pass them out. You're too intimidating, Callum."

Cassie grinned at his expression of mock outrage and dropped her phone in the cup holder beside her seat. "That will be a nice surprise for the next passenger."

Anna strolled to the front of the bus. With a smile, she handed one phone to the bus driver, who tucked it into the same pocket of his shirt that held the twenty dollar bills. This had been a lucrative journey for him. Then she passed another phone to a raggedly dressed college student, who was barely keeping his eyes open, and tucked the last one into the open zipper pocket in a backpack on the rack above a sleeping woman.

A minute later, the bus exited the highway and pulled into the driveway of the Hampton Inn. It took approximately eight seconds for the four of them to disembark. Callum saluted the bus driver, who waved and turned the bus back onto the road. A shuttle bus waited in the valet parking area, and passengers were starting to file onto it, coming from the hotel.

"Ten minutes to the airport, ma'am." The driver spoke in response to a woman's question, having come out of the shuttle bus to help load the passengers' luggage. "When's your flight?"

"6:30."

"We'll have you there in plenty of time."

"Too bad we can't fly from here to San Francisco," Cassie said.

Callum shook his head. "Anna and Meg have no ID. I thought about it, but even with Jones's help, we have no way to accomplish that particular miracle. If all goes well, I'll be back within the hour, and we could be on the plane to Britain by noon." He kissed Cassie goodbye and joined the line of waiting travelers.

"Let's get inside," Meg said.

It was shortly after five in the morning and breakfast was being served in the small dining area off the lobby. A talking head for the local news channel gave way to a video of an apartment building on fire. Meg glanced towards the front desk, but the lone clerk on duty was being besieged by guests checking out.

"What do you think?" Anna said.

"I have cash," Cassie said. "I can pay for breakfast."

"Not to be either clandestine or a thief," Meg said, "but paying for breakfast is going to draw attention to us."

"Not eating is going to draw attention to us." Anna gazed toward a row of plastic cereal dispensers. "I could eat something sugary and artificial if you twisted my arm."

Meg feigned a shudder.

Cassie surveyed the lobby and then tipped her head towards the breakfast area. "Get a table by the window, close enough to the television to hear what the announcers are saying. I'm going to email Mark." She sounded as authoritative as Callum.

Neither Anna nor Meg begrudged her the right, since she did work for MI-5, and the three women drifted away from each other. Anna and Meg wandered towards the cold cereal, and Cassie made her way towards a computer and printer set up near the lobby fireplace.

The food on offer was standard hotel breakfast fare: pastries, cold cereal, bagels, and waffles. Meg forwent the sugary cereal in favor of a bagel and cream cheese. The coffee looked unappealing, so she opted for orange juice. It might be processed to within an inch of its life, but she hadn't eaten an orange in seven years. There were some things even the Queen of Wales couldn't get.

"Carbohydrate heaven." Meg took a bite and made a face. The bagel didn't taste as good as she remembered. Admittedly, it wasn't a New York bagel. "I was hoping we'd have a chance, despite all the travel, to run down a pizza before we leave this world." Meg was glad for the duffel bag at her feet with its precious cargo of tomato seeds and potatoes.

"I haven't thought about not eating carbohydrates in years," Anna said. "I suppose whether or not I eat them hasn't been at the top of my list of concerns."

"Back home, we eat what's available and are thankful for it," Meg said, watching one of the patrons dump a half-eaten waffle into the garbage, followed by a full plate of pastries.

Cassie arrived three minutes later, got herself a bowl of cereal, and sat down, wrinkling her nose at the colors in Anna's bowl. "How is it?"

Anna made a so-so motion with her head. "Sweet."

Cassie pulled her chair around so her back was to the wall and the front door was directly in her line of sight.

Meg pointed at her with her knife. "Did you go to spy school?"

For a second, Cassie looked startled. Then she grinned. "I did."

"I noticed Callum was trusting you with more stuff than I expected," Meg said.

"He is a control freak," Cassie agreed, starting to eat her bran and raisins.

"I chalked up your driving to the fact that he isn't used to driving on the right side of the road, but that isn't it, is it?" Meg said. "Or not entirely."

Cassie smiled into her bowl. "I got a very high score on the driving test—higher than his—even with driving a car that had the steering wheel on the wrong side."

Anna took two more bites of the pink and orange cereal and then abandoned it in favor of a waffle, which she coated with butter. She picked up the container of (fake) maple syrup and put it down again. She saw Meg watching her and shrugged. "I thought I missed sugar. Turns out, I don't like it as much as I thought I did."

Meg wasn't enjoying eating what was available either, whether because of the flour processed to within an inch of its life, the sugar, or the oddly bland flavors. A few of the criticisms Meg had heard leveled at medieval food were that spices were rare and the food rotten and unflavorful. Meg had never eaten rotten food nor seen anyone else eat it, and the critics were missing something important: butter made from cow's milk where the cow had eaten actual grass was a very different food from the pat in a foil wrapper Meg had spread on the other half of her bagel. She wished she'd had a chance to eat more of what was being served at Cassie's aunt's house.

"He's here." Cassie stood up.

It was a matter of a few seconds to gather up the duffel bag and two backpacks and toss the remains of their meal into the trash. Cassie led them out the door and walked straight to the black car Callum had rented. As before, Anna and Meg got into the back seat.

"How did it go?" Cassie said.

"It was easy," Callum said. "No questions asked. We need to swing by another Wal-Mart, get new mobiles, and then we're in business again."

"Anna and I will buy them this time while you circle the block," Cassie said. "And we'll pay cash."

"How much cash do you have?" Meg said.

Cassie shot Meg a sardonic look. "Lots. My husband plans for every contingency." She looked at Callum. "Though I don't think even you believed Anna's and Meg's arrival was imminent or you might have done things differently from the start."

"I didn't." Callum sped out of the parking lot, following the directions to the Wal-Mart given to him by the GPS in the car. When they reached the store, its parking lot was packed, just as the one in Eugene had been.

Cassie and Anna got out. "We'll be as quick as we can."

"I don't see any parking spaces anyway," Meg said to Callum. "Is it turning out to be a good thing or a bad thing that we're fleeing across America on Black Friday?"

Callum gave a laugh, circling through the parking lot at two miles an hour. "I'll let you know when we finally reach that plane."

Meg sat back in her seat and closed her eyes. She didn't want to feel tension in her shoulders any more. She didn't want to be scared that men in a black SUV would pull up beside them and point their guns. When Llywelyn had been ill and she'd brought him to Aberystwyth, whatever happened, she'd found comfort in the fact that she'd had no choice. This time it had been Marty's choice, and he'd paid for it with his life. Meg hated what he'd done to Anna. She hated how her children and grandchildren had been forced to witness what he'd done to Anna. But she would never have wished him dead.

Then again, justice being what it was in medieval Wales, he might have paid for his actions with his life anyway.

And with that, tears pricked at the corners of Meg's eyes, partly because she was so tired, but mostly because she had allowed herself to think about Llywelyn again for more than a few seconds. She knew—because she knew him—that he would be going out of his mind with worry for her and Anna. He'd told Meg what it had been like when she'd disappeared at the beginning of her labor with David twenty-three years ago. Meg's absence had torn him apart, as it had ripped away her own heart. He'd spent as many years searching for her as she had for him.

At least this time he knew where she'd gone. At least he knew now that she would do everything in her power to return to him and the children. But he had to be hating his own impotence every second they were apart. Hopefully, with David beside him, he would find a way to keep busy.

Callum tapped his fingers on the steering wheel. "This is taking too long."

Meg peered out the window, but no sirens wailed and no police cars turned into the parking lot. "The store's just crowded."

Wal-Mart's cameras might be on a closed-circuit, but that didn't mean the ones in the parking lot were. Fortunately, since it wasn't yet seven in the morning, it was still dark. They could hide among the huge number of people and cars. If it had been any morning but Black Friday, the parking lot would have been all but deserted, and they would have had a much harder time keeping a low profile.

Callum grunted, which Meg took to be dissatisfied agreement, and before Meg started to actively worry about them too, Cassie and Anna came out the front entrance of the store. Callum pulled around the end of the parking lot, cruising slowly, and stopped before he reached the end of the row of cars. Anna saw him, tugged on Cassie's arm, and hurried over, both women taking long, confident strides. Meg felt a burst of admiration for her daughter, who was handling these difficult circumstances with such grace.

"Any problems?" Callum said as Cassie and Anna opened their doors and sat in their seats.

"Not that I know of," Cassie said. "We got the same deal you did, and Anna and I bought the same phones, though we went through separate registers." She shot Callum a worried look. "I hope that's okay."

"It should be," Callum said.

"It's a question of how omnipotent the U.S. government has become," Anna said. "I can't say it looks good from here."

"Hundreds of people all over the United States are buying these phones today," Meg said. "Buying them in two separate transactions was a great idea."

"I will never again say that I hate Black Friday," Cassie said. "I have never shopped on this day. We always avoided it." Then she held up a prepaid mailer envelope. "I also wondered if you would object to me using this?"

"What is it for?" Callum said.

"It's so I can mail the truck keys back to my grandfather," Cassie said. "By the time he gets them, we'll be long gone, or we'll be in custody. It won't matter if someone knows we were once in Medford."

"Okay," Callum said, giving in far more easily than he might have. And then he explained why. "I'm sorry we involved him. I wish I had been smarter about finding another vehicle."

"Short of renting one, which would have been a trick in Pendleton, Oregon on Thanksgiving night, I don't see what choice we had," Meg said. "No matter whose car we borrowed, if they caught our images at Mission Market or the truck stop, they would have traced us to Art."

Cassie grimaced. "I think it's actually our fault—Callum's and mine."

"How so?" Anna passed a phone to Meg and started opening a second herself.

Cassie twisted in her seat to look back at them. "Assuming they picked up the flash of your entrance into this world at the same time Mark did, seeing Callum and me on those cameras shortly thereafter, with a posse of searchers, was like blowing a horn and announcing, 'they're here!'" Then she looked over at Callum. "You understand that my grandfather isn't regretting helping us, right? No matter how much trouble we've caused him?"

Callum gave a jerky nod.

"What do you mean by that?" Anna said.

Cassie busied herself with the phones in her lap. "My grandfather would have been offended if we hadn't asked him for help. On the reservation, we look out for each other, never mind who might be in trouble with the law. That's why so many men volunteered to look for you. It's a dangerous world out there."

"We're grateful," Meg said.

"It would be the same at Llangollen," Anna said. "People protect their own."

Cassie nodded. "Here's what my grandfather wants in return: for David to fund an expedition to the New World himself, instead of leaving it to the Spanish in two hundred years. He wants us to make sure it turns out better."

"That won't be easy," Meg said. "Ninety percent of the native peoples who were here before Columbus died after 1492. Mostly from disease. Is it better to leave it for later, or to 'discover' the New World now hoping we can handle the side effects?"

"Creating the United States of Britain is one thing," Anna said, "but we'd be changing history on a way bigger scale. Maybe there'd be no U.S."

"Maybe," Meg said. "But how responsible are we for something that might or might not happen five hundred years from now? We've already changed the course of British history irreparably. I don't think we should worry about the U.S." She laughed. "We're sitting here running from a government that feels pretty totalitarian to me right now. We have the ideals, and most of them aren't even reality in this world. Maybe we can make something better."

"All those deaths, though," Anna said. "I can't even wrap my mind around a 90% mortality rate."

The conversation had carried them back onto the highway. Callum seemed to be handling driving on the right side of the road without any trouble. He hadn't contributed to this conversation at all, but then, as a Scotsman, it wasn't his country's future at stake.

"My grandfather understands there might not be a right answer," Cassie said. "But we've got to come up with something *better*."

12

November 1291

David

Given what his father had looked like when David had forced him into his bed in the early hours of the morning, he'd been prepared to tell him that there was no way he was continuing with the army towards Maentwrog. But when Dad appeared shortly before noon, he seemed like a completely different person from the man David had put to bed.

"What are you looking at?" Dad said when he caught David staring.

David hastily cleared his expression and deflected his father's question. "I gather you slept well?"

"Strangely enough, I did." Dad swung his arms back and forth, loosening his shoulders. "I'm not in my dotage yet, you know."

"You've mentioned that before," David said, and then opted for the truth. "I don't know when I've ever seen you as gray as you were last night, except when you've been ill."

"I might have lost a step or two, but I make up for it in cunning." He shot his son a wicked grin, again belying his earlier exhaustion. "I've been thinking about our friend Madog."

"I'm listening," David said.

Dad took a bite of mutton, chewing hard, and then swallowed. David had learned to eat mutton for breakfast, but he was suddenly envious of Anna, who might be getting cheerios. If she was safe. Worry for her and Mom had David's stomach clenching, and he put down his buttered roll, no longer hungry.

"I've decided that I know what this is about," Dad said. "And it isn't about his ancestral lands in Meirionnydd. Or at least only peripherally."

"Okay," David had no clue where this was going.

"It's about gold."

David had grown fond of gold in the last three years since he'd become King of England. If land meant power, so did cold, hard cash. And in the Middle Ages, gold *was* cash. "What gold?"

Dad snapped his fingers at one of the pages standing near a doorway that led to a corridor off the great hall. "Bring me the map on my desk. The big one."

"Yes, my lord." The page bowed and dashed off, returning a minute later with a two foot square piece of parchment.

Dad whipped it out of the boy's hand and laid it on the table, using two cups, a pitcher, and a knife to hold down the corners, which wanted to roll back up. It was a map of Gwynedd, one drawn by Mom and Bronwen, from their own memories and using the maps of this time as reference. Distances were hard to gauge in the Middle Ages, and drawn coastlines didn't always translate to geographical maps like this one.

Latitude was easily determined by the angle of the sun, but longitude was harder. Two years ago, David had printed out an internet account of how navigators had worked out longitude. Upon his return to this world, he'd presented the various options to the scholars at Cambridge and Oxford, who'd shared it with their counterparts on the Continent.

The working out of how to determine longitude, particularly at sea, was one of the greatest collective scientific endeavors in history. David didn't want to short circuit the advancements that came with those efforts, so, as in that other world, the British crown was offering a considerable prize for the person or persons who came up with a workable system that could be implemented on land and sea. GPS, sadly, wasn't an option. But a working chronometer? David was counting on it.

"I know you are hoping that your mother returns with a survey of the mineral deposits in Wales," Dad said. "I will be interested to see how accurate such a map could be, and if our finds match your world's."

It hadn't occurred to David that the resources below ground might be different in this universe. It didn't seem like they should be. He gestured to the map in front of them. "What does this map tell you?"

SARAH WOODBURY

Dad planted a finger on Carndochen, a second at Cymer in Dolgellau, and a third at Harlech. "These three castles. What do you see?"

"If a man were to control those positions, he would control all passage in and out of that region of Meirionnydd," David said.

"Very good," Dad said. "More to the point, Carndochen and Cymer are also locations where gold has been found. I have sent men several times to survey the area, using local men as guides, but other than a few rocks and flecks of gold sifted out of the river, they have found nothing productive. It's my guess that Madog has found more, perhaps a great deal more."

"Could he keep such a find a secret?" David said.

Dad looked at him.

"What?"

"This is gold, son," he said gently. "The man who finds a vein of it running through the earth would want to keep that knowledge to himself, wouldn't he?"

David nodded, reorienting his thinking from a global to a local scale. "He might need help extracting it, however. He might tell his lord under the pledge that he would share the profits."

Dad's mouth twitched. "Where Madog is concerned, that would be a good way to get oneself killed, but a peasant might not know that."

"Can I ask you a question?" David said.

"Of course." Dad rolled up the map and slipped the tie around it.

"Many barons in England have behaved similarly to Madog and Rhys," David said. "Some have supported my enemies, and I have taken their lands—like you did with Madog. Others, like Rhys, you have left in place, though with a much diminished patrimony. Why the difference, and how did you decide how to deal with each one?"

Dad scoffed. "You ask me this question, but it is no less than what I have been asking myself." He pressed his lips together for a moment, thinking. Then he said, "Taking Rhys's circumstances first, I never meant to bicker with either him or his cousin, Wynod. In the early days of my rule, when I was trying to conquer all of Wales and hold off the English at the same time, I gave more land to Wynod's father than to Rhys's. Rhys's father abandoned me immediately. Wynod's remained faithful—for a while."

Dad sighed. "It was a purely political calculation, and one I believed at the time I had to make, though clearly we are harvesting its fruits now. Twenty years later, Rhys surrendered to Edward early in the 1277 war. Wynod did too, a little more rapidly than I might have hoped, though he'd had little choice, given the enemies that surrounded him. He returned to my side in 1282, however, and I forgave him his lapse."

"Didn't Mom say that in our old world Wynod stood by Wales after your death?" David said.

"He was the last to surrender after Dafydd was captured," Dad said. "Your mother has also told me that even Rhys regretted his allegiance to Edward before the end."

"And that is why you were more lenient with him," David said, comprehension dawning. "You hoped that by returning his lands to him, you could mend the rift between you."

"Obviously, my attempts have failed in that regard," Dad said. "I won't take lands from Wynod to augment Rhys's, and he cannot forgive me for it."

"What about Madog?" David said.

"His is a different situation entirely," Dad said. "His father sided with my brothers against me at Bryn Derwin in 1257, and I deprived him of his lands as a result. He refused to swear fealty to me, lived off the largesse of King Edward until his death, and Madog himself was born in England. I didn't even know that Madog spoke Welsh until he showed up at Brecon in the company of Rhys last year."

"Could be that Rhys is using him," David said.

Dad guffawed. "If Madog doesn't realize that, he is a fool."

Then Ieuan came through the door to the great hall and strode toward the dais. "Whenever you're ready, my lords."

Ever since the company had arrived in the early hours of the morning, messengers and scouts had been flowing in and out of Aber in a steady stream, some confirming information Dad already knew, others adding to it, and a few correcting bits of misinformation. One of the most important tidbits had been brought as a by-the-way from a villager who'd fled from Carndochen to Dolwyddelan in the night. Dad's castellan there had sent a pigeon a half hour before, reporting that the vast majority of the men in Madog's army were from southern Wales.

For all Madog's claim that he was fighting for his ancestral lands, Madog's supposed people hadn't flocked to him. They were flocking to Dad instead.

"We're ready now." Dad rose to his feet, the map still in his hand, and headed for the exit. On his way out the door, he handed the map to Ieuan.

"What's this?" Ieuan said to David as he stopped beside him, watching Dad tromp down the steps to where his horse waited.

"It's a way to secure the peace, once we've won the war," David said.

Ieuan didn't open the map, just tapped the parchment against his leg, observing the men with David. They looked as ready as they could be, especially given the short notice. "It's the war I'm concerned about," Ieuan said. "It may be that Madog has no men of his own, and his father's people haven't rallied to him, but that means we're facing bowmen from Deheubarth. They don't miss."

Welsh archers were renowned throughout Europe for the power and accuracy of their bows. Archery, unfortunately, was not a skill that David had mastered in the nine years he'd lived in the Middle Ages. His father had believed wrestling and sword fighting were more important. David could pull a bow, but that was all that could be said for his skills. Ieuan, on the other hand, like David's wife, was a master.

"I am reluctant to fight other Welshmen too," David said. "It would be my preference to give them the chance to defect back to us before this war gets more out of hand."

Ieuan didn't quite roll his eyes, but his mouth twisted. "They are traitors, my lord."

"They go where their lord points," David said. "Many may feel that they don't have a choice but to fight for Rhys and consequently for Madog. But I'm not interested in making any more permanent enemies. Nor is my father. We always have to make peace out of war, and it's never an easy task."

"It hasn't been so bad in England since Valence's death," Ieuan said.

"True, but he was a foreigner to the English in the first place, many of the men who fought with him this last time were from Ireland, and his Norman peers didn't like him much either. He'd lost the war before it had even started, though none of us knew it at the time."

More rebellions like Valence's—and Rhys's—were precisely the kind of threat that could derail David's plan for a united Britain before *he* even started. He could handle the messiness of democracy. He didn't need to be the King of England, provided nobody else was king either. Madog and Rhys, however, wanted to carve away their little slices of Wales for their own benefit and set themselves up as absolute rulers.

Wales' problem had always been a lack of the administrative infrastructure that any government needed to maintain itself. When it had a strong king, all went well. When he died, however, either his sons fought over the carcass or, even if the transition went smoothly, the new ruler might not be as capable a leader as his predecessor. The history of both England and Wales was riddled with such instances.

Having a Parliament helped, but it didn't solve the problem. If an idiot sat on the throne—and had the traditional power of the throne—he could wreak all sorts of havoc. King George III, the man who lost the American colonies, was certifiably insane. That wasn't any way to run a country.

Nor, quite frankly, was this.

When the former Soviet Union broke up, it was because Russia had conquered its neighbors and held on to them by force. It wasn't any surprise that when change came, their colonies wanted to rule themselves. The same was true for Scotland and Wales in that other world. They'd been conquered and held by force. In the world David came from, even after seven hundred years, many Welshmen resented English rule.

But a democracy was different. When a region agreed to abide by the law of the land, it couldn't throw a fit or threaten to take its bat and go home when things didn't go its way. When that happened, things got nasty (e.g. the American Civil War). If Rhys and Madog objected to Dad's rule, they should have gone to Brecon and made their case before Parliament. Because they hadn't done that, Dad was going to have to put them down instead.

So it was that Dad and David rode out of yet another castle. The ranks of men had swelled to three times their original number. Every man in North Wales who could ride a horse had ridden it to Aber. The rest marched. They couldn't make the full distance to Maentwrog today, but if the weather remained fine, they could reach it by tomorrow. And then Dad would see about taking Harlech back.

At Bangor, the company would turn southwest and take the road to Caernarfon. A small motte and bailey castle that a Norman had built centuries ago lay eight miles from Bangor and defended the western end of the Menai Strait. Dad planned to rest there. No Norman had controlled the castle since before the time of Owain Gwynedd, and Dad had shored it up since 1282, taking advantage of its prime location. It was after they reached Caernarfon that Dad and David would go their separate ways: David to take the more southwestern road to Criccieth, and Dad to travel due south to the muster at Maentwrog.

David still didn't like it. He still thought it was a waste of his skills and men to send him to Criccieth. He spent most of the journey to Bangor organizing his reasons as to why he should ride to Maentwrog too. David had actually opened his mouth to voice them when a scout burst from the trees to the south of the road.

"My lords! My lords!"

They reined in. The scout's horse danced and spun as he struggled to get the animal under control. Ieuan dismounted and caught the bridle, putting a hand on the horse's forehead to calm it. The others gathered around.

The scout took in a breath. "Sire, I bring information of Madog's movements in the south. He has split his force and has left just enough men at Harlech to maintain the siege. He marches even now towards you."

"He's looking to confront us directly?" David said.

"We should have known that we couldn't catch him by surprise," Carew said.

"And he should know that he can't catch us by surprise." Dad's brow was heavily furrowed. "What is he thinking?"

"Madog can't maintain the siege if we come behind him," Ieuan said. "It makes sense for him to challenge us if he thinks he can stop you before your army has fully gathered."

"He marches with many men, my lord. More than I see here." The scout gestured to the cavalry behind them. "He has passed Maentwrog and continues north on the road to Caernarfon."

"He marches through Beddgelert?" Dad said. That was the same road south that Dad had intended to take from Caernarfon.

"My lord." Carew lifted a hand to Dad, who nodded at him. "If Madog chooses the ground and the timing, and has more men than we have, I can understand his daring. If he meets us on the road to Maentwrog, we will have only cavalry and whatever footmen can catch us by the time we reach his position."

"We should go around," Ieuan said. "Take the western road."

David scoffed a laugh. "Or we could all ride to Criccieth and relieve Harlech by sea."

"Or we could end this tonight," Dad said.

There was a moment's pause. David saw the eyes of some of the others shift from Dad to him. They were waiting for him to speak. *Cowards.*

David sighed. "Which is exactly what Madog would expect you to decide."

"Good." Dad's eyes lit. "We shall be utterly predictable ... except where we're not."

David studied the expressions on the other men. Cadwallon looked eager for anything, but that was his normal state. Justin tugged on one ear. He would go wherever David pointed and not question what he asked of him. Samuel's face was impassive. His father had taught him to keep his feelings to himself.

Ieuan and Carew, however, had years of experience in battle. Ieuan was rubbing his jaw, thinking hard, while Carew tapped rhythmically on the hilt of his sword with his left hand. Nobody was leaping about with enthusiasm at Dad's suggestion, but neither were they arguing with it.

"We need to keep our eyes on the goal," Carew said. "Is that Harlech or—"

"Defeating Madog is the goal," David said, "just as defeating Dad is his."

Dad looked at David, eyebrows raised. "So you do support confronting him?"

"Isn't it my job to play devil's advocate?" David said. Some of the men frowned, perhaps not sure of that particular phrase, so he hurried on, "You are right that we can deal with the army in front of Harlech at our leisure once Madog is taken care of. I'm just concerned that he has all the advantages. We need to create some for ourselves."

"We would need eyes and ears," Carew said.

David turned in his saddle, gazing around him at the trees that encroached the road. They were only a few hundred yards past the crossroads at Bangor where three paths had met: the first led back to Aber and was the road they'd taken to get here; the second, the road they were on now, led to Caernarfon; and the third headed south into the mountains, to Dolbadarn, Dad's fortress in western Snowdonia. The decision they made in the next few minutes would determine which road they took—and possibly the course of the future of Wales.

What was happening right at this moment was very similar to what David had faced with every war he'd fought in the Middle Ages: he had access to hours-old information about the movements of his enemies and no way to communicate with his allies in a timely fashion. David had never grown used to it; it was a stupid way to fight a war, but in the Middle Ages, it was the only way. They were going to have to decide what path to take—right here, right now—and live with the consequences of that decision.

Dad nodded. "I need to know where they are, how many men they have, and as much as possible about what they're planning."

"We need to know who Madog has left at Harlech, too," David said.

Dad looked at him. "What are you thinking?"

"If Madog does this right—no guarantees, of course—he will have left his tents and pavilions in plain view, so Evan will have no idea that the bulk of his army has left the field," David said.

Justin nodded. "Evan won't know that he could sally forth and break through those lines."

"He could relieve his own siege—" Ieuan was nodding too. "We have to get a message to him."

Dad turned in his saddle and surveyed the men who followed him. He had a *teulu* of fifty, all trusted, all capable of finding a way to Harlech alone if need be.

"Four would be enough," David said. "In a little boat, with Madog on the move, they might be able to slip up the back stairway unnoticed."

"We'll address that in a moment." Dad faced the messenger. "Of Madog's two thousand men, how many are spearmen and archers, and how many are horsemen?"

"No more than two hundred on horseback." The scout's manner turned matter-of-fact. "The rest are on foot."

"That means he can't move them far," Cadwallon said. "Or he can try, but we can move much faster. He must have left Harlech almost at the moment he laid siege to it."

"Two hundred horsemen." Justin tapped a finger to his lips. "Would he bring them all?"

"Cavalry are no use in a siege," David said. "Say he leaves a minimum of two hundred at Harlech. Most should be bowmen.

That leaves him with all of the cavalry and well over a thousand archers and spearmen with whom to march north."

"Where will they seek to confront us?" Justin said. He knew very little about the lay of the land in Wales, but he'd studied the maps.

David knew the road to Beddgelert well. At one time, he and Math had ranged all over Gwynedd for precisely this reason. It was what every lord worth his salt did with his days: exploring the countryside and making sure that he knew every creek, every trail through the underbrush. It served not only to keep his men sharp, but meant that one day, if needed, he could make decisions like this one with full knowledge of the landscape.

Ieuan scanned the mountains to the south. If not for the clouds, Mt. Snowdon would have loomed above them, fewer than ten miles away. "Madog might seek to defend the crossing at Beddgelert."

"Or later, when the road narrows to nothing at Aberglaslyn," David said. "That would get my vote."

"We need to know for sure." Carew bent his gaze on the messenger. "How much of what you are telling us have you yourself seen?"

The scout's eyes went wide, but he answered steadily enough. "Three of us saw him cross the river at Maentwrog and trailed after him until he started up the road to Beddgelert. At that point, I circled around to the north. Once I was clear of them, I rode as fast as I could to warn you."

Dad straightened in his seat, resolve in his eyes. "We'll take the road to Dolbadarn and flank them over the Nantmor. And we'll do it tonight."

Nobody told him he was crazy.

"We can steal every available man from Bangor and Dolbadarn. And send word to Dolwyddelan so that when Math reaches the castle, he will know what we undertake," David said.

"He'll come late," Ieuan said. "And he'll find either clean-up work or, if we've lost, the need to finish what we started."

"At least he'll have warning about what he's riding into." David checked the sky. It was technically early afternoon, but here at the end of November, the daylight was already fading. "If we do as you plan, Dad, we'll be working entirely in the dark."

"So will they," Dad said.

"We cannot assume Madog is going to make a mistake," Ieuan said. "He has had more time to plan than we have. He won't assume we'll walk into his trap unawares."

"Nor can we assume he'll walk into ours," Dad said, "but that doesn't mean we won't lay it just the same."

13

November 2019

Anna

The cut on Anna's neck was starting to scab over a bit. With a damp paper towel, she dabbed at the blood that had dried on her neck.

Mom came out of one of the bathroom stalls and studied the wound. "It looks okay, hon. You can hardly even tell it's there."

Anna looked down at her hands, surprised they weren't shaking, and ran them under the warm water from the tap. The bathroom was freezing. They had crossed the border into California a bit ago, and Callum had deemed it safe enough for a five-minute break at a derelict gas station in the tiny town where he'd chosen to stop. Anna could forgive him the cold temperature since the gas station had no cameras.

"How much farther, Mom?"

"An hour, Callum says."

Anna closed her eyes. "I wish we were there."

Mom put her arm around Anna's shoulders. "We will be."

They returned to the car. Callum had stocked up on water, diet soda (Cassie's preference), and junk food. Anna was too tired to be excited about it, but she took a bag of potato chips anyway. Then Cassie's phone beeped at her.

"I thought we weren't calling anyone?" Anna said.

"She's Skyping with Jones," Callum said in a low tone. "The mobile phone company records it as a use of the internet rather than a phone call, and that means it's less traceable."

That sounded good to Anna until Cassie said, "What do you mean we're not going to make San Francisco?"

Anna couldn't hear Mark's response, but Cassie shot Callum a worried look. He mouthed, 'speakerphone!' at her, and she pulled the phone down from her ear and pressed a button.

"I'm tired of riding blind, Jones," Callum said. "What's happening?"

"Nothing on our end that should concern you right now," Mark said. "I can bring you up to speed when you get here."

"At least you're still saying 'when'," Callum said, "not 'if'."

"We're going to get you here," Mark said, and there was a grim quality to his voice that hadn't been in it until now. "But it doesn't help that a warrant has been issued for your arrest. It's gone nationwide."

"What the hell?" Callum said.

"Why?" Cassie said.

"Why isn't the question," Mark said. "It's who issued it."

"Then who?" Callum said.

"The FBI. Anna is wanted for questioning regarding the disappearance of her brother," Mark said. "The three of you are what they're calling 'known associates'. That seems to be the best they could come up with."

"They could have charged me with Marty's disappearance," Mom said.

Typically, she was willing to take the pressure off Anna because she was her mom. Anna rubbed her shoulder. "Whether me or you, it hardly matters," she said.

"Isn't there a statute of limitations on something like that?" Mom said.

"Not on murder," Mark said.

Anna didn't know whether to laugh or to tear out her hair. She leaned forward to speak into the phone. "So it's our own government that wants us?"

"So it seems," Mark said, "but your government at times can hardly be distinguished from the private contractors it hires. Half the police forces in your country are now privately owned. Who's to say where it ends?"

"That's crazy!" Anna said. "When did that happen?"

"Cities were strapped for cash. Detroit went bankrupt, and that was only the first of many," Cassie said. "Most forces are staffed by veterans like Callum who came home from the Middle East needing a job. Policing for a private company was familiar and paid well."

"How does a city police force make money?" Anna said.

"By arresting people, of course," Callum said. "Tickets, fines, confiscated materials."

Mom snorted. "That sounds remarkably like the medieval inquisition that David is trying so hard to counter."

Callum glanced in the rearview mirror at her. "Much like it, yes."

Anna looked from Callum to Mom. "You mean like what happened to the Jews? Trumped up charges or search and seizure, legal or not, so the authorities could confiscate their property?"

"Land of the free and home of the brave," Cassie said in an undertone.

Anna waved a hand. "Okay, regardless of all that, how are we getting to that plane?" She didn't want to ignore other people's pain, but they had Mark on the line and were digressing.

Mark cleared his throat. "I was getting to that. George Spencer, from the consulate in San Francisco, is going to meet you at the car park for the Solano County Fairgrounds."

"Wait a minute." Mom took out her phone and accessed the map function. Anna was surprised Mom knew how to use it. Maybe she'd acquired a smartphone in the eighteen months she'd been here after Anna and David went to Wales. Anna would have had no idea where to start.

Cassie, meanwhile, started pressing buttons on the dashboard. "Got it," they both said at the same time.

"We're ten miles out," Cassie said.

"He's a bit farther, but he'll be there when he can. You need to get off the highway and keep a low profile until he can find you."

Anna leaned over to look at Mom's phone. "There's a Six Flags there."

"What's that?" Mark said.

Anna spoke louder. "Six Flags. It's an amusement park. Is it going to be open today, or will we be the only ones in the parking lot?"

Cassie puffed a laugh. "This is Black Friday, remember? Believe me, it's open."

"What does Spencer look like?" Callum said.

"Thin, average height, balding brown hair, wicked sense of humor," Mark said.

Callum laughed. "Got it."

Ten minutes later, they found themselves stuck in a mile-long traffic jam to get into Six Flags, and twenty minutes after that, they pulled into the parking lot of the fairgrounds.

"The traffic must have been better coming from the south," Mom said.

"Why's that?" Anna said.

Mom tipped her head to the right, pointing to the black SUV that had just pulled in. "Do any of you drive anything but black SUVs?" she said to Callum.

He opened his door. "Apparently not."

"We have less than a minute." A man looking very much as Mark had described leaped from his vehicle.

"What happens after a minute?" Anna said as she got out of the car too.

"I just dropped off my son and his two friends at Six Flags,"
George said. "If either your vehicle or mine is being tracked, a
detour into this car park could look like a shortcut—"

"—or it could look like a meet." Callum dumped the duffel
bag from Wal-Mart into the open rear door of the SUV and got
into the front seat.

"It's been twenty-seven seconds by my count," Cassie said.

"Is it likely someone is tracking you, George?" Anna said.

George eyed her. "You're Anna?"

She nodded.

"I always assume someone is tracking me." George shook
hands with Callum. "Jones taught me that."

The three women piled into the back seat while George
climbed back into the driver's seat with Callum beside him and
drove off.

"What about the rental car?" Anna said.

"Our office will take care of it on Monday," George said.

Callum nodded, removed the battery from the key fob for
the rental car, and dropped both it and the fob into the glove box
of George's SUV. He closed it with a snap. "Monitoring George,
who has diplomatic immunity, would be illegal, but our
adversaries don't seem much concerned about legality today."

"George, do you know the specifics of what we face other
than the warrant for Anna's arrest?" Cassie said.

Anna still couldn't quite get over the fact that she was a
wanted woman and wondered what people who had known her—if

they heard about it—would think when they learned of her new criminal record.

"I know only that she's wanted," George said. "I, of course, haven't been to the office today, so I have no notion that any of you are fugitives from the law, or else I would never have picked you up. My task is to get Director Callum to his airplane, as ordered by the Home Office. The individuals accompanying him are neither my problem nor my concern."

Callum turned to look at Anna, who was squashed on the bench seat between Cassie and Mom. "They don't know it, but you're our ideal culprit, and your crime is perfect."

"How so?" Mom said.

"For starters, it isn't even a crime. Anna's wanted for questioning in David's disappearance, but they have no body and no evidence of foul play—only that he was last seen with her. The order to apprehend her will be seen by local police as urgent but not that urgent."

Cassie nodded. "If Anna were to be seen, the police would follow her, but they wouldn't shoot. She isn't armed and dangerous. She's wanted for questioning."

"I guess that's something," Anna said, unable to keep from sounding morose. Being a fugitive might sound adventurous from the comfort of a living room couch, but it felt a lot less fun in reality. She was tired, hungry, and scared. If she hadn't been with Mom, Cassie, and Callum, she might have curled up into a ball like a hedgehog.

"Running from the law isn't as much fun in the living as the telling, is it?" Mom elbowed Anna in the ribs. "When I told you about our flight across Wales three years ago I made it sound less bad than it was."

"You managed to make it sound funny, but I knew it was scary." Anna had thought that and more besides. She and Math had talked about Mom's trip at length. Talking about it made it easier to think about something like that happening to the two of them. And it could have, if Marty had chosen his target a little differently.

Anna glanced at Mom. Math was one of the most competent men she knew, and he wouldn't have begrudged Anna her superior knowledge of the modern world, but it would have grated on him to be so helpless. On the whole, it was better that it was Mom and Anna who had come here. "How does driving in the dark across the Elan Valley compare to this?"

Mom's eyes got a distant look. "Your father was ill, so that added to the worry, and he and Goronwy were relying on me to get them through it. I can't say this is better, though." She leaned forward and put a hand briefly on Callum's shoulder. "I didn't know then as much as I do now about who was chasing us. I would have preferred to keep my innocence, quite frankly."

"Hopefully today will be a little less adventurous than that day." George glanced at Mom in the rearview mirror. "I have the same security clearance as Jones does."

"How do you know Jones?" Callum said. "Not that I want to appear ungrateful for the assist from the consulate."

"We're cousins." George was silent for a minute as he navigated between cars that were going more slowly than he wanted. Once away from the Six Flags' exit, the traffic thinned considerably. "He's filled me in on the salient points."

"Do we have a plane?" Cassie said.

"The British government have requested that Director Callum return to Cardiff immediately," George said. "Getting you a plane wasn't a problem."

"And the rest of us?" Anna said.

George dipped his head slightly. "The plane is going. Like I said, it's a small matter to take on a few more passengers." George reached into his breast pocket and removed two red passports, which he handed to Callum. "Your guests are diplomatic couriers, traveling at the behest of our government."

"Thank you." Callum passed the passports back to Mom and Anna. "I can't thank you enough. I owe you a favor."

George gave a laugh. "One you may regret. As it is, my son thanks you for his surprise trip to Six Flags with two friends." He shot Callum a look Anna couldn't interpret. "It might cause an international incident when the American government discover you flew out of Oakland with a fugitive."

Anna stared at the elaborate golden seal on the front of the passport. Opening it, her name was revealed to be Anna Llywelyn. Sudden tears pricked the corners of her eyes. Blinking them away, she leaned in to look at Mom's passport. It said Marged Llywelyn.

"It's Black Friday, as we've been reminded repeatedly this morning," Callum said. "Everything is working a touch more slowly than it might be otherwise."

"Let's hope it continues—" George stopped as the SUV buzzed at him. He pressed a button on the dashboard. "Hello?"

"Good morning, Mr. Spencer." A woman's voice came on the line.

George cleared his throat. "Good morning Consul-General. How may I help you?"

"An agent from Homeland Security for California stands before me," she said. "He has informed me that the imminent threat level for San Francisco, specifically the airport, is now at red."

"How unfortunate," George said.

"He has apologized for whatever inconvenience this might cause us."

Everyone else in the vehicle remained absolutely silent.

"He has also informed me that all bridges in and out of San Francisco are being monitored, and all cars searched."

"I imagine that is going to cause many people some difficulties," George said. "Do we know the specifics of the threat?"

"No," she said, and Anna could almost hear her eyeing the agent in her office. "But he expresses his condolences for our losses at GCHQ."

Then a man's voice came on the line, clearly American. "Your Consul-General informs me that a top agent in the Security Service was to be flying home to England today."

George didn't answer immediately, and Anna could hear rustling in the background. Then George said, "Was that a question?"

"No," the Consul-General said. "Please come straight to my office once you reach the consulate."

"Given what you've told me about the bridges, I may be very much delayed," George said.

"As I would expect, Mr. Spencer." The Consul-General ended the call.

Mom leaned forward. "So, that means—"

"We proceed as planned," George said.

"But the airport—" Mom said.

"We're going to Oakland," Anna said. "That's what you said earlier, right?"

For the first time since they'd started driving, the lines of tension around George's mouth eased, and his expression lightened.

"The Consul-General knows that too, doesn't she?" Callum said.

"She does," George said. "But for some reason, Homeland Security doesn't know that we charter private planes out of Oakland as well as San Francisco."

"Since when?" Cassie said, laughter in her voice.

George looked at his watch. "Since the call came in from the Home Office last night. But again, it's Black Friday. It may be the paperwork hasn't sifted through the proper channels yet. In fact, I'm certain that the office we're supposed to notify is closed today."

The four passengers relaxed into their seats. For the first time since they'd entered Art's truck nearly twelve hours ago, Anna found her breath coming easily. She hadn't realized how tightly she'd been holding herself. "How long until the airport?"

"Ah. Funny you should ask." And now George actually grinned. "It's coming up on our right just now."

Anna looked where George pointed to a sign that said, "Private Departures."

"Thank God," Mom breathed from beside Anna.

Half an hour later, as the airplane's engines roared to life and the jet headed down the runway, Anna cracked the lid on her bottle of water. They had an eleven-hour flight to Cardiff. She'd never been very good at time zone math, but Callum said they'd arrive around six in the morning tomorrow. They wouldn't have made it to the Middle Ages, but at least they'd be in Wales. It was a start.

14

November 1291

David

Anna and Mom had been gone for a day and a half. David was really glad that he'd slept at Aber, because nobody was going to be getting any sleep tonight. It was past midnight and they'd been riding or walking, with only a brief rest at Dolbadarn, since they'd left Bangor nearly twelve hours earlier.

To David's huge relief, the word that had gone out from Aber had borne fruit. Men had begun to trickle into the ranks since midnight, swelling their army from the four hundred foot soldiers who'd gathered by the time they'd reached Dolbadarn, to eight hundred, and since they'd come down the road off Mt. Snowdon, the numbers had reached a thousand. Northern Welshmen were known for their spears, but every man knew how to use a bow if he had to. Before the sun rose, they might have the opportunity to use both.

By the time they set up camp between two little lakes to the east of Beddgelert, they had a much better idea of what Madog intended. Beddgelert sat at the head of a narrow gap between two hills that ran for a mile from Beddgelert to Aberglaslyn. Madog had arrayed his forces on the bottom slope of the Nantmor, facing northwest and guarding the entrance to the Aberglaslyn valley.

Madog's intent, as far as they could tell, was to launch his attack as soon as Dad's force exited the gap. When they'd speculated about where Madog might set his trap, Dad had assumed that he would descend from the sharp peaks rising up on either side of the gap, fall upon Dad's small force, and create a very effective killing zone at the river bottom. It was what every Welshman worth his salt would have planned, but that didn't seem to be what Madog intended.

Admittedly, the terrain was steep and difficult, and the swiftly flowing river that split the valley meant that Madog's men could attack only from the eastern ridge. Still, bowmen placed upon the west side of the river could have mowed down Dad's cavalry at six arrows a minute. Even in the dark, it would have been an uneven fight, which Dad likely would have lost.

Madog, however, appeared to be looking for a straight-up fight on a field of battle. Madog's men were well placed on the Nantmor above a field, which would put Dad's forces at a disadvantage because of the little warning he'd have (were he unaware of Madog's plans) and the small amount of room to maneuver.

David would have said that it was an excellent arrangement if a far better one hadn't lain a quarter of a mile away. Dad had spent many minutes puzzling over the disposition of Madog's men until he remembered that even if Madog's blood was Welsh, he had been trained in war by Englishmen. He didn't understand bows, and it seemed that Rhys's sons, if they were, in fact, in attendance, hadn't been able to impress upon Madog how he might ambush Dad more effectively.

David meandered through the ranks of men, stopping at a group of ten who clustered together, sorting their arrows. Fortunately, winter hadn't closed in yet, and in American terms David thought the temperature was roughly forty-five degrees. With his armor and thick wool cloak, he wasn't chilled. Nor would the men be. Wool was as common as rain in Wales, and all of the men were dressed for winter, in thick cloaks, tunics, and breeches. A few didn't wear shoes, but David thought that was by choice. Archers often fought with only one shoe to be sure of their footing. They were lucky it wasn't raining because that froze the hands and made it hard to aim an arrow.

"Where are you from?" David said to the men.

"Dolwyddelan, my lord," one of the men said. "My name's Cadoc."

"Thank you for coming," David said. Dolwyddelan was only seven miles as the crow flies from Beddgelert, but because of the rough terrain, they had to have come at least twice that distance to reach this spot. It was the same distance Math was going to have to travel if he was going to join the fight. David hoped Math had received the message and was even now coming their way.

Another man growled. "I don't like this Madog."

"His father ruled these lands before my father took them from him," David said.

"He never ruled here." The man waved a hand. "That was to the south."

"And even if he did," Cadoc said. "Madog speaks no Welsh, I hear. My sister married a man from Meirionnydd. If Madog rules there, I fear they'll be tithing to a bloody Norman from England next." He looked hastily at David. "No offense meant, my lord."

"None taken," David said.

That seemed to please them, and with a nod, David moved on, intending to speak to another group of men, but then the first man, Cadoc, spoke to David's back. "It must be hard living among foreigners, my lord. Just as long as you don't get too used to them."

David turned back, trying not to smile because the man was serious, and he didn't want to appear mocking. "I am, and always will be, a Welshman. I took the throne of England so no more Normans could plant their boots in Welsh soil. I live among the English so you don't have to." The words had come out before David had really thought them through. He hadn't meant to be so startlingly honest.

"You took a Welsh wife," Cadoc said. "Didn't think you were going to."

There were nods all around. It went without saying that discussions of David's personal life had taken place up and down the length of Wales since his father acknowledged him as his son; David had a brief image of the men sitting in a tavern, nodding over his decision to marry Lili.

None of them had any notion of the division that decision had created in David's family. It was still astonishing to David how stubborn his father had been about it. He'd actually wanted David to take Lili as his mistress. She might have been willing, but it had been David who'd refused. He'd figured out before he was sixteen—before his mother explained it to him in no uncertain terms—that his station as the Prince of Wales meant that all he had to do was crook his finger, and he could have any woman he wanted. Which to David meant he couldn't have any.

"I hope your mother and sister are well." This comment came from a boy no older than William.

David canted his head in silent thanks. "I do too. It's hard to have them gone."

"But they're safe, yes?" he said.

"They are safe; I am certain of it." David rested his hand on the boy's shoulder, nodded again in what he hoped was a reassuring manner, and continued on.

William, whose Welsh was perfect, had been shadowing David this whole time. He made sure they were out of earshot before he spoke. "They don't think much of Normans, do they?"

"No, my friend, they do not." And if William was only discovering that now, he wasn't as smart as David had always thought.

William looked down at his feet, thinking it through. They didn't have much light to see by other than a few sputtering torches and campfires carefully tended to keep from smoking. They'd posted dozens of men on the heights to the west and south of the camp to give warning if any enemy scouts came this way. So far, Madog had sent scouts north along the road to Beddgelert, the direction from which he believed Dad would come, but he hadn't sent his men this far east.

"I suppose I always knew Welshmen from Gwynedd felt that way," William said. "It's different in the March."

The March was the border between England and Wales which had been fought over the by the Welsh and the Normans for two centuries.

"The Welsh and English rub along fine when they understand each other better," David said. "My own *teulu* is proof of that. But these Welshmen live far from the border. And if it makes you feel any better, they think Welshmen from the south are foreign too."

That prompted a smile from William. "Madog is very sure of the trap he has laid, isn't he?"

"It seems so, and that worries me," David said.

"Are you worried that we've got it wrong?" William said.

David stopped walking and turned to look at him. "Yes."

"What would happen then?"

"Then we may die."

William swallowed hard. "We may die anyway."

"That's true." David started walking again. "Still, Madog can't hide his men any more than we can truly hide ours. Our current advantage is that we know where his men are, and he only thinks he knows where we are."

William chewed on his lower lip. He seemed about to speak again, but then he raised a hand to someone beyond David. David turned to see Samuel waving an arm above his head. William and David wended their way through the men and entered Dad's tent. Cadwallon, Ieuan, and Carew were already there.

"It's nearly time," Dad said.

David contemplated his father and decided that it was his duty to air his objections one last time. "I don't like you putting yourself in harm's way like this."

"Nor does anyone else," Carew said.

Dad shot Carew a quelling look, which Carew pretended not to see, rocking back and forth on the balls of his feet. "In fact, none of us want to see either of you leading your companies."

"Leading from the rear isn't leading," David said, though modern leaders would disagree. At some point—and David wasn't sure when in history this had happened—kings and rulers had started appointing men other than themselves to lead the actual fighting. It was probably when kings stopped being warriors. And it made sense not to sacrifice the brains of the operation to a stray arrow. But it also meant that the men ordering the death of other men never got their hands dirty, and that wasn't how David worked.

"You are too valuable to risk," Carew said. "Madog is a petty lord. He isn't worth your life."

"We've discussed this already," Dad said. "Madog's scouts cannot be completely incompetent. They will have reported to him that I rode from Aber and intended when I left to take the road through Beddgelert. It is why he set up his ambush here. Consequently, I'm the best person to lead the company that rides through the gap. All men know what I look like, and what's more, Madog hates me. My presence on the field has a better chance of upending his reason and encouraging him to behave recklessly."

David put up a hand. "Madog knows me too."

Madog had come to David's court at Winchester when he'd summoned all his lords to him, and then he'd gone to Brecon when Dad had summoned the Welsh Parliament.

Dad shook his head. "How do you say it, son? *I can sell this.*" He turned to Cadwallon. "We can, can't we?"

Cadwallon nodded, rather more vigorously than David would have liked.

Dad smiled and then brought his attention back to David's face. "My men will be loud and arrogant, riding through Beddgelert with torches blazing. We want Madog and his men looking forward, unaware that you and Ieuan are leading companies by different roads."

Beddgelert lay two miles west of where Dad's company was currently camped. Dad, riding with Carew and Cadwallon, would lead his two hundred cavalry to a small track between two ridges that would allow him to skirt Beddgelert to the north and bring him onto the road about half a mile above the village. He would then ride south through the town, across the bridge, and into the gap, following the eastern bank of the river Glaslyn.

Madog's army would be waiting for him on the other end of the gap, arrayed on the western-facing downslope of the Nantmor. Dad would be caught between the river and the narrow passage behind him, with no way forward, sideways, or back.

That was Madog's plan. The counter plan—as proposed by Ieuan—had two additional components. Ieuan was to lead the spearmen and bowmen on foot over the top of the mountain between here and Aberglaslyn. In turn, David was to take the rest of the cavalry around the back of the mountain and come in at the southern end of the valley, effectively catching Madog's men in a pincer movement. He would drive into the back of Madog's force before Dad and his men were slaughtered.

"This had better work," Ieuan said, echoing David's thoughts.

"It was your plan," David said. "Don't tell me you're getting cold feet."

"It seemed like a better plan when it was I who was the bait, not the king," Ieuan said.

"I have done this many times before." Dad looked at David. "Did you know your mother saved my life by warning me of an ambush farther south on this same road?"

David blinked. "I did not know that."

"It was a long time ago," Dad said. "That time it was Goronwy who rode through the gap and I and my men who fell upon our enemy. It will be the same again."

All this small talk, this banter of words that made it sound like they were planning an expedition to look at the standing stones on Anglesey, was, of course, a front, a cover for the truth that lay beneath: they were going to war and no man knew if he would come out the other side as whole as he went in.

Depending on how the next few hours went, history might view this fight as a little war, inconsequential in the broad scheme of things. David hoped that was the case. But men had already died—at Carndochen, Cymer, and Harlech—and no matter how effectively they surprised Madog, men were going to die today. One of them might even be him.

"Make sure your bowmen position themselves higher up the mountain than Madog's bowmen," David said to Ieuan. He knew better than to tell his brother-in-law his job, but he couldn't seem to help himself. "It'll be like shooting fish in a barrel with us as the fish if you don't."

Ieuan nodded and refrained from sneering or otherwise calling David to account for his mother-henning. Then the tent flap flipped up, and Justin poked his head inside. "My lords, two more scouts have returned."

"What do they say?" Ieuan said.

"Madog's men remain settled in at Aberglaslyn," Justin said. "They have extinguished their fires and their torches and wait for us in the dark."

"They're going to have a long wait." Ieuan chewed on his lower lip. "Could this be a cover for movement to a different position? Perhaps they intend to ambush us in the gap as we originally feared?"

Justin shook his head. "The messengers report no such movement. Two more scouts remained behind to watch, and I will send the others out again."

"What about Madog's scouts?" Dad said. "Surely he has many too."

"We spied two men at the bridge at Beddgelert," Justin said.

"That's all?" Ieuan said. "What about farther north?"

"None that the men have encountered," Justin said, "but I report only what I was told. Madog appears to have no intention of facing you until Aberglaslyn. Those two scouts will give him plenty of warning of your approach."

Dad nodded. "They will run as soon as they see our torches to warn Madog that we are coming. I wondered if he might post a small force at the bridge, but he must want to lure us into a false sense of security, and make us believe we have a free road until Maentwrog."

Now William's brow furrowed, and he turned to David. "May I speak, my lord?"

"Of course," David said.

"You are riding to war. You would have scouts patrolling ahead of you," he said. "Why would Madog think you wouldn't discover his army on the hillside?"

"He believes me in my dotage," Dad said.

William looked nonplussed.

"If he does, he's an idiot." David scrubbed at his hair with one hand. "Maybe Madog is an idiot, but I'm pretty sure that Rhys's sons are not."

"What I fear is a second force coming behind us and blocking the road back to Beddgelert once King Llywelyn has crossed the bridge," Cadwallon said. "Such a force might be encamped to the west of the Nantile Ridge, opposite this position."

"Have the scouts checked that location?" David said.

"Yes, my lord," Justin said.

"And found nothing?" Carew said.

"And found nothing," Justin said, "but in the dark and moving quietly, with the fog that has begun to creep in, they could be a hundred yards away, and we would never know it."

"Have our scouts check again," David said. "We must be sure. At the very least, if something is amiss, a lone man can warn my father before he reaches Beddgelert, even if the rest of us are already on our way."

"Yes, my lord." Justin bowed and departed. Dad gazed after him, rubbing his chin, and then he nodded as if he'd decided something.

His expression made David wary. "What is it?"

"Madog's movements are dependent upon mine. He wants to surprise me with battle. That is all very well and good, but it is our movements that worry me. Once I cross the bridge at Beddgelert, my force will be as vulnerable as any force I have ever led. Even if we traverse that mile at a walk, if you have fallen behind, we will arrive at Aberglaslyn before you and be defeated. And if we are wrong, if Madog intends to descend on us from the cliffs above the gap, I would prefer to take that distance at a gallop."

Ieuan's jaw remained tight. "We will do what we promised. But no rider could reach either of us in time, no matter how fast he rode or how important the message."

"Sound your horn when you cross the bridge, Dad," David said.

Dad raised his eyebrows. "That will ensure that Madog, too, knows that I am coming."

"His men will have warned him already."

Dad's expression turned thoughtful.

David continued speaking. "Not all horn calls are the same. Some are for setting forth. Others are for battle. I'm not suggesting a war cry. It would be natural for you to sound your horn to call the people of the region to you. If anything, such an act would reassure Madog that you know nothing of his movements."

"Would Madog know the difference between one call and another?" Samuel, who would be riding as part of David's company, had been keeping silent in one corner.

"His men would. The sons of Rhys would." Cadwallon stood with his arms folded across his chest. "Who are these men that they would support Madog's rise against you? This is treason. How do they not see it?"

"It's only treason if they lose," David said.

"It doesn't matter who they are," Dad said, cutting off further discussion. "We will answer that question after we defeat them."

As when they departed from Aber, the others took his statement as a dismissal. Bowing and nodding, they left the tent to prepare their men.

David stayed behind and turned to meet his father's eyes. "It does matter. If there are Welshmen among Madog's men who might be loyal to you under different circumstances, and we gain the upper hand, we must give them the opportunity to lay down their arms."

David's father studied him for a moment and then gave a quick nod of his head. "I agree. If we can."

15

November 2019

Meg

Once the plane had taken off and was level, Meg pulled out her phone and waved it at Callum. "Can I call my sister?"

"Call her," he said.

"Wait!" Anna put out a hand to her mother. "You can call from an airplane? Since when?"

Meg looked up in mid-dial. "They've had the technology for a while now, even if they wouldn't let you do it." She bit her lip. "You were gone, sweetheart. I think I read the first article about it during the year and a half I had to live without you."

Anna unbuckled and came over to Meg with her arms out. "We never talk about it, you know."

Meg hugged her back. "What don't we talk about?"

"About that time." She released Meg and returned to her squashy airplane seat. Meg had never flown in such a comfortable plane. The seats were leather, roomy, and soft, and arranged more in talking groups than in rows.

Meg sat facing backwards with Anna across from her and Cassie to one side. Callum had sat beside Cassie for the few minutes it had taken to lift off, but as soon as he had given Meg permission to call her sister, he'd pulled out his own phone. He was talking on it now while pacing the aisle, which ran beside the left windows for the full length of the plane. Private planes were definitely the way to go.

"That's probably because it's a time I generally pretend didn't happen," Meg said.

"We talk about what happened to David and me all the time but never what it was like for you, other than that you missed us," Anna said.

Meg rubbed her forehead with two fingers. "When we get home, I will give you the blow-by-blow, as much as I can remember. I promise." She held up the phone again. "This airplane has what amounts to a mini-cell tower. It will communicate with cell towers on the ground."

Cassie nodded. "It operates on a frequency that doesn't interfere with terrestrial cell phone use or the airplane's avionics."

Meg shot Cassie a grin, impressed with her excellent techno-speak.

Anna looked from Cassie to Meg. "They can do that?"

"Guess so." Meg put the phone to her ear, again with her heart in her throat. When she'd last phoned her sister, Elisa's kids had been sick with chicken pox, and none of them had been able to see Meg. At the time, she'd felt like Elisa hadn't wanted to see her either, but having nursed her own twins through a bout of chicken pox two months ago, Meg could better understand how truly rotten they had all felt. Certainly it had turned out for the best that Elisa hadn't tried to fly across the Atlantic with Ted. MI-5 had begun its pursuit of them within a few minutes of Ted's arrival at Aberystwyth.

And now here Meg was again, reaching out to her sister while in the process of fleeing the country without a chance to see her. Just a few minutes to talk to her on the phone.

"Hello?" A deep voice, one Meg didn't recognize, answered after two rings.

Meg was momentarily stumped, thinking she'd dialed the wrong number or perhaps her sister's number had changed, but decided to carry on. "Is Elisa there?"

"Sure, just a second." The voice went away and, belatedly, Meg realized that it had belonged to Christopher, her nephew, who was now seventeen years old.

"Hello?" Elisa said.

Meg let out a short breath. "Hi Elisa. It's Meg."

"Oh dear God," she said.

"I named my daughter after you." Meg didn't know where those words had come from, but all of a sudden out of all that had happened since Meg had spoken with Elisa last it seemed like the most important thing to tell her.

"Th-th-thanks—" Elisa stuttered a bit more, starting sentences and stopping them while Meg fought tears and couldn't speak at all. Then Elisa said, "Where are you?"

Meg swallowed hard, fighting for control. Anna, who'd been watching her steadily, moved to her mother again, this time crouching in front of her. Anna held out her hand for the phone, and Meg gave it to her.

"Hi, Aunt Elisa. This is Anna."

"You're there too!" Elisa spoke so loudly Meg could hear her even without putting the phone on speaker.

"Yup," Anna said. "Just give Mom a second. She's going to come back on."

Meg breathed deeply, looking up at the ceiling and wiping the tears from her cheeks with her fingers. Anna was still talking, exchanging more pleasantries about her kids and Elisa's, but still watching Meg's face as she spoke.

Then Meg nodded, and Anna gave the phone back to her. "Hi Elisa. We're in an airplane, flying across the United States."

"Are you coming to see us?" Elisa said.

"We can't." Tears threatened again, and Meg struggled to hold them in. "I'm sorry, but we can't. I'm a little surprised that you don't have Homeland Security beating down your door already."

"Are you in trouble again?" Elisa said.

"I guess so. It seems so," Meg said, "though it's hard to understand why."

"Hard for me too, though after what Ted went through in Wales, I suppose we should have expected it." Elisa had turned matter-of-fact, and it helped Meg to get her emotions under control. "Where are you flying from and to?"

"We ended up in Oregon," Meg said and gave her sister a brief rundown of the last twenty-four hours. She felt, under the circumstances, she owed Elisa at least that, and she didn't want her sister to be surprised if the government showed up and was playing with a different deck of cards than she was.

At the end of Meg's little speech, Callum, who'd finished his conversation, made a 'give it to me' motion with his fingers, and Meg handed the phone to him.

"Elisa, this is Callum. We'll be leaving U.S. airspace within the hour, so I'm less worried about Homeland Security than I was." He paused, listened, and then said, "No, I don't think they'll send fighter jets after us. This is a diplomatic flight. If the American government wants to make trouble, they'll do it once we're on the ground in Wales." Then he listened some more. "Yes, they will discover Meg and Anna were here. That might not happen today, but it will definitely happen in the next few days." More listening and then, "You are free to tell them whatever you need to." He'd been pacing around the small space but finally sat down beside Meg, leaned close with the phone between them, and turned up the sound.

"Are you sure?" Elisa's voice bellowed out of the speaker, and Callum hastily turned the volume down once more.

"Yes," Callum said. "I'm going to give you back to Meg."

Meg took the phone but didn't put it to her ear right away. "Is it really okay just to talk?"

"Go ahead." Callum smiled. "You may not get another chance for a long time, and you might as well use up your minutes."

Tears pricked Meg's eyes yet again, but she returned to the line. Unlike three years ago, Elisa sounded confident about her own life and happy to hear about Meg's. They talked for an hour, and when Meg finally hung up, the tears were back, but this time she was crying because she was happy.

It was six in the morning, U.K. time, when the plane touched down at Cardiff airport. Naturally, it was raining.

Meg peered out the rain-spattered window. "What's in store for us today, Callum?"

"I hope you're not thinking about the last time we were in modern Wales together," Callum said.

Meg glanced at him, hoping he wasn't offended. He'd changed into a suit, tie, and trench coat—the uniform of an MI-5 agent—which George had arranged to leave on the plane for him. The women were still in their two-day-old jeans, t-shirts and sweaters, and winter coats. It wasn't as if Meg hadn't ever worn the same underclothes multiple days before washing, but as the Queen of Wales, she didn't often have to.

"I don't blame you for being worried." Callum leaned over Cassie's shoulder, looking at the scene before them. A single SUV waited on the soaked tarmac. "I'm hoping that's Jones."

"And if it isn't?"

He pressed his lips together.

"Are we getting to avoid customs here too?" Anna said.

"You have the red passport," Cassie said, "and Callum is still the director of the Project, for a few more days anyway. Given the explosion at Signals yesterday, you two are small potatoes."

"For today, arresting the organization behind the bombing has to be the primary concern of the Security Service to the exclusion of everything else," Callum said.

Meg nodded. While she didn't know anyone involved, she could feel Callum's sense of loss. She wouldn't have wished what had happened on anyone, even if it meant that they were flying (quite literally) under the radar.

The airplane door opened, and the four companions filed down the steps to the waiting SUV. As it turned out, Mark wasn't there to greet them, but Callum cordially lifted a hand to the man who was. Of a more lithe build than Callum, and with skin that bespoke some African ancestry, he stood ramrod straight and wore his suit and trench coat like a uniform, just as Callum did. He also held a truly enormous umbrella. As they approached, he moved it so that it covered all of them.

"Agent Jeffries." Callum shook his hand. "Good to see you again." He turned to Anna and Meg, waving a hand back and forth. "Anna, Meg, meet Agent Darren Jeffries of MI-5, formerly of the Project."

Darren nodded his head. "A pleasure to meet you." Then he looked at Callum. "Jones sends his greetings."

"I hoped he'd be here," Callum said.

"He couldn't get away," Darren said.

Callum looked warily at Darren, who simply opened the passenger side door and gestured everyone inside.

"Should I be concerned?" Callum said, getting into the front passenger seat.

"Director Tate knows you've arrived. I am to drive you directly to the Office."

Callum's lips twisted.

"Given the current crisis—" Darren cleared his throat, "—he told me you would understand the urgency."

"Oh, I understand," Callum said.

Meg sat with a certain amount of reluctance and ended up in the middle seat between Cassie and Anna. Cassie noted the stiffness in her shoulders and leaned in to her. "It's okay. This is going to be okay. The Project is all but shut down. Nobody should be worrying about you at all."

"I hope so," Meg said. "I'm tired of running."

As at Oakland, they'd ended up in an area of the airport set aside for charters and private planes. Darren had to drive through a guarded gate to get out of the airport, but he was waved through with a brief flash of his ID and nothing more. It was a far cry from the security lines in the public sections of every airport Meg had been in since 9/11, and she said as much.

"This is the secure part of the airport," Callum said. "You're with the British government now, and its agents come and go as they please."

He wore a self-satisfied smirk. Meg had known that he'd been frustrated by their journey across Oregon and California, but now he was back on his own turf. It was exactly how Llywelyn had felt when he, Goronwy, and Meg had arrived back in the Middle Ages after fleeing from MI-5. They'd come through the time vortex in England, which wasn't exactly home to Llywelyn. Still, the change in his manner had been palpable. He'd been sure of himself and his place in the world again.

Darren turned right and headed east. While Meg had long since grown used to walking and driving on the left, it was still weird for her to see vehicles constructed with the steering wheel on the right. In medieval Wales, if a person crossed paths with another person while walking or riding (or charging into battle), he always went to the left. The idea was to put your sword arm between you and the other person.

In addition, a right-handed person held a horse's reins in his left hand, so under gentler circumstances, passing on the left allowed one man to greet another with his right hand. At some point—and this must have been a strange cultural shift—three-quarters of the world had started traveling on the right. Meg didn't know why.

Since it wasn't even seven in the morning and still dark, there was hardly any traffic. When the city center didn't appear after a few minutes, Meg leaned forward to speak to Callum. "Where are we?"

"The airport is ten miles from the city center," Callum said. "This isn't eastern Oregon. They didn't have enough room to build it any closer in."

He was trying to keep things light, but Meg was too tense to laugh. She sat back, feeling as helpless as she had ever felt in her life. And she'd been helpless plenty of times. She gazed out of the window. After twenty-six hours in the modern world, she was growing used to it by now: the traffic and the lights, even the food.

"Ma'am?" Darren glanced at Meg in the rearview mirror. "I apologize for my role in what happened to you at Chepstow. I'm glad to see you well. I hope King Llywelyn is too."

"He is, last I saw him. Thank you," Meg said, touched by his concern.

"I saw you fall," Darren said. "You and Director Callum."

Callum glanced at Darren, his mouth twisting in a wry smile. "Seeing is believing."

"Yes, sir," Darren said.

Callum looked out the window. "It was for me too."

"That must have been something of a shock to see, Darren," Meg said.

"Yes, Ma'am," said Darren. "Once Director Callum returned, I was happy to work under him on the Project. I was reassigned back to MI-5 proper two months ago."

"Just as well now," Cassie said, keeping her voice low. "Callum has more contacts throughout the intelligence services than he had before. The staff *believe*, you see, even if the Prime Minister doesn't."

Meg put a hand on Anna's leg. She'd been entirely silent since they'd left the plane and hadn't talked much while they were on it. "How are you doing?"

"I haven't been to Cardiff since you took me here after David was born. I have no memory of that trip at all."

"Sometimes I wonder if I shouldn't have found a way to live and work in Wales," Meg said. "Though work visas for historians are kind of thin on the ground."

"It's okay, Mom," Anna said. "Hindsight is 20-20. You taught David Welsh at least."

Meg had tried to teach Anna too, of course, but they'd been at odds for much of her teenage years, and Anna hadn't been interested. Although Meg had never said as much to her, the year and a half they'd been separated—with Anna and David in the Middle Ages and Meg in the modern world—had been good for their relationship. Anna had learned her mother's secrets and figured out that Meg was human and could make mistakes. By the time they saw each other again, Anna had grown up enough, and missed her mother enough, not to task her with her failings and to forgive her for them.

After another ten minutes of driving, Meg could see the lights of Cardiff ahead of them. The SUV crossed several bridges, and then Cardiff Castle rose on the left, surrounded by a high wall. The SUV stopped at a traffic light. It always felt absurd to sit at a light when there were no other cars in the vicinity. Callum looked back at Cassie, nodded, and pressed a button on the door beside him. Her door unlocked, and Cassie reached across Meg to poke Anna. "Come on, ladies, let's go."

"What-what are you doing?" Darren turned in his seat, a bewildered look on his face.

"Tate just needs Callum. As of Monday, I don't even work for them anymore." Cassie slung her backpack on her back and tugged the large duffel out of the rear compartment. Callum handed Meg his backpack.

"You don't want what's in it?" she said.

He patted his coat pocket to indicate that he had everything he needed. "I'll call you as soon as I know more and we have a plan."

Five seconds later, the three women stood together on the sidewalk, the light turned green, and Darren and Callum drove away. Cassie and Anna each grasped a handle of the duffel bag and hung it between them.

"I don't like being separated from Callum," Cassie said, "but this is for the best. Unless Mark told him, or Darren did, Director Tate doesn't even know that you guys are here. Better to keep it that way as long as possible in case someone remembers why MI-5 cared about you in the first place." She started across the street.

Meg and Anna belatedly followed, with Anna trotting a few steps to catch up since she was attached to the handle of the bag.

"Are we worried about someone following us?" Meg said.

"You can't understand the kind of bureaucracy a government is until you've worked for them. We're hoping that the right hand doesn't know what the left is doing," Cassie said.

"What about the Americans?" Meg said. "By my count, we may have three different agencies after us."

"How do you figure that?" Anna said, looking back at her mother.

But Cassie knew what Meg meant. "The CIA used to care about you. That's one. It may be that the Dunland Group-turned-CMI still does. An agent from Homeland Security was in the Consul-General's office before we boarded that plane in Oakland. There may be others."

"Would Homeland Security have revealed all to the CIA in the last eight hours?" Anna said.

Cassie laughed. "Not unless inter-agency cooperation has improved enormously in the last three days. Anyway—" she surveyed the street corner, "—it looks to me like we're alone." She started walking down the street they'd reached. "Come on. Let's get inside."

"Inside where?" Meg said.

"Ah." Cassie grinned at her. "This is where the fun begins."

"What's that supposed to mean?" Anna said.

Cassie didn't answer—just shot Anna another mischievous grin, heading into a deserted pedestrian shopping mall with cobbled streets. All the buildings were at least a hundred years old, three or four stories tall, with a shop at street level and apartments and offices on the upper floors. They passed a Subway and a

Burger King. America had made big inroads into Wales since Meg was last here.

Cassie led Meg and Anna to an alcove with a key code by the door. She punched in some numbers, and the door unlocked.

"Callum and I planned ahead," Cassie said. "All intelligence agencies have safe houses, and this is ours."

"The Project's?" Meg said.

Cassie glanced at her. "No. Ours."

They hurried down a narrow hallway, taking several lefts and rights, before exiting that building into an enclosed courtyard. Then they went through an archway, up several flights of steps to another long corridor, and finally stopped at a wooden door made of solid oak with another keypad beside it. This one also required Cassie to press some buttons before it opened, and then she stuck her face up to it.

"Retina scan," she said.

The door lock clicked, and they entered.

"Oh, wow." Anna dropped the duffel bag to the floor.

"Thanks." Cassie shut and bolted the door.

The apartment was a corner one, spacious and full of light, with hardwood floors, ceramic counters, and lots of polished chrome gleaming from the spotless open-plan kitchen.

"This is incredible!" Meg said. "How did you afford—" She stopped, deciding it was crass to ask about money.

"We didn't," Cassie said, answering the question anyway. "I don't know if Callum ever told you, but his father worked for the U.S. State Department and was a bit of a spy himself, though he would never say how much. This apartment belonged to him. He bought it off the record and off the books through a shell corporation back in the 1960s."

"How fortunate that he set this up in Cardiff," Meg said.

Cassie smirked. "He had safe houses in London and Paris too. And somewhere in Bulgaria, of all places. It's a good thing the corporation pays the taxes, because they're ridiculous." She stopped, grinning at the stunned looks on her friends' faces, and then added, "In case you hadn't realized, Callum is from what you might call 'old money' on both sides of his family. When David made him Earl of Shrewsbury, he wasn't the first lord in the family tree."

Anna laughed and, for the first time since they'd left Rhuddlan, it sounded genuine. "That explains a lot. He probably has more right to the throne of England than David does."

"Being an American, I pumped him for any memories of hanging with nobility growing up, but he's pretty close-mouthed about the whole thing," Cassie said. "I can tell you that Callum's mother is descended from James Stewart, who happens to be Callum's friend back in the Middle Ages."

"James Stewart, the fifth high steward of Scotland?" Meg said.

"The very same."

"I bet he never mentioned it to James," Meg said.

Cassie shot Meg another grin. "Callum didn't know about it then, just that he was related to the Stewarts. After his mother died, he'd boxed up her papers and stuck them in a closet in the

London safe house. It was only after we returned that I started going through them, and we discovered she'd done his whole family tree."

It may have been a strange conversation to be having while on the run from multiple governments, but Meg thought it explained a few things about Callum. And maybe more than a few things. It could be just the historian in Meg projecting, but he seemed like a person who'd been raised in a family with deep roots—and deep pockets—in the past.

"You might be wondering why we didn't take David here to recoup after he was abducted," Cassie said.

Anna crouched beside her duffel, unzipped it, and began to lay out its contents. "Actually, at this point I wasn't going to second guess you."

"David was ill. He needed the hospital." Meg said. "You guys did your best. Nobody doubts it." She glanced at Cassie, and the look on her face was one of relief.

"Not even David?" Cassie said.

Meg looked at her more closely. "Have regrets been eating at you?"

Cassie nodded and shrugged at the same time. "I've tried to ignore them, but I wish we'd made different choices from the start. Then David wouldn't have almost been killed, and Callum and I wouldn't have had to spend the last two years here."

"If you hadn't made those choices, you wouldn't have reconnected with your grandfather. Or been here to help us." Anna held a potato in each hand and looked up at Cassie. "How long do you think we have until Callum gets back to us?"

"The poor man should be busy for a while. But we have our cell phones." Cassie took out hers, waved it, and concluded in a singsong voice, "And nobody can track them."

Anna watched her sourly. "You're awfully cheerful for someone who hasn't slept since yesterday."

"I got some sleep on the bus and plane. Enough to stay awake for a while longer." She studied Meg and Anna. "I think we need to make a pact."

Meg came closer so the three women surrounded the duffel bag Anna had stopped unpacking. "What kind of pact?" Meg said.

"We're going back to the Middle Ages, right?" Cassie said.

"Right," Anna said, speaking for both her mother and herself.

"We need to be prepared," Cassie said. "Last time, it was a disaster from start to finish for Callum and me, though I'm glad David made it fine. We're not going to let that happen again. Nobody is going to get left behind."

"How can we possibly ensure that?" Anna said. "Sometimes—like when Mom jumped off the balcony at Chepstow, or David got Bronwen to almost wreck her car in Pennsylvania—we can control what happens. But half the time it just happens."

"You two have to promise not to leave us, not for any reason, no matter how compelling it feels at the time," Cassie said. "I'm not saying David didn't do the right thing two years ago. A bullet wound isn't something to mess around with. But if you're going home, we're coming with you."

"You both are really truly sure?" Meg said.

At Cassie's fervent nod, Anna added, "Callum too?"

"Yes," she said. "You can ask him, but he's already said he's sure. We'll take the risk, and we're not Marty."

"You came the same way as Marty, though," Meg said.

"I'm not the same person I was then. Neither is Callum."

"Okay," Anna said. "But I think the person you're really talking to is Mom. Because I'm not sure that I even have the genes for this."

"What are you talking about—" Cassie broke off as her phone rang.

She stared at the screen for a second and then answered. "Hello?"

Meg couldn't hear the other side of the conversation, but Cassie mouthed, "Mark." She listened for a few seconds before saying into the phone, "Slow down, slow down. What's going on?"

Meg leaned close, but then Cassie made a disgusted sound at the back of her throat and put Mark on speakerphone.

His voice filled the room. "I'm telling you, it's all gone sideways."

"Can your phone be traced?" Cassie said. That wasn't the response Meg would have made to Mark's assertion, but given how far they'd come since Rhuddlan, perhaps it was the most important question she could ask.

"You people are costing me a fortune in tech," Mark said. "This is my third mobile of the weekend, same as you."

"Where's Callum?" Cassie said.

"He won't tell me," Mark said. "He and Jeffries are on foot, heading your way, but they may not make it that far."

Meg peered out the window to the street below. Many more people were moving along it now that the sun was up. As it turned out, Cardiff did wake early, even on a Saturday.

"He was supposed to be at a meeting at the Office," Cassie said.

"He never made it. This was all a ruse." Regret leaked from every syllable Mark spoke. "Director Tate never wanted Callum's help with the disaster at Signals. The whole thing was a setup to get you out of the United States and out of the American government's clutches so Tate could have you here."

"Right where you wanted us," Meg said.

"Not me! But yes, this is all about you and Anna." Mark's laugh was bitter. "When Jeffries rang to say that he and Callum—and only he and Callum—were two minutes out from the Office, Tate's surprise made Callum suspicious."

"How did he get away?" Cassie said. "Why is he still with Darren?"

"I'll let him tell you that," Mark said.

Meg thought back through everything that had happened in America. "What about your friend George? Was he in on it?"

Meg could hear Mark's hesitation when he spoke. "The Consul-General told him to give you every assistance. She didn't tell him why."

"To screw the Americans, that's why," Anna said. "And us, I guess."

"The minute Callum reaches us, we should just leave," Meg said. "If some poor guy hadn't been flying the plane, we could have crashed it into the ocean and been done with all this."

"I keep telling you, we can't return without what David needs," Anna said. "Not if we can help it."

"I'm working on that," Mark said.

Meg had forgotten for a moment who they were talking to.

"That's why Callum called me first. That's why I'm also coming to you."

"I do *not* want another chase through the streets of Cardiff," Cassie said. "Where are we meeting?"

Anna had already started repacking the duffel. Cassie headed off with the phone tucked to her ear, still talking to Mark. Meg stared out the window, finding her anxiety rising and falling with every breath. The budget cuts to the Project made sense now. The powers-that-be had wanted her family when they were in front of them, but they didn't want the expense of waiting for them between trips. Callum's group hadn't made any headway in duplicating what they could do, so the government had decided to focus on watching for their re-entry and then springing into action. It was just Tate's bad luck that Meg and Anna had come into this world in such a remote place—and that Cassie's and

Callum's loyalty to Meg and her family trumped their loyalty to any modern government.

Cassie returned with the phone put away, carrying two swords and a finely woven mesh bag nearly the size of a backpack. Meg didn't ask what was in it, and Cassie didn't explain. With some maneuvering and distorting both ends of the duffel out of shape, she managed to fit all the items inside the larger bag.

"That's what you meant by being ready," Anna said.

"It's time to go," Cassie said. "If there's anything else you want or need, now's the time because in an hour we could be gone."

That sounded very good to Meg.

Anna nodded her agreement. "Let's go home."

16

November 2019

Callum

Callum clamped down on the string of curses that were running through his mind at his own government's betrayal. "Whatever impulse prompted you to notify Director Tate that we were close—"

"He requested that I ring him as you exited the airplane, but his mobile was busy so I left a message and didn't speak to him directly." Jeffries shrugged. "It seemed reasonable to try again. Honestly, sir, I didn't know."

At the next traffic light, only a few blocks from where the women had left the SUV, Jeffries had rung up Tate. Cardiff Castle had still been in view to the west, perched on its motte, and they'd just passed City Hall. Because the light had turned green as Director Tate had answered the call, Jeffries had pulled to the side of the road to speak to him. Callum had insisted he put Tate on speakerphone.

"Sir," Callum had said. "This is Director Callum."

"Callum!" Tate said. "I trust your flight was smooth?"

"Yes, sir. I apologize for arriving at such an early hour and on the weekend too."

"Early to you; late for many of us here."

"Yes, sir."

"I understand that not only Cassie but several guests accompanied you on your flight," Tate said.

At that point, Callum had glanced at Jeffries, who leaned across the gearbox to whisper, "I didn't tell him. Jones asked me not to."

Once Jones had brought in George Spencer to produce Anna's and Meg's identification, Callum had accepted that he'd opened his plans to his own government. Callum hadn't seen a way to counteract that, not if he wanted Anna and Meg safe in Wales; it had seemed like an acceptable risk.

When Callum didn't respond, Tate spoke again, "The Consul-General in San Francisco let me know that you had successfully rescued our two time travelers from the Americans. That was good work. I'm looking forward to meeting them."

"Of course, sir," Callum had said. "I'm sure we can arrange that later today."

His answer had prompted a pause of several beats from Tate, who'd then said, "They aren't with you?"

"No, sir. Not at the moment."

Jeffries had then made a slashing motion with one hand across his throat, but Callum hadn't needed his warning to know that something wasn't right.

"I'm sorry, sir, but it looks like there's trouble ahead of us," Callum said. "An accident, I think. If you'll excuse me, Jeffries and I will be along shortly." Callum closed the connection and moved for the door handle.

Jeffries opened his door at the same time Callum did.

"What are you doing?" Callum had said.

"Coming with you, sir."

"You can't," Callum said. "It could be your career."

"It could be yours too, sir," he'd said. "Besides, I'm not doing anything wrong—just walking with you to get a cup of coffee."

"You should take me in," Callum said.

"I'm not going to do that, sir," he'd said. "And the only way you're going to stop me from coming with you is to shoot me."

Since Callum hadn't brought his gun with him, that was going to be a little difficult. Callum studied Jeffries for more time than he had to spare and then decided he could tag along, based on nothing more than the few interactions he'd had with him, and the fact that Jones thought well of Jeffries. "Leave the keys and mobile phone in the vehicle. Do you have anything else on you that's traceable?"

"No, sir."

Callum eyed him. "Did you discuss a plan with Tate in advance in case I scarpered? You'd come with me in hopes I'd lead you to the women?"

"No, sir." Jeffries remained calm. "It's a good plan. Either way I come out on top."

"Exactly." Callum laughed. "No point in going down with the ship."

"No, sir," Jeffries said, and then a worried look came into his dark eyes. "It isn't right, sir."

"What isn't?" Callum was tempted to ask Jeffries to stop calling him 'sir', but since he knew it wouldn't do any good, he didn't bother.

"Any of this."

"I'm sure Tate would say it's just business, to use the American expression." Callum set off across the street, ignoring horns that honked at him. "Come if you're coming. I'm calling Jones." Callum wanted to speak to Cassie too, but she was safe at the flat. Jones needed to get out of the office and get his arse down here with those plans David wanted. Then the four of them could be on their way to the Middle Ages.

Callum spoke into the phone, telling Jones what had happened, what he planned to do now, and what he needed from Jones. Jeffries hurried after Callum. "Where are we going, sir?"

Callum held up one finger to prevent Jeffries from interrupting his conversation with Jones. He spoke into the phone, "How long do you think we have before they send the troops after us?"

"They might give you a quarter of an hour to come quietly," said Jones. "They may still have hope of that."

"Text me if you hear more. I need you to ring Cassie now and tell her what's happening. I'll ring her myself with a meeting place as soon as I have one." Callum disconnected.

"We need to do this fast," he said to Jeffries.

"Yes, sir."

Callum frowned, deciding he had to try. "Please stop calling me 'sir'."

"Aren't you a lord in the Middle Ages?" Jeffries said.

"The Earl of Shrewsbury," Callum said. "How did you know that? I kept it out of my file."

"Jones told me."

"The man has too loose lips," Callum said.

"So, I'll keep calling you 'sir', if that's all right."

The food shops were beginning to open. Awnings for the ethnic grocery shops had been raised, and of course, coffee and tea had been available since five, even on a Saturday morning. Although the safe house was very close, Callum didn't dare go to it, not only because he didn't want Jeffries to know about it, but in case they were being followed.

They headed back through old town Cardiff, coming into it from the opposite direction from which Cassie, Meg, and Anna had entered it. Near the entrance to a coffee shop with a line snaking out the door, Callum stopped to ring Cassie himself.

She picked up immediately. "Where are you?"

"Not far. Where are you?"

"Safe," she said. "We want to be with you."

"Come to Hadley's Coffee Shop on Queen Street," Callum said.

"Mark said that Darren is with you. Why?" she said.

"I couldn't get him to leave."

Jeffries' mouth twisted in a wry smile. "I heard that." He raised his eyebrows and pointed into the shop with his chin.

Callum nodded. "Coffee, cream, one sugar."

"Got it." Jeffries disappeared inside.

Callum could have ditched Jeffries then, but he had begun to think that he might prove useful—and seeing as how currently his only ally was Jones, he couldn't be as choosy as he might otherwise have been. Besides, when Cassie and Callum had arrived here with David two years ago, both Natasha and Driscoll, whom Callum had called friends, had proved to be traitors. Jeffries deserved at least the benefit of the doubt Callum had given them.

Callum watched him through the window of the coffee shop. So far all Jeffries had done was order. What he hadn't done was surreptitiously borrow someone's mobile to ring Tate.

Callum's mobile buzzed with an incoming call. "Hang on, Cassie."

He switched calls.

"Where are you?" said Jones.

Callum told him about the coffee shop, his eyes still on Jeffries' back. "Did you get the maps?"

"It took longer to print them than to access them. I'm bringing them, but I'm on a bus," said Jones.

"Which bus?" Callum checked his watch. "How long?"

"Twenty minutes."

"Too long," Callum said.

"No choice," said Jones. "Number 25."

Jones knew that would mean something to Callum. Memorizing bus and train tables was child's play to an MI-5 agent. "All right," Callum said, accepting what he couldn't change. "The bus turns the corner by the castle. We'll catch it there." He hung up.

Jeffries returned with the coffee. "I should have parked the car somewhere else."

"The last thing anyone at the Office wants to do is hunt us down," Callum said. "Right now, they're still hoping you'll bring me in, and that they'll get to Meg and Anna that way."

"If Director Tate rings my mobile, he won't get an answer," Jeffries said.

"And he still won't know where you are or what you're doing." Callum took a sip of coffee.

"Why are we standing here in the open?" Jeffries said.

"Because we're in a surveillance blind spot," Callum said.

Jeffries turned his head sharply to look at Callum. "How do you know that?"

Callum didn't deign to dignify the question with a reply.

Jeffries ducked his head. "You must have stashed the girls around here somewhere. Even you aren't that omnipotent."

"What do you mean?"

Jeffries waved a hand. "You know, the way you came out of the debacle after Lady Jane's death smelling like roses."

"That was then, clearly," Callum said, "given what's happened to the Project since."

"Yeah, but—" Jeffries took a long drink of his tea, "—you'll end up all right even after this. You always do."

Callum eyed him. Jeffries' words should have sounded resentful, but his tone was more admiring than anything else. Jeffries noticed Callum looking at him and shrugged. "Why do you think I'm here instead of turning you in?"

"That is oddly honest of you," Callum said. "I hope you're not in for more of a ride than you bargained for."

"I didn't join MI-5 to keep an eye on snot-nosed terrorist wannabes or harmless Welsh nationalists. We should be out in the field rounding up the men who bombed GCHQ. Why is Tate wasting resources chasing down you and the girls?"

"I can't answer any of that," Callum said.

"Neither can I," Jeffries said, "but if anyone is going to find those answers, it's going to be you, not Tate."

"I fear your confidence has been misplaced," Callum said.

"We'll see," Jeffries said, "but I'm guessing this blind spot isn't here by accident."

Callum smiled into his coffee. It was true that several cameras between here and the safe house had been routinely vandalized as soon as they were fixed, some multiple times, until their owners had given up and moved them to slightly different locations without the same angle of vision.

Jeffries' optimism could not have been more different from Callum's own assessment of his situation. The last few months had been discouraging in the extreme. One of the most difficult things for Callum to come to terms with was how spectacularly he'd failed in his mission. Cassie argued that he'd done the best he could, but from where he stood, that was irrelevant. Callum had felt like he was in one of those internet memes where 'You had only one job!' was written over the top of a toilet that had been installed upside down.

Callum's job may have had many moving parts, but it was still one job: to protect David, his family, and his interests in the modern world. In September, Callum had sat in the Permanent Secretary's office, listening to him explain why the Prime Minister no longer felt the need to fund his department, and had looked into the face of utter failure.

Recent events, however, had Callum reexamining that assessment. First of all, because the funding had been cut to nothing, when Meg and Anna had come through into this world, only Jones had been on duty to see it. If Callum's office had been fully up and running, everybody from the Prime Minister on down would have known about it right away. Callum's strictures would have safeguarded Meg and Anna, but the two women would have been on display, and who was to say that the Prime Minister wouldn't have swept aside Callum's carefully laid plans at the last moment?

Like Director Tate had hoped to do today.

Second, the demands of Callum's job had made it difficult to get away last Thanksgiving, and he had feared that he was going to miss this year's celebration in Oregon. Because his department had been dismantled, however, when he put in for leave, nobody had cared how long he asked to be gone. From the look on the Permanent Secretary's face, he might have given Callum time off until Christmas if he'd asked, since he was being transferred back to MI-5 at the new year anyway.

Third, and more personally, the upheaval of the last few months had ensured that Cassie and Callum felt far less obligation to their jobs or their employer than in the past. Callum saw now that there was more than one way to serve his country, and he was beginning to think that MI-5 might not be it. He and Cassie could return to the Middle Ages with light hearts.

Provided they survived the journey.

17

November 1291

David

David had never had any delusions regarding his role in war and his ability to fight in it. Raised on the assumption that all the fighting he would ever do was with a plastic light saber or in a computer game, he'd ridden into his first fight beside Bevyn when he was fourteen hoping for little more than survival.

He had wanted to win, of course. He had wanted to make his father proud, but he'd had no delusions that if he was brave enough or fought hard enough, somehow they would win. It was only after he'd lived in the Middle Ages for a few years and fought in more battles that he'd started to understand what it took to win. And for the most part it wasn't bravery, at least not his bravery, or only if by 'bravery' one meant the ability not to turn tail and run.

David's bravery in battle wasn't going to save them. Subterfuge, on the other hand, or the ability to think several moves ahead of his opponent ... now that was a different story.

Justin and David crouched behind some scraggly bushes, looking up the valley towards Aberglaslyn. Thick fog surrounded them thanks to a sharp downturn in the temperature of the air compared to the river and the valley. The fog was turning out to be a godsend, however, hiding their slow approach to their current location.

Fog was not without its drawbacks: sound carried better, so they had to be even more careful to stay quiet; and David couldn't see a thing beyond his nose. He'd rock/paper/scissored Ieuan for Uncle Ted's binoculars and won. David had them in his hand, awaiting the moment he was able to see anything through them.

A scout had reported that Ieuan and his men had reached their position too, roughly half a mile to the north of where David's men were hiding. Ieuan was to be the anvil to David's hammer. David just hoped that Madog and his army really lay between them, because however much the scouts assured him that they were there and in the numbers advertised, David couldn't see them. His desire to remain in control of any situation was being tested.

Justin put a hand on David's arm and tipped his head towards a shadow that had emerged from a stand of trees downslope from them. "Scout."

"We can't allow him to stumble upon us by mistake," David said.

"I'll take him." Justin gathered himself, ready to spring up and descend on the scout.

"No. Wait. If he gets close, kill him, but just watch him until I get back." David wriggled away and ran the fifty feet to where his men had gathered in the trees near the path they'd come in on.

William stood holding the reins of both his horse and David's. When he saw David, he started forward. "My lord—"

David held up his hand to stop him and tried to look reassuring at the same time. "I need an archer."

"I'm an archer, my lord." One of the Welsh riders stepped forward while at the same time tossing the reins of his horse to a compatriot. His name was Afan, and to say that he was an archer was to seriously understate the case.

"Come with me," David said.

David and Afan crawled to where Justin still waited, trying to hurry and yet be as quiet as possible. To David's ears, they were making an awful lot of noise, but with the coming of day, the wind had risen and was rustling the branches in the trees around them.

"Is he still there?" David threw himself onto his stomach beside Justin. He didn't bother pulling out his binoculars again because they still couldn't see farther than the stand of trees that hid the scout.

"There's two of them now," Justin said. "The second is still hidden among the brambles. You were right to wait, my lord."

David couldn't see the one in the trees but believed he was there. "Can you take him?" he said to Afan.

Afan had settled at David's shoulder, on the other side from Justin. "Either of them, my lord. Or both." His eyes flashed.

David had offended him with the question, but he'd had to ask it. "Justin, work your way around to the right. Afan, be ready to loose an arrow the instant Justin appears to take the nearest man down. We can't give the second scout time to shout a warning."

Justin disappeared into the bushes to the right, and Afan retreated towards the left to a position that would allow him to stand to shoot, but still hide him from the sight of the scouts. Another ten minutes and the sun would fully rise; at that point, it would be a lot harder for both sides to hide, no matter how gray the morning. They needed to get the scouts before then.

Or rather, his men needed to kill them. There wasn't much point in pretending otherwise. Though Bevyn wasn't with David today, he felt his old mentor at his left shoulder, speaking urgently in his ear as he had before that first battle at the Conwy River when David was fourteen years old, reviewing what he'd taught him all those years ago at Castell y Bere. David hadn't learned everything he needed to know about life in the Middle Ages from Bevyn, but he'd learned how to fight. Bevyn had taught David to do what was necessary because it was necessary. It was a legacy that, regardless of the disagreements that had come between the two men in the past, David could be grateful for now.

David kept his eyes on the first scout they'd seen. The man crouched low, hurrying from the original stand of trees where his friend waited, up the slope towards David. The scout was only fifteen yards away when Justin stepped out from behind a gorse bush. Before Justin could even move against the man, Afan had loosed his arrow from the left. David heard the dull thud of it hitting flesh.

David was on his feet in an instant, racing down the slope towards the trees eighty feet away. He slid the last distance on the fallen bracken and wet grass, barreling into the second scout, who was hit but not dead. The arrow protruded from the left side of his chest. Afan had missed the center of his mass, though it was still a spectacular shot from where Afan stood to where the scout had been standing in the dark under the trees.

The man scrabbled with his hands at his waist. At first David thought he was going for a blade, but then David saw the horn slung on a leather strap around the man's torso. Even if David hadn't tackled him, he wouldn't have had enough breath to sound it, but David gave him points for trying.

David ripped the horn out of the scout's hands and threw it down the slope. It was only then that he truly looked at the man. He was young—David's age or maybe a little younger. And he was dying; they both knew it.

David clasped his hand in his. "It's okay. It's going to be okay."

"You."

David bent closer as the man tried to speak again.

"We didn't think you would come too."

"It was just luck that I was with my father at Rhuddlan," David said. There was no harm in telling him that, since he would never be able to tell Madog.

"No! No!" The scout came to himself for a second, finding strength he shouldn't still have, and grasped David's shoulder with his free hand. "Not you. Not luck. Not for you." His eyes widened. "We didn't know. Tell Madog—" He held himself still, and for a second David thought he was going to speak again, but then he couldn't. He was dead.

David sat back on his heels, cold swirling in his belly. Men had died in his arms before, but he'd never held an enemy to his last breath, never witnessed the kind of deathbed confession you see only in movies, and he didn't know what the man had meant for him to understand or to tell Madog.

Afan spoke from behind David. "Madog didn't come all this way to defeat you, my lord. He wants only your father."

David turned to look up at him. "Is that what you understood from what he said?"

"You are the King of England," Afan said. "The only reason Madog is free to wage war against your father is because England no longer threatens Wales. Your very life protects us. Every Welshman knows it. Madog knows it."

David didn't know how to respond. What the scout had said had occurred to him before, but he hadn't ever heard anyone else articulate it. David looked back to the scout and reached out to close his eyes. Then he wiped his bloodstained hands on the scout's cloak and stood.

Justin had come up beside Afan and had been listening. He'd just killed a man for David, a Welshman fighting a war for Wales, but even he was nodding. "We all know it."

A horn call sounded in the far distance, reverberating down the valley. "That's your father," Afan said.

Although Dad's company had dawdled on the way to the bridge to give Ieuan and David time to get their men in position, Dad's intent was to ride the mile from Beddgelert to Aberglaslyn at a canter. That would bring the lead horses to the head of the valley in no more than ten minutes. The road along the river was only wide enough for two horses to ride abreast, which meant that the company would stretch out for a quarter of a mile. David was regretting this plan more and more by the second.

"We should move." He backed off their position and ran to his horse, finding his hands shaking—not so much from fear as adrenaline. He put the binoculars away in the saddlebag.

William was right there beside David, fastening down the straps. "Is it time, my lord?"

"It's time." David caught William by the upper arm. "I know you fought for me at Windsor, but you've never been in a cavalry charge. You stay to the back or your father and mine will have my head, you understand?"

"Yes, my lord." William nodded, but David wasn't entirely confident he'd obey. William was his father's son and had a fine sense of honor. As shown by the fact that he was David's squire in the first place, he had a knack for letting his honor lead him into trouble.

David didn't have time to press William further and hoisted himself into the saddle. Two minutes later, the company was moving. It was half a mile from the spot where they'd hidden themselves to the top of the valley where David's father would emerge, and to David it felt like he'd hardly settled himself into the saddle before the roar of hundreds of men's voices split the air.

"Madog's men are charging!" William's voice went high with the same excitement and fear that was inflicting everyone.

David made a guttural sound deep in his throat. "And hopefully Ieuan and Dad are too." But he couldn't tell from here.

Justin pulled his horse up beside David, eyebrows raised.

David nodded. Justin was his captain. It was his job to command the men.

All Justin had to do was look back at the riders and jerk his head once in the direction he wanted everyone to go, and they were off.

The company surged down the hill into the valley. The fog still hovered close to the ground, but with the coming of the day it was thinning, and there was enough light to see by—at least to prevent the men from driving their horses into the river by mistake. At a gallop, a horse can cover half a mile in two minutes, and they were the longest two minutes of David's life before his horse came around a hillock, the slope gave way to a flat field, and he could see the battle before him.

The only good thing about Dad's position had been that the river flowed from high to low, as rivers do, so that he'd been descending out of the gap when Madog's forces charged into his. The two armies—if one could call Dad's numbers an army—had met at a low spot in a farmer's field on which only stubby November grass grew.

A man to David's right screamed in pain, an arrow sticking out of his shoulder. More arrows rained among David's company, hitting men and horses alike. But they were charging, and David disciplined his mind to focus on what was ahead of him and not that his men were falling around him. Or that he might fall too. A second rain of arrows came, indicating that Madog's bowmen were getting into a good rhythm, but the third barrage came haphazardly. And then the arrows ceased to come at all.

There was no point in glancing up the hill to see what was happening, not if David hoped to live through the next few minutes. But he spared a thought for Ieuan's bowmen, who must have found, if belatedly, good ground from which to shoot. It could only be they who were keeping Madog's bowmen occupied with themselves instead of David's men.

Justin had pulled a little ahead of David and was the first to reach the rear of Madog's force. The spearmen were pressing forward, taking on not only Dad's cavalry but Ieuan's footmen, who had surged from the path along the draw that ran between where Madog's men had waited and where Dad's company had emerged. None of the foot soldiers on either side were in what one might call a uniform, but everyone on David's side wore a red kerchief, either tied around necks or upper arms. Madog's men wore a plain linen band.

Madog's men were less organized than Dad's. Good.

The armies met in the chaos that accompanies any battle once the two sides are joined. It was only toy army men who deployed in squares and lines. As David swung his sword into the back of a man who'd been late to turn at his approach, he banished all thoughts from his mind but the necessity of staying on his horse and not dying. David's company had completely surprised the men at the back of Madog's army. Their focus had been forward towards Dad's cavalry, who'd ridden into the valley from the north, and Ieuan's spearmen, who had formed up on the slope above the field to the northeast and were fighting behind their tall shields.

Madog's men fell before David's riders, as footmen almost always fall before cavalry, no matter the unevenness of the numbers.

Overall, Dad's forces were far fewer—Madog could have had up to fifteen hundred men on foot alone—but if every one of David's horsemen still in the saddle managed to take on a single footman and win, those casualties would be enough to make the rest of Madog's men turn and run.

David had divided his cavalry into thirds, each with a leader. David's contingent followed him up the middle of the field. He'd been keeping an eye out for his father all the while he was fighting, and it took another minute and three more deaths for David to find him. Dad was still seated and had three of his own men hemming him in and preventing more than one of Madog's men at a time from reaching him.

Whatever Dad might say, war was a young man's game. David spurred his horse towards him. Another third of David's men had driven through Madog's ranks to the west along the river and had managed to circle all the way around the enemy force and link up with Dad's company.

It looked like Dad's men had been holding their own too; victory was possible. David was sure, in fact, that his side was winning, right up until he fought his way to Dad's side and turned to look back the way he'd come. At David's arrival, Dad's guard pushed outward, creating a small pocket of space for the two men to confer.

Dad grunted a greeting. "Where's their cavalry?"

David had been so focused on what he had to do that he hadn't registered the giant missing piece of the puzzle. "Could Madog have left them at Harlech?"

"Unlikely," Dad said. "That's not what the scouts reported."

David stood in his stirrups, his eyes sweeping over the field. The fog had thinned some more, such that visibility was a hundred yards instead of twenty. No horsemen appeared. It was surely too much to hope for that Madog had already gone down, but David didn't see him either.

Slightly panicked at what could be a major miscalculation on their part, David raised his sword above his head, calling his men to regroup around him. Most of them had swept through Madog's lines and turned to face back the way they'd come like

David had. Ieuan was doing a good job of holding his own on the hill. Madog's spearmen had fallen back to regroup too. David needed his men to head back through them. They needed to win this now.

But as it turned out, there was no *now*. At the moment David tasted the possibility of victory, a horn call echoed from the southern end of the field.

Madog had come.

David's only comfort was that Madog had left his charge a little late. Instead of riding into the rear of David's cavalry, which was now forming a line ten men deep at the northern end of the field, facing south, Madog's own spearmen were between him and them. Madog's spearman had noticed this problem too. Most of them scrambled to get out of the way, not towards Ieuan's spearmen, who held their position on the hill, but west towards the river.

David's sword went into the air. He stood in his stirrups and lifted his voice to his men. "Forward!" Then he pointed his sword at the opposing cavalry, which had started to materialize out of the fog. Though Madog didn't have more horseman than David did, his men and horses were fresh.

David urged his horse into a trot. He slashed at the heads and shoulders of the spearmen who were foolish enough to stand their ground or slow in getting out of the way. Dad's guard had formed up around him to David's left, though Dad would never allow them to ride into Madog's force in front of him. Like David, he wore his shield on his left arm and held the reins loosely in his left hand, though he was mostly controlling his horse with his knees. Cadwallon rode on Dad's right to protect his unshielded side.

Justin rode to David's right, and David could hear him cursing steadily, something about condemning Madog, the fog, and all Welsh traitors to hell. But then Dad raised his hand, and the line slowed. Still eighty yards away, Madog had risen to stand in his stirrups and had ripped off his helmet. Even from this distance, David could see the slash of a grin that split his face. He whipped the helmet around in a circle above his head, calling his men to action, and then tamped it back down on his head. Back in the saddle, he looked straight at Dad and cupped his hands around his mouth. "Do you surrender, Llywelyn? You must know that you cannot win!"

Calling David's father 'Llywelyn' was an insult, of course. He was the King of Wales, a fact which Madog was plainly telling him that he didn't acknowledge.

Madog was working from a position of strength. He had the greater numbers. Out of the corner of David's eye, he could see Madog's spearmen gathering themselves by the river, prepared to renew the fight they had thought lost. The cold feeling that had sat in David's stomach since the scout had spoken of David's lack of luck turned to solid ice.

David swallowed hard. Their plan had failed. What Bevyn would say about the disaster when he heard about it didn't bear thinking about.

"Fight or run," Dad said.

"We can't run," David said. "If we run, all of Ieuan's men will die. And after that, Madog will chase those who survive all the way to Aber."

Dad nodded. "Then we fight."

David ripped off his helmet, as Madog had done a moment ago, but David tossed his aside so his men could see his face and take courage from his defiance. Then he stabbed his sword above his head. "Cymry!"

From the hillside to David's left, Ieuan's men heard his call. Whether or not they understood the bravado behind it—and the desperation—they roared their approval. David spurred his horse, riding towards Madog as fast as his horse would carry him and outstripping Dad within twenty yards.

Without hesitation, the men followed David down the center of the field, and if they questioned his choice of fighting instead of running, they didn't show it. David could tell where Madog was by the white plume on his helmet. Shouts and calls came from behind. Except for Justin and Samuel, coming up on the far right, David was getting ahead of his men.

But he had formed a plan. It might be a crazy, foolish plan, but cutting off the head of the snake might be their only chance to win this battle. David had seen the reckless look in his father's eye a moment ago, and David thought that Dad had seen this one chance too. He might say David was more valuable than he was, but David was younger and stronger. This fight belonged to him.

"I'm counting on you to watch my back, Justin. You know what to do. We've practiced this many times." David sheathed his sword.

"My lord! What are you doing?"

"What I must." David didn't spare Justin another glance. Madog was only twenty yards away now and bearing down on David as fast as David was racing for him.

"My lord, but—"

David headed his horse to Madog's right, which wasn't the usual way of doing things in the Middle Ages. As David intended, it caused a momentary hesitation in Madog's horse. Instead of David's sword clashing with Madog's, David bashed his shield into Madog's shield and used his greater size and strength to drive Madog's shield down and away. More than that, as David's left arm swept downward, he launched himself at Madog.

David hadn't played football in years—and hadn't liked it much when he did play—but he'd rehearsed this move with a practice dummy and his own guard so often he'd dreamt about it. David's chest hit Madog's left shoulder and upper arm. Letting go of his shield, he wrapped his arms around Madog's shoulders, and they fell together off the other side of Madog's horse. Madog's right side hit the ground with a horrible crunch, and he lost his grip on his sword.

The fall knocked the wind out of David and did worse to Madog. As Madog lay momentarily stunned, David scrambled to his feet, pulled his sword from its sheath, and kicked Madog's sword out of range of his groping hand. It would have been expedient at that point for David to turn Madog onto his back like a turtle and drive his sword through Madog's heart, but the rules of warfare were such that David couldn't kill him when he was down. They were knights after all. He had to give Madog a chance to surrender.

As David had fallen on Madog, the front lines of the two forces had met with an awful crash. Though David was only peripherally aware of anyone but Madog, he could tell that Justin and the men of his immediate guard were doing their jobs, circling around the pair and allowing David to take on Madog without fear of being attacked from behind.

David did not take chivalry so far as to give Madog back his sword, however, and Madog moaned and struggled to rise. He got first to his knees and then to his feet. His helmet was askew, and he tugged it off, revealing a mop of black curly hair, soaked with sweat and pressed to his head. David pointed his sword at him, not willing to give Madog any more time to think. "Do you surrender?"

Madog gave a mocking laugh, weaving on his feet. Dad was right that he was short and thin—not a soldier by nature, David guessed, but someone who'd taken on that role out of pride and necessity. David could understand it, even if he couldn't condone its manifestation here.

"Tell your men to stand down," David said.

"And if I do, what then?" Madog said.

"This war will end here, and you will receive justice according to the laws of this land," David said.

Fighting continued in other parts of the field, but the soldiers in the vicinity—both David's and Madog's—had stepped back from each other in order to watch the exchange. That was a medieval tradition too: to have the two lords who led their troops fight one another in single combat to determine the outcome of the war. In fact, David had counted on it.

"Like it ended with Valence?" Madog choked on his own laughter. "Where I dangle by the neck at the end of a long rope?"

"It is you who brought this rebellion on us, Madog," David said. "You don't have the right now to set the terms of your own surrender. But I will give you the same terms I gave Valence: a trial before a jury of your peers—"

A horn call rang out from the southern end of the field, the same direction from which Madog's call had come. It was the third call of the day and the sweetest sound David had ever heard.

"Math!" He shouted the name to the skies.

Justin laughed, and Carew called from David's right. "God favors us, my lord!"

Math must have marched through the night from Dolwyddelan, taking the mountain paths between ridges that only local Welshmen would know, to arrive here at this moment. Madog's men were now caught between them.

David directed his gaze again to Madog, knowing he was gloating and unable to stop himself. Madog looked away for a second, eyeing the men around him—and then he threw himself at David, a blade pulled from his boot flashing in his hand. David's shield arm came up to block the knife, and with a thrust, he skewered Madog through the gut with his sword.

As Bevyn had taught him.

18

November 2019

Anna

Cassie hurried Meg and Anna back out through the maze of corridors. They were more heavily burdened than before. Cassie and Anna each carried a backpack over her shoulder, and this time Cassie and Mom held the giant, bulging duffel bag between them.

"How far to the coffee shop?" Anna said.

"A few blocks," Cassie said. "We have to go the long way around, though, because we want to avoid surveillance cameras." She glanced over at Anna. "Don't worry, Callum and I planned ahead."

"Clearly," Mom said.

Cassie led them through a stairwell, and they came out on a different street than the one they'd come in on. "I don't know if I can explain what it's been like, being left behind." She walked rapidly across the cobbled road and entered another doorway on the other side.

"You don't have to, Cassie," Mom said, "I know all about it."

"I guess you would." Cassie took a left and then a right through another maze of buildings.

"When David was born, Mom did everything she could to get back to Dad," Anna said. "She couldn't."

"Your mom's life was never in mortal danger," Cassie said.

"True," Mom said, "but I'm not so sure how this would have worked if it had been. David was still a baby. He wasn't ready."

"We saved Dad's life at Cilmeri," Anna said, "but if you had brought us back sooner, Dad wouldn't have gone at all."

Mom's expression turned brittle. "Now that I couldn't promise you. The man is stubborn."

Cassie's lips twitched in a quick smile before she took the lead again. "I think I need to explain anyway."

Anna certainly wasn't going to stop her.

"Callum and I had to make plans because we didn't know how soon you would return, and we wanted to be ready when you did."

"That explains the safe house and all the rest," Mom said.

"Exactly," Cassie said.

"Is that why you two haven't—?" Anna stopped. She'd been about to ask one of the most personal questions possible.

Cassie made a 'hm' sound. "Were you going to ask if that's why we haven't had kids yet?"

They'd crossed another street and passed through several basements before taking a set of stairs back up to street level. A wooden door blocked the way.

Before she opened it, Cassie leaned against it. "This isn't the Middle Ages, Anna. Waiting two years is nothing here. But yes."

Anna was still catching her breath, but she ducked her head in acknowledgement of that sacrifice. "Thank you for telling me."

"I wouldn't want you to mention it to Callum." Cassie looked from Anna to Mom. "Ready?"

"Ready," Mom said.

Cassie opened the door, and the three women stepped out onto another cobbled street. Callum and Darren stood two feet away to the right, half-hidden underneath a large green awning.

"Hey," Cassie said.

"Hey yourself." Callum took the duffel from Cassie and slung it over his shoulder. It clashed with the proper look of his suit, tie, and trench coat. He was bigger than any of the women were, though, and he hadn't exactly let his hard won medieval physique run to fat. "Any trouble?"

"Not that we know of," Cassie said. "I gather we're catching a bus?"

"The 25." Callum checked his watch. "We have five minutes to get there."

"Then we should go." Cassie looked back at Mom and Anna. "This is where it gets tricky. The bus stop is at the end of this street in the exact spot where we got out of Darren's car. We should walk determinedly without running. Anna, could you walk with Darren as if you know him well?"

Darren and Anna looked at each other. He shrugged. Anna nodded.

"Meg, you and I will stay together, and then Callum can bring up the rear," Cassie said.

"We may have to bunch up to cross the street, but otherwise, don't stop for anything," Callum said. "We'll be in the open and vulnerable."

Darren lifted one arm, eyebrows raised, and Anna moved close enough so he could put his arm across her shoulders. She kept the backpack slung over her left shoulder, and she put her right arm around his waist. It was awkward and weird to be walking this way with a man she barely knew. Math would just have to forgive her. If she ever told him. Maybe it would never need to come up.

"There it is!" Up ahead, the bus swung around a corner. It was an orangey-yellow and turquoise double-decker—not the London red—and faces peered down at Anna from the top level. Darren raised a hand to warn the traffic that they were crossing, and they dashed across the street. The others hustled along behind. Darren ducked around the front of the bus so it couldn't leave before they got on it unless it ran them over, and they entered through the folded front door.

The bus driver, sitting at the front of the bus to the right, didn't even look as Darren dropped a handful of coins into the meter. Five adult tickets spat out.

"Another month and this wouldn't have worked," Darren said. "The buses are going to stop taking cash."

"Yeah, and our cards would be a big fat neon sign for MI-5." Cassie crowded onto the top step, her hand in Callum's, and looked past Anna down the length of the bus. "There's Mark."

Mark looked exactly as a computer nerd should. He was in his early thirties, of average height, semi-balding, with extra padding around the middle, glasses, and rounded shoulders from too many hours spent in front of a computer. He, too, wore a backpack, and as the companions filed down the crowded aisle towards him, he made room for them to stand around him. At the front of the bus, the seats were arranged with their backs to the windows, but where Mark stood, they were in rows, two seats to a side with an aisle down the center.

Mom found a seat on the left in the first row next to the window, and Callum heaved the bag off his shoulder to lean it against the seat beside her. Anna took off her backpack and dropped it onto the seat itself, and then she sat with her back to the window, right in front of Mom. Everyone else remained standing, holding onto a floor-to-ceiling pole or the bar above their heads.

The bus hadn't moved, and Cassie peered towards the front, standing on tiptoe to look past the other passengers that crowded the aisle. "It's okay. The bus isn't going because the light's red."

Anna shifted in her seat, anxious with the wait. She was glad to be moving, though Callum hadn't actually said what the plan was and where they were going next. A few seconds later, the bus started forward, drove a short distance, changed lanes in order to take a right, and then passed in front of a large white building on the left.

"That's the courthouse," Cassie said, pointing, "and that's City Hall beside it—" She broke off. "My God!"

People had begun exclaiming all around the bus. A woman screamed.

Anna had been looking at Cassie but now twisted in her seat, half-kneeling to look out the window—at the exact moment the front façade of City Hall ballooned outward in an explosion of yellow and red. Rubble, flames, and even vehicles that had been parked in front of the building shot up and outward. A second later, the percussion wave hit the bus, rocking it and throwing the passengers around.

If Anna hadn't been holding onto the back of the seat, she would have fallen into Mom's lap. As it was, Cassie staggered, and her backpack whacked into Callum's arm. He caught her around the waist. "Christ."

A few people had burst from the front doors of adjacent buildings. Others ran down the sidewalk, trying to protect their heads from falling debris. The bus had been slowing in order to stop at the bus stop in front of City Hall, but the bus driver stepped on the gas instead, ignoring the people gesturing frantically from the bench at the bus shelter, desperate to get away quickly.

All around, people were screaming both to get off the bus and for the driver to go as fast as he could. Then the bus skidded sideways, coming to a halt as a light pole crashed down across the road in front of it. The bus couldn't go any farther forward, so with some jerky back and forth starting and stopping, throwing the passengers around in their seats as if they were ping pong balls, the bus driver managed to turn the bus around. He didn't even bother to drive on the left side of the road as he should have, but accelerated back the way he'd come, heedless of the panicked traffic coming at him.

Callum and Anna crossed to the opposite side, pressing close to the window. Smoke billowed from the ruined City Hall, and Anna tried to make out what was happening through it. The bus driver, having just passed the near corner of the courthouse, yanked the wheel sharply to the right to avoid an oncoming car.

And then the courthouse exploded too.

Anna couldn't say who screamed first—her or Mom or everyone on the bus together—but there was no other possible reaction. No human had any power over the mountain of stone and the wave of hot air the explosion sent hurtling towards the side of the bus. Anna put up her hands in a futile attempt to protect her face and—

Heart-stopping terror.

The black abyss.

More screams.

And Callum's quiet voice, saying, "Here we go again."

19

November 1291

David

I t was a double-decker bus.

It was a freaking double-decker bus, bursting out of nothingness to the right and driving through Madog's men, to come to rest on top of Madog himself, squashing him like he was a wicked witch and this was *The Wizard of Oz*. Except that he was already dead because David had killed him.

"Sweet Mary, mother of God." Samuel had clearly learned to curse like the Christian soldier he'd once pretended to be. "My father has hinted over the years but—"

"Nothing could have prepared you for the truth," David said. "I'm sorry I didn't reveal all to you sooner, especially after Callum disappeared."

Samuel nodded, but David didn't think he'd really heard him. Like everyone on the field, he had eyes only for the bus.

If Bronwen were here, she might have said, *"Like you couldn't have shown up twenty minutes earlier?"*

In that initial charge, Dad had taken his men down the left side of the field, David had taken his directly up the middle at Madog, and Carew had ridden up the right. Like David, Dad had dismounted during the fight, but David caught sight of his plume. He stared at the bus too. David thanked whatever intuition had urged him to leave Madog where he lay and return to where Samuel held his horse, or else he would have been squashed too. William, wherever he'd disappeared to, would be even more starry-eyed after this.

All around the giant vehicle, horses reared and men scattered. David found himself swallowing down the semi-hysterical laughter filling his throat at the incongruity of the giant turquoise and orange bus invading a medieval battlefield. The laughter didn't last long, however. There were dead and wounded to see to, not to mention an entire army that had just learned it was defeated—first by the death of its leader, then by the arrival of Math, and now by the appearance of a modern bus.

David gestured to Justin, who'd surfed up beside Samuel. "Don't look at it; don't think about it. Just do your job. We need to contain and control Madog's men. Now."

"Yes, my lord," Justin said.

David caught his arm. "If some run, let them go rather than shooting them from behind. These are Welshmen."

"Yes, my lord."

David nodded. "I will explain about the vehicle later."

The bus had split the field in half. On this side, the only side David could see, those of Madog's men who'd seen him fall had lost the will to fight already. The front ranks had thrown down their arms, and David's soldiers had already begun rounding them up. Ieuan's force lay just behind David to his left, and they too were corralling Madog's spearmen. David didn't know what had become of Madog's archers or Ieuan's, but as long as no more arrows flew down from the heights to harm anyone, he wasn't worrying about them at the moment.

While Justin raised his hand to those men who were still mounted, calling them to him, David loped towards the folding door nearest to him, which lay about two-thirds of the way down the length of the bus. Before he reached it, it opened, and Callum swung down. He wore a suit and trench coat but held his sheathed sword in his left hand.

"My lord," he said.

Emotion rose in David's throat, preventing him from speaking. He shook his head. Callum grinned in response to David's muteness like he'd caught David out in the biggest practical joke imaginable. Then his eyes flicked past David's shoulder. Samuel had followed David, and the big soldier was goggling at Callum.

"Glad to see you're still alive too, Samuel." Callum said, still grinning.

"Where is—" David finally managed to get two words out.

Callum's attention swung immediately back to David. "We're all here. We're all safe, though the bus driver didn't make it." Callum had been holding onto the metal railing that ran along the steps of the bus, and he swung back to let David past him. David came up the steps and then stopped, rendered speechless again by what he saw: Mom, Anna, and Cassie, thankfully, but also two dozen other people in various states of disarray. They stared at him. It had been a bumpy ride, apparently.

"Hi," David said in American English. "Welcome to the Middle Ages." Because, really, what else was there to say?

A small sea of faces looked back at him, and David realized only then what they must be looking at: him. He held his bloody sword down at his side, but his hair was matted and possibly bloody too (though the blood wasn't his), and he wore the full armor of a medieval king.

And then David *whuffed* as Anna barreled into him and wrapped her arms around his waist.

"Thank God! Thank God, we made it back. I don't ever want to do that again," she said.

David hugged her, though since he still held his sword in his right hand, it was an awkward embrace. Then Mom was there too, and Cassie.

"We've lived a lifetime since you left." David eased his hold on Anna. "I suspect you have too."

"Math—?" Anna began.

"Math and Dad are here, but I don't want you going out there to find them yet. You've landed in the middle of a battle." While all the windows on the north side of the bus were intact, many on the south side were broken. David bent to look towards the southern end of the field where men and horses still seethed in places, but most of the fighting seemed to be waning. With the loss of Madog and the arrival of Math, there wasn't anything for Madog's men to fight for. As David watched, another group of men threw down their arms rather than die for a lost cause.

Mom peered at David through the lenses of a new pair of glasses. "Have we ruined everything?"

"Oh no! This was right where you needed to come in," David said. "It couldn't have gone better if you'd planned it."

While they'd been talking, the crowd had grown. People had come down from the upper level, which was accessed by a metal staircase at the rear of the bus. Callum moved to block anyone from exiting the vehicle, with Samuel filling the doorway behind him.

"It was a pretty rocky transition. We haven't had a chance to do more than talk to a few people." Mom gestured towards the front of the bus. A man was lying across three seats that faced inward. "The bus driver's gone. A rock came through his window and hit his head."

"I'll get some men to move him. He can lie with our dead." David turned to Callum. "How many people are we talking about?"

"At least forty, my lord," he said.

David put a hand on Callum's shoulder and shook him. "I missed you."

"What's happening out there?" Callum said.

"A rebellion led by one Madog ap Llywelyn. The tide had turned, and then you showed up to seal the deal." David stepped away from the women, moving with Callum to the rear door. Several passengers at the front of the bus were struggling to open the front door, but they were having difficulties because it was jammed. That was a good thing, because they weren't going to be any happier out there than in here, once they discovered what faced them. Someone was going to have to explain to them about their new reality—and convince them once they'd been told.

Cassie saw David looking towards the front of the bus and started forward. "Wait! Don't do that." The people in the aisle gave way before Cassie. David didn't blame them. They had a dead man two feet from them, a battlefield outside their window, and Cassie's face held a particularly determined look. David wouldn't have stood in her way either.

"What are we going to do with everyone?" David said to Callum, leaving Cassie to handle the tourists up front. David had become better at delegating tasks. Managing forty modern people was going to be a monumental one, which David neither could— nor wanted to—take charge of.

One of the men who was trying to open the front door raised his voice to Cassie. "Who do you think you are?" He sounded like the worst kind of aggressive American.

David glanced through the open door behind him. His men were milling around the bus. Then Dad appeared out of the crowd.

"I've got to go," David said to Callum. "I need to deal with what's going on out there."

"I know." Callum looked down at himself. "I'd help, but I'm not dressed right, except for—" He pulled the sword a few inches out of its sheath. "Look what we brought. I have yours too."

"Please tell me bringing a double-decker bus back here wasn't part of the plan," David said.

"No," Callum said. "Though we had every intention of returning, we didn't mean for it to happen this abruptly."

David swept his eyes around the new arrivals one last time. "I don't even know where to start with them."

"We've got this, David, at least for the moment," Anna said from beside Mom. "Do what needs doing."

David reached out to clasp her hand briefly and then released her to step off the bus. Without a doubt, this was the craziest thing that had ever happened in all their time traveling. And there'd been plenty of crazy things. It was bad enough to have brought Marty or Callum to the Middle Ages, but an entire busload of people? David hadn't even had the chance to ask Anna or Mom how they'd accomplished it.

Dad put a hand on the railing outside the bus doorway, and David stepped off the bottom step to stop in front of him. He looked at David, his eyes questioning, and David nodded. "They're here. They're fine"

"It's just cleanup work on the field." Dad put a hand briefly to his heart but was surprisingly subdued considering David had just told him that his wife had returned from the twenty-first century in a double-decker bus.

"Did you speak to Math?" David said.

"Briefly. His men are helping to round up Madog's men and see to the wounded. They're fresher than any of our men."

"I'm on my way." David made to move past his father, but Dad stopped him with a hand to his upper arm.

"We might have lost, Dafydd."

"I know," David said.

"It was only because of your heroics that we didn't."

David wasn't quite sure what to say to that. He didn't even know if it was true, given the arrival of Math and the bus.

Then Dad added, "It's been too long since I lost a battle. I'd forgotten what it felt like to stare death in the face and not flinch."

David nodded. "We'll talk later. Mom's waiting for you."

David didn't want to talk about this right now, but Dad was right. Yet again, the time travel option had been a force in a victory. They hadn't counted on it—it hadn't even occurred to David that Mom and Anna's return could in any way assist them—but it had come through for them anyway. The battle had been all but won, but the arrival of the bus had sealed the deal.

He didn't know what to think about that. He didn't know whose hand lay over him. He put his trust in God. He spoke to his people about Avalon. But the truth was that he didn't know why any of these things happened to his family. David really hoped that the answer wasn't an omnipotent robot living in a hidden base on the moon.

William held David's reins, and as David mounted, he saw Mom and Dad embrace inside the bus. He looked away, already thinking about what came next, but then he looked back, registering the way Dad was listing to one side. David hadn't noticed it when they'd been speaking. Then Mom put her hands to either side of Dad's face, talking to him intently. David decided he could leave him to her for now.

He looked at William. "Are you injured in any way?"

"No, my lord."

With Justin and William, David rode around the bus to the southern end of the field. Men and horses, dead and wounded, lay everywhere, reminding David strongly of that first evening in Wales when he and Anna had rescued Dad from the English ambush. That day, the dead had littered the ground. The minivan had run over the last four enemy soldiers, but Dad's men had already been dead, having fallen while defending him. As it had then, bile rose in David's throat, but he swallowed it back. It was a good thing he hadn't eaten in a while. He was the King of England. It was no longer forgivable for him to lose his breakfast on the ground.

While their captains herded Madog's men to one side of the battlefield, forcing them to sit in rows near the river with their hands on their heads, Math and Carew conferred with each other fifty yards from David.

Taking in the scene, David had to acknowledge that they'd been arrogant and reckless. Together, he and Dad had committed themselves to dying—and their men to dying. David couldn't pretend it meant nothing. Even now, with victory assured, his knees shook at the thought of what could have been, and he was glad that he was mounted so nobody else could see them tremble.

David should have known he was fooling no one but himself.

"*What* were you thinking?" The look Math gave David as he approached could have split wood. Math dismounted, and David did the same, the better to face their disagreement head on.

Math hadn't said 'my lord'. He didn't take David's hand or embrace him. He was angry, and he sounded like Bevyn, who might have ripped David up one side and down the other had he been here.

"We did what we had to," David said.

"That's your defense?" Math turned on Carew. "You condoned this action?"

Carew's nostrils flared. "We thought we had the advantage, or as much of one as we were going to get against a larger force."

"We were supposed to come behind Madog's army at Harlech!" Math said.

"Madog's army wasn't there," David said, working up to a more proper defense of their actions. "It was they who set up the initial ambush."

"And you who walked into it!" Math said. "You're the King of England! You have the responsibility not to be stupid!"

David rubbed his chin with one hand, studying his brother-in-law. David didn't see how this conversation was going to turn fruitful, given that Math's criticism—though entirely valid—was after the fact. David didn't say that to him, however. It wouldn't accomplish anything but cut Math down and throw David's own weight around. He didn't want that kind of relationship with his brother-in-law. Whether or not Math could ever forget it, David didn't want to play the King of England with him.

"I killed Madog."

Math snorted his derision, but then he pressed his lips together, preventing himself from berating David further.

David looked away to gather his thoughts. Then he met Math's gaze again. "As I said, it seemed like a good idea at the time. The alternative to meeting Madog here was to bypass his force and continue on to Harlech, but that would have done us little good if he'd continued north and taken another castle—Aber, for instance."

Carew cleared his throat. He had been listening to the conversation, but his eyes hadn't left the bus, and he used the opportunity to change the subject. "My lord, if you could give me a word for that ... *thing*?"

"It's called a bus. It runs on burning naptha," David said, hauling out the old explanation. "There nothing magical about it."

"Except how it arrived," Carew said.

David's lips twisted. "Except that." He turned to look at the bus with Carew. "Though I would also say that magic is merely something for which we don't yet have a proper explanation."

"Your mother and sister went to Avalon," Justin said. "You said so earlier."

"So I did, and so they did."

"Then that is all the explanation we need," Justin said.

David made a noncommittal noise. That might be the case for Justin—and David's most loyal followers—but not everyone was going to feel that way.

William had retreated a few paces during Math's excoriation of David, but now he moved closer, his eyes wide with excitement and expectation. "May I enter it?" The adrenaline rush of the battle, and the fact that he'd lived through it, was still coursing through his veins.

"If there's time," David said. "We have many wounded."

William nodded, not at all deflated, and David looked back to the bus, wondering if they'd be so lucky as to have a real doctor on board.

"My lord," Math said, his tone under control and back to being an advisor and brother, "none of us are physicians, and we have a more pressing task. We must see to Rhys's wayward offspring."

As one, the companions turned outward, looking away from the bus for a sign of the two brothers.

"Did they fall with Madog under the bus?" William said. From the way he said 'bus', David had a feeling it was going to be a staple of his vocabulary from now on.

"I know the brothers by sight," Carew said, "and I didn't see them when Madog fought King David. I don't see them now."

"Deciding the battle was lost, would they have run?" David said.

Among the Welsh, this wouldn't have been a strike against them but purely a practical matter of staying free to fight another day.

"They still hold Carndochen and Cymer," Math said. "If nothing else, one of those castles could provide a temporary refuge until they flee south to their father."

"If Lord Rhys is as smart as I think he is, he'll pretend he knew nothing of Madog's plans," Carew said. "Mark my words."

David nodded. That was medieval-speak for *I called it!* Rhys wouldn't be the first father to hang his sons out to dry when a king tasked him with treason. Gruffydd ap Gwenwynwyn, whose son, Owain, had plotted with Dad's brother, Dafydd, had seen the error of his ways in a similar fashion. Oddly, David found that he missed the gruff old soldier, who'd died a few years ago of old age and without an heir. He would have had a few choice words to say about today's events.

Good Norman that he was, Justin was looking offended at the notion that the brothers would have abandoned their men if they thought the battle was lost. David put a hand on his shoulder. "I didn't say that Rhys and his sons wouldn't be called to account for their sins, only that Carew was right about the manner by which Rhys would try to weasel out of punishment. My father will see to him. You'll see."

William was horrified too. "Madog is dead and what might Rhys lose? A castle? A few acres of land?"

"Politics." Justin shook his head.

Math laughed. "Son, it is the blood in every nobleman's veins."

20

November 1291

Meg

Meg wanted to laugh and cry and shriek all at the same time. When that corner of the courthouse had come flying towards the bus, Meg barely registered what she was seeing before it hit. Death, really, because it would have rocketed right through the bus. And here she was, held tightly in Llywelyn's arms where she belonged. It was as if she'd been holding her breath for two days and hadn't known it. And all of a sudden, between one instant and the next, all was right with the world again.

"*Cariad.*" Llywelyn kissed her temple.

Meg wanted to fall to the ground with him and never stop kissing him, but she couldn't in front of all these people.

Llywelyn smiled into her eyes, reading her mind easily. "You brought back more than a few visitors, my love."

"Believe me, it wasn't our intent."

"I wouldn't have chosen for you to fall into the middle of our war either," he said. "You could have been killed."

Meg didn't want to hear that, but it seemed obvious that he and David had gotten themselves into a dangerous situation—a life-threatening situation. When David had come to the Middle Ages at fourteen, he hadn't been a soldier, but his father had turned him into one as quickly as he could. It had literally been a matter of life or death. While David's dream was to create a new country—a united Britain—and fighting this so-called 'little war' might be the first step towards the fulfillment of that dream, Meg's wish for her son and husband was that they might no longer need to go to war at all.

Llywelyn pulled a bit away from Meg so he could see her face better. The movement made him wince and lean slightly to his left, as if he was protecting his side.

"What is it?" Meg framed his face with her hands, not hiding her sudden rush of fear for him—as well as the tears that were forming at the corners of her eyes against her will.

Llywelyn brushed the tears away with his thumbs. "I am well, *cariad*. David too."

"Then what's wrong?" Meg put her hand down at his side.

He winced again. "It's nothing. The time for worrying is past."

She didn't believe him. Something was wrong with him, though none of the blood on him was his. Adrenaline could mask a lot of ills, however. It would soon be wearing off—for him and for every other man here. She made a mental note to make Llywelyn address whatever was hurting him the moment she managed to leave this bus.

Llywelyn kissed Meg's forehead one more time, looking in her eyes to let her know he wanted to do a lot more than that, and then disappeared back outside. They'd been apart for two days, which had been a lifetime for both of them, but compared to their previous partings, it was nothing. Meg knew that he would find them a quiet moment before the end of the day to hold each other properly and talk, but it couldn't happen in front of all these out of place and terrified people.

Then Anna tugged on her sleeve. "I'd say we have a lot to worry about at the moment."

Meg turned to look at the crowd that had gathered around them. Llywelyn had meant his words to be for Meg alone, but Anna wasn't wrong. Meg raised her hand above her head and waved it, but when that didn't catch the attention of more than one or two people, she cupped her hands around her mouth. "Hey!"

The talking stopped, and everyone looked at her. Those who'd traveled on the upper level of the bus had come down, the last stragglers sitting on the steps of the stairs. Cassie had gotten the obnoxious American under control by whispering urgent words in his ear that had caused his face to pale. When she returned to Meg's side, she didn't tell Meg what she'd said, and Meg didn't ask.

Meg began: "I can't tell you how or why this has happened, only that you have fallen into the middle of a medieval battlefield. That should be obvious to you by now given the carnage outside these windows. Now, Callum—" Meg put a hand on Callum's arm, "—hasn't been letting you off the bus because the battle was ongoing and you'd only get in the way. I still need most of you to remain on the bus so we can figure out who you are and where we go from here, but for now I need a show of hands of anyone who has medical training or experience."

"Who are you?" The questioner was a well-dressed man in his mid-fifties, with distinguished graying hair and a thickness to him that spoke of too many restaurant meals.

Callum made a dismissive motion with his hand, but Meg said, "I am the Queen of Wales."

Several people blinked, but the response was something less than Meg might have hoped. Shock was still the order of the day. The overweight businessman sputtered and was joined by the obnoxious American, a much larger man with broad shoulders and a thick chest.

"I got this, Mom." Anna stepped towards the two men. "What are your names?"

They didn't know to whom she was speaking, which may well have been Anna's intent. Each shot the other an uncertain glance, and then the taller man stuck out his chin. "Mike."

"I'm Gordon Hardin," the older man said, clearly with the expectation that it should mean something to his listeners. Success in business had obviously made him think he was smarter than everyone else and deserved adulation. Several people on the bus murmured, but Meg didn't catch their words and his name didn't mean anything to her.

Anna plowed on. "Okay, Mike and Gordon. Here's the deal. You have time traveled—well, if you want to get technical, you've world-shifted—to the Middle Ages. And at least for now, you're stuck here with us."

A woman of about forty, who was sitting near Anna, raised her hand like she was in school. "How do you know this?"

Meg appreciated her restraint since at least she was polite. But even as the woman spoke, her eyes tracked to the scene outside the bus. Meg might have asked her, *how could you not know this*, but since both Meg and Anna had spent their initial hours in the Middle Ages uncertain about where they were—and then not wanting to admit where they were—Anna was understanding and answered her civilly.

"I've lived here for the last nine years. We were visiting your world when that building exploded and sent us back here." Anna held up her hand again. "Yes, to get this out of the way, if it's anyone's fault you're here, it's mine. Sorry. I can't help when the time traveling happens, and this time I took all of you with me."

Meg couldn't believe Anna was saying that—taking the heat for Meg and for all of them. She wanted to protest. She would have if it wasn't already too late and would have complicated matters even more.

"Of course, we'd probably be dead if we hadn't come with you," Cassie said.

Anna shot her a grateful look. "True."

While Gordon muttered something Meg didn't catch, Mike elbowed the two people standing between him and Anna out of his way and stalked down the aisle towards her. "How do we get home?"

"We don't." Meg moved to stand beside Anna. "And let me say this once: if you speak to my daughter in that tone of voice again, I will see you in chains."

Mike clenched his fist and waved it in Meg's face. "Don't you threaten—"

Two seconds later he was face down on the floor, taken down so quickly Meg hadn't seen who'd done it. Not Anna; it was a total stranger, who'd been sitting next to Mark and Darren. Callum edged his way past Anna and Meg to where the man knelt with his knee in Mike's back. Darren had risen too. His hand rested under his jacket at the small of his back. Meg recognized the stance. It meant he had a gun back there. Meg was glad he hadn't drawn it.

Callum nudged Mike with the toe of his shoe. "We'd appreciate it if you'd stop being such an ass."

The man twisted his neck to look up at Callum and gaped at him—who wouldn't if those words had been spoken to him in Callum's fabulous upper crust accent—but then he started sputtering again.

Ignoring Mike, Callum held out his hand to the stranger. The man wore fatigues and had a crew cut, so it didn't take a genius to realize he was military. "I am Lord Callum, Earl of Shrewsbury, lately of MI-5. Who are you?"

"Peter Cobb, sir." He shook Callum's hand.

"Thanks for your help." Callum tipped his head to Darren, who moved forward to help Peter manhandle Mike to his feet, his arms twisted up behind his back.

Mike started shouting obscenities at the treatment, but Darren and Peter held him tightly and headed him out of the bus, to the shocked silence of everyone else on it. Even Gordon had stopped his protests and was staring at Anna and Meg with wide eyes. Before Callum exited, he turned back to look at Mark. "Help Meg and Cassie take inventory, will you? We need names, histories, skills. We've got to figure out who these people are, and what we're going to do with them."

Mark gaped at him for a second, and then his expression cleared. He stood, opened his backpack, and took out a notebook and pen. Then he held out the backpack to Meg. "What's in there is for David."

She didn't take the backpack. "Keep it and give it to him yourself when you get a chance."

He took another step towards her. "The first time Callum talked about coming here, for about five seconds I thought about asking to come with him. But I'm not a soldier! Did you see that bloke who took down Mike? That's who David needs."

Cassie shook her head. "You heard Callum. He's already given you a job, one he trusts you to do better than anyone else on this bus. More even than me."

Mark snorted. "Not more than you." He turned to Meg. "Or you."

"I'm the Queen of Wales, Mark," Meg said, "and Cassie is the Countess of Shrewsbury. Callum should have phrased it better when he spoke to you. He should have asked us to help *you*."

Anna put her hand up and waved it at the muttering crowd one more time. "Medical people? Do we have any?"

Three people raised their hands.

"Yay," said Anna in an undertone. And then louder. "Do any of you speak Welsh?"

Two of them nodded. That was a good start, though medieval Welsh was going to take some getting used to and initially would be incomprehensible to them. At least they would know some of the mechanics and how the language was structured.

Meg nodded at Anna. "Go ahead. That's your thing. I bet there's a first aid kit by the driver's seat. We have men out there who need help."

The people who'd raised their hands seemed eager to get off the bus, until they reached the bottom step and stood on it, temporarily frozen at the sight of what lay before them. Anna gestured them forward.

Meg turned back to Mark, content to leave the medical situation to her daughter, and sure that she should. All of the time travelers had struggled at one time or another with how to occupy themselves intellectually in the Middle Ages—a time when the vast majority of women weren't educated at all, and the range of professions for women was sharply limited. While caring for her

SARAH WOODBURY

two-year-olds was a full time job currently, so was being the
Queen of Wales.

Under other circumstances, Meg would have been out
there nursing the fallen, regardless of her skill or lack thereof, but
at the moment, the forty lost and scared twenty-first-century
people were the higher priority. If Mark took on their welfare long-
term, he would be occupied for many months to come and be
doing them all a great service.

"So, Mark," Cassie said. "What do you want us to do?"

Mark cleared his throat and surveyed the people on the
bus. They'd quieted in the last few minutes and now watched Mark
intently. Cassie raised her eyebrows, still waiting, but with a smile
hovering around her lips.

Mark took in a breath and handed the pen and notepad to
Cassie. "The job, I guess." He nodded to the crowd before him.
"Let's start with everybody's names."

21

November 1291

Callum

While the bus had been crossing that black expanse, Callum had spared a single moment for regret. But almost immediately his sense of responsibility had kicked in, along with an unexpected wild and irrepressible joy. The feeling had startled him with its intensity and left no time for fear. He hadn't admitted until the bus crashed into the battlefield how very much he'd missed the Middle Ages.

He wasn't much pleased about arriving in a bus full of modern people, however. The others were trying to be matter-of-fact about it, but that was going to take them only so far. There were elderly people on the bus, college students, and obnoxious Americans. Callum counted six kids ranging in age from three to fifteen. Anna and Bronwen, wherever she was at the moment, were going to have their hands full dealing with whatever medical issues they'd brought with them.

And they had just given David yet another headache he didn't need.

Callum hadn't even begun to think about what he'd left behind in Cardiff: a destroyed courthouse and City Hall; MI-5 and the Project in disarray; and a world blown all to hell. He had meant to leave it behind, but not like this. He'd meant to say goodbye.

With the help of Samuel, who was larger even than Mike, Jeffries and Cobb dragged the ugly American out of the bus. The dead men who lay not only under the bus but all around it had the desired effect of shutting Mike up the instant he saw them.

As they hauled him across the field to where Ieuan and some of his men had corralled those of Madog's men who weren't overtly injured, Callum took the opportunity to quiz Cobb about his credentials. As it turned out, he'd served in Callum's former unit and was coming off a stint in the Middle East. He peripherally knew Jeffries. That shouldn't have been surprising since the community of veterans in Cardiff was small.

Madog's men sat in rows with their hands on their heads. The fog that had covered everything twenty minutes ago was burning off, leaving mist behind. Heedless of the wet grass, they plunked Mike down at the end of one row. Samuel stood over him. He'd taken up his role as Callum's lieutenant without missing a beat, though his eyes had a wild look to them that belied his calm exterior.

"Who's this?" Ieuan gestured to Mike. He hadn't blinked at the appearance of Cobb or Jeffries. Callum wouldn't have blamed

Ieuan if he'd at least wondered more about Jeffries, whose coloring was rare indeed in medieval Wales.

"His name is Mike," Callum said, clasping Ieuan's proffered forearm and clapping him on the shoulder with his other hand.

Ieuan raised his eyebrows.

"That's all I know about him except that he spoke insultingly to Anna and Meg and implied that he might hit them."

That prompted a growl of anger from Ieuan, as Callum knew it would.

In the past, Ieuan and Callum had communicated in a hodgepodge of English and Welsh but, in Callum's absence, Ieuan's Middle English had become a thousand times better than Callum's Welsh. Now, for the benefit of Jeffries and Cobb, Callum switched temporarily to modern English. "Lord Ieuan is one of King David's chief advisors and his wife's brother."

"What language were you speaking with him?" Cobb said.

"That's 1291 English," Callum said.

Cobb's face blanched, but then he got his expression under control. His hands went behind his back. Callum recognized the stance immediately. Cobb had just put on his mission face.

Callum nodded his understanding. "This is just another mission. Treat it as such."

"Yes, sir," Cobb said.

Though Callum had harbored doubts about Jeffries, his fellow agent had been in the game from the moment he and Callum had abandoned his car, so Callum kept his gaze on Cobb.

"You could return to the bus now if you like, or you could stay with me. I myself am an advisor to the king and must speak to him now that we've dealt with Mike."

"Was King David the kid who got on the bus right after it crashed?" Cobb said.

"Yes," Callum said, "and he hasn't been a kid for a long time."

"Yes, sir," Cobb said. "If it's all right with you, I'll stick."

Before turning away, Callum lifted a hand to Ieuan. "I can't tell you how good it is to see you."

"Glad to have you back where you belong," Ieuan said. "Where's my pizza?"

Callum laughed. "We didn't bring any with us, but we did bring the next best thing: ingredients. By next year, you might be able to make your own."

Ieuan smiled. "I'll hold you to that."

Callum stepped close to Samuel. "While I confer with the king, could you go back to the bus? Cassie is there with Queen Meg and Princess Anna. I'd like someone I can trust protecting them. With all this—" he gestured to the chaos of the battlefield, "—anything could happen."

"Of course, my lord."

Callum gripped Samuel's shoulder. "It's good to see you, Samuel."

Samuel brought his hand up and gripped Callum's upper arm, neither man finding it possible to speak.

Callum cleared his throat and turned back to Cobb and Jeffries, who'd been following their conversation without comprehension. "Come with me, both of you."

Mike had been watching them too, though they'd all moved too far away for him to hear what they'd been saying. Now, he called out, "What about me? You can't leave me here!"

Callum looked back at him. "Before long, you will be given the opportunity to rejoin your companions from the bus. In the meantime, I suggest you consider your behavior and modify it to reflect your current circumstances."

Mike's expression grew confused.

Jeffries leaned in. "I'm not sure he understood what you said, sir."

"He'll learn, or he won't," Callum said.

Cobb, Jeffries, and Callum strode across the stubble field towards David, who was meeting with Carew and Math. David saw him coming, and even though they'd greeted each other earlier, David took two steps towards Callum and then embraced him, lifting him off his feet in the process, which was no small feat.

Carew and Math came after him, grinning too.

"I hadn't realized what a calming influence on our young king you'd had until you'd gone," Carew said, clasping Callum's forearm in greeting. "It's good to see you again."

"It's good to be back." As Callum spoke to Carew, he glanced out of the corner of his eye at David. Math, of course, knew that David was from the twenty-first century. Ieuan had been there. But Carew wasn't yet party to that level of truth. And then Callum decided that it didn't matter that he wasn't. Whether they called the place they'd come from the twenty-first century or Avalon, it was a different world. It might as well *be* Avalon. The double-decker bus sitting in the middle of the field was proof enough of that. Callum could feel it rising up behind him, drawing everyone's eyes, even as they directed them away again, as if they were having trouble looking directly at it.

Putting a brave face on what had to pass for the truth, Callum looked at it with Carew. David, however, was looking at Cobb and Jeffries. Callum had forgotten them in the few moments it had taken to greet David.

He gestured with one hand. "Sire, may I introduce you to Peter Cobb and Darren Jeffries."

David stuck out his hand to each man in turn, and they shook. "Sir," they both said.

"Sire," Callum corrected them. "'My lord' in a pinch."

They bowed their heads and repeated in unison, "Sire."

David smirked and clapped each man on the shoulder. "You'll do just fine." He looked past them to the bus. "I can't say the same about everyone else."

"We put one of the Americans—Mike—with Madog's defeated soldiers," Callum said. "I'm hoping it will force some sense into him."

"What about those guys?" David pointed to where Anna, wearing jeans and the purple parka she'd borrowed from Cassie's aunt, was conferring with three modern people and three medieval people.

"Those are medical people." Callum decided not to worry about what people might think about the oddity of Anna's clothing.

And then he had more important concerns.

Three riders appeared from over a rise at the south end of the field. David wasn't wearing his helmet with its red plume, but the lead rider must have recognized him even from that distance because he made a beeline towards him. "What's this?" Callum stepped in front of David, automatically resuming his role of protector.

David put a hand on his shoulder. "Harlech, I hope."

Callum gave him a questioning look. He hadn't known there was a problem with Harlech, but the messenger soon answered his unspoken question before David had to.

"Sire!" The lead rider threw himself off his horse and went down on one knee before David. "I bring word from Harlech. We are besieged by—" His mouth dropped open as he finally noticed the great looming bus behind the king.

"By Madog ap Llywelyn," Carew said dryly. "We know."

"Did Sir Evan send you?" David said.

The man managed to get his expression under control, though his eyes kept straying towards the bus. "Yes, my lord. He requests aid to relieve the siege."

David frowned. "Has there been no sign of the messengers we sent to you?"

"I left Harlech by sea in the night," the man said. "We had not received word from you by then."

"That's no surprise, I suppose." Math bent his head to the man, who remained kneeling because David hadn't given him leave to rise. "Are our men mustering at Maentwrog?"

"Yes, my lord. We rested briefly there. They are waiting for the king."

By 'king', he meant Llywelyn, not David. Callum felt the medieval world settling in around him once again. It wasn't as if he hadn't been gone for two years, but more that he'd put on an old shirt that he'd unearthed from the bottom of a trunk. It was foreign and familiar at the same time.

David surveyed the field. "It might feel like this war is over, but it isn't. We need to gather every man capable of riding."

Nobody questioned that decision, even with the long night they must already have had to have fought a battle here at dawn.

Carew dismissed the messenger and his companions with a wave of his hand.

They bowed and headed for the river where horses had been picketed. While the companions had been talking, Llywelyn's men had swung into action like a well-oiled machine—not to prepare for battle, but to manage the aftermath. Cooking fires were already burning. Men were hauling water from the river, and those who were healthy were moving among the fallen, bending to aid those who could be saved. Villagers from Beddgelert and Aberglaslyn were present too. At times like this, the Welsh were one big family, and if Callum knew David at all, Madog's injured men would be receiving the same care as Llywelyn's own.

"If I am to serve you, my lord, I need armor and a horse," Callum said.

David's expression turned grave. "Sadly, neither should be difficult to acquire, even in your size. I need you to stay here, though."

"Stay here?" Callum said.

"You made one kind of example of Mike, Callum. Cobb and Jeffries will be of another kind." David stepped closer. "This is a nightmare. These people are stuck here forever. Every member of our family is finally here by choice. *Every one.* But we have to acclimate forty people who aren't here by choice and can never, ever return to what they knew."

"Conscripting them might not be the best idea we've ever had," Callum said.

David's eyes went to Cobb and Jeffries, who were standing side by side like cardboard cutouts, with their feet spread and their hands behind their backs. "Can either of you ride?"

"Yes, sire." They spoke together, but Callum saw a flicker of unease in Jeffries' eyes that might indicate he wasn't telling the exact truth.

"This is the deep end of the pool," David said.

"Sink or swim, sir," Cobb said.

Callum nodded, understanding as few could.

David spun around and headed back to Math and Carew, moving with them to mount his horse in preparation for the next stage of the war. Callum didn't feel dismissed. David was telling him that he believed him competent to whatever task faced him, and he needed to be getting on with it.

Callum looked towards the ad-hoc camp where he, Jeffries, and Cobb would find ownerless horses and armor salvaged from men who would never need them again. If they could find nothing in their sizes, they could scavenge from among Madog's men, though the noblest among them were still underneath the bus. Callum canted his head towards Cobb and Jeffries. "Until further notice, you two should consider yourselves my lieutenants."

"Yes, sir," Jeffries snapped off a salute.

Cobb followed Jeffries' example. "It's an honor, sir." His shoulders, if possible, got even straighter. "You have been an inspiration, sir."

Callum narrowed his eyes at him. He was the Earl of Shrewsbury and had been the director of the Project, so he was used to some admiration. But the inspiration part was new to him. "In what way?"

Cobb cleared his throat. "You traveled here three years ago and returned. You completed the mission, no matter how long it took."

Callum glanced at Jeffries, who shook his head as if to say, *I didn't tell him!*

"How do you know that, Cobb?"

"Common knowledge in our unit, sir."

"My mission was classified."

"Not so much, sir."

Callum shook his head. The time travel miracle had not only brought them to the right place, but it looked like it had also brought at least some of the right people with them.

22

November 1291

Anna

Anna watched David out of the corner of her eye as he personally eased the passing of two different men, clasping their hands in his and holding on until the light faded from their eyes.

"It's kind of him to take the time," Math said, coming up behind Anna and circling her waist with his arms.

She turned and put her arms around his neck, bending her wrists back so she wouldn't get the blood that was on them in his hair. He kissed her hard, and then she pressed her face into the hollow of his neck. They stood together unspeaking because speaking wasn't necessary.

They stepped back from each other, not wanting to part but knowing they both had work to do. And then Math grinned—that wild, wicked, gorgeous grin he didn't often show and usually only to her—and he wrapped her up in his arms again in order to swing her around. "Thanks be to God you returned safely."

"You knew I'd come back, right? That shouldn't have been a question."

"The only question was *when* you'd return." He set her down. "The bus is a nice touch, though your brother could have done without it."

"We can't seem to avoid complications," Anna said, her heart lighter than it had been in two days. A little balloon was trapped inside her chest, and she floated along with it.

Then Math and Anna each took a breath, coming back to the reality of the field and the wounded men who lay around them in rows. One of the modern medical people, a twenty-something named Rachel, looked up from where she was wrapping a cloth around a man's leg wound. She was one of the two medical personnel who spoke Welsh, and she seemed to be doing remarkably well for a woman so out of place and time.

While Anna and Math had greeted each other, David's head had remained bowed for a few more moments, and then he straightened and came over to them.

"Every time," he said. "Every time, I swear that I will find another way to solve our problems rather than lose men in battle."

"Avalon hasn't done it," Anna said, even as she was horrified at herself for implying Avalon was real. "Nobody could ever censure you for not caring about the men you lead."

David's hands clenched into fists, and he tipped his head back to look up at the sky, breathing deeply and gathering himself for what lay ahead. Then he brought his head down again to look at Math. "It's time to go."

Anna put an arm around David's waist one more time and hugged him. "A king isn't much good on the remains of a battlefield except to get in the way anyway."

He snorted. "You're trying to get rid of me."

"I'm trying to make you feel better about doing what you have to," she said.

Math canted his head, indicating the southern side of the field where the soldiers were gathering yet again. It was a wonder that some of them weren't falling off their horses from exhaustion. Nobody had slept; nobody was going to sleep for a good long while.

So after one look back, which was all David allowed himself, he left. Duty warred with duty. Anna knew her brother well enough to know how hard it was for him to leave the wreckage of the battle behind him.

Ieuan and Math went with him.

But not Papa.

When Anna didn't see Papa's red-plumed helmet—a match to David's, though David's feather had a black tip—poking up among the men as they rode away, she scanned the battlefield looking for Mom. Papa hadn't been injured when they'd come in on the bus. Maybe he'd felt more of an obligation to stay than to go.

Then Anna spied Mom, still in the wool coat she'd borrowed from Cassie's aunt's house. She blended in among the medieval people around her better than Anna did in this purple parka. Anna wasn't regretting wearing it, however. The coat was filled with down and was really warm. It kept the winter chill away nicely.

Mom was bent over someone on the ground, but as Anna watched her, she stood abruptly, looking this way and that. When she spied Anna looking at her, she waved her arms high above her head, calling Anna urgently to her. Anna's heart rose into her throat. She grabbed Rachel's arm. "Please come with me."

Rachel tied a last knot on a bandage and stood. "What is it?"

"I don't know, but I'm afraid—" Anna couldn't articulate what she was afraid of because it was too awful. She started across the field, picking up the pace as she got closer and saw Papa lying on the ground. His eyes were closed, and his mouth was open, his breath coming in gasps. Mom must have wrestled him out of his mail tunic, because it lay beside him, and he wore only his shirt. Cadwallon stood sentry above him, his face drawn and white.

"I thought he was fine! He said he was fine." Anna fell to her knees beside her father. She couldn't see any blood, so her thoughts went instantly to his heart. He was past sixty now. Anything could have gone wrong with him.

"He just says it hurts. I'm not even sure what *it* is, or that he knew it was this bad before he realized he couldn't ride," Mom said. "And even then, he passed it off to David as saddle soreness."

"Did David believe him?" Anna said.

"His father ordered him to go," Mom said, "and David agreed that he shouldn't leave what was happening at Harlech to be sorted out by someone else."

Rachel knelt on the opposite side of Papa from Mom and Anna. "I need you to translate," she said to Mom, who nodded and sat back on her heels.

"Sire," Rachel said.

Papa turned his head slightly and opened his eyes to look at Rachel.

"Are you having trouble breathing?"

Mom translated, and Papa shook his head and nodded at the same time. "Just hurts." His voice came as barely more than a whisper.

Rachel seemed to understand what he said, but Mom translated into English anyway. Rachel opened her backpack and removed a small black case. She unzipped it and pulled out a stethoscope. She glanced at Mom, who'd clasped her hands in front of her lips. "I'm a doctor."

Anna put a hand on Mom's shoulder and leaned in to whisper. "She's actually a surgeon, though still in residency."

"Thank God," Mom said.

Rachel listened all around Papa's heart, lungs, and abdomen and then pressed gently on Papa's breastbone.

"Hell!" He jerked upward and twitched away from her hand.

A number of men had clustered around them by now, and Papa's exclamation deepened the looks of worry and fear on their faces.

"Did you fall from your horse?" Rachel said.

Papa's breathing eased back to shallow as he tried to master himself. "I don't remember."

Cadwallon made a small movement with his hand, and everyone looked at him. "The king's horse stumbled and threw him moments before—" he gestured helplessly towards the bus, "—it appeared." Cadwallon seemed to fear that someone would blame him—or perhaps he blamed himself—because he continued, "None of Madog's men got near the king, and when I helped him to his feet, he said not to fuss over him."

Rachel's eyes narrowed, and this time she felt at Papa's head, probing with her fingers and watching his face for indications of pain. Then she sat back on her heels and spoke to Mom and me. "I'd love to do an x-ray, which I realize isn't possible. I think he has several broken ribs and a concussion."

"So his heart's okay?" Anna said.

"Is there some reason to think it might not be?" Rachel said.

"He had pericarditis three years ago," Mom said.

Rachel's brow furrowed. "How did you take care of that?"

Anna didn't want to tell her that *sometimes* they could time travel by choice, but she would find out eventually, and it was better not to lie. "Mom jumped off the balcony at Chepstow Castle with Papa and ended up in modern Aberystwyth."

Rachel's only reaction was a slight widening of the eyes. Then she turned back to Papa. "In the past, I would have bound your ribs, but to do so can prevent you from taking deep breaths and, particularly in your case because you aren't a young man, it could lead to pneumonia. You aren't going to want to move, so I won't bother warning you not to move abruptly."

Mom translated what Rachel had said, and threw in a, *"you'd better listen to her,"* of her own at the end. Papa reached out a hand. Mom clasped it and leaned in to kiss his forehead. When she spoke next, there were tears in her voice. "I'd thought I'd come back only to lose you."

"You're not going to get rid of me that easily." Papa's voice was soft and breathy, but there was humor behind it.

Two of Papa's men levered him to his feet, and then they and Mom walked *very slowly* with him to his tent, which had been set up near the river. No movement was going to be comfortable for him for a good long while. The two women watched him go, and then Rachel looked intently at Anna. "I was worried that he'd punctured a lung. I'm not seeing that now. If he has internal bleeding, we'll know in the next few hours. Same with the head wound. Under these conditions, I'm not sure I can do anything about any of it."

Anna studied her for a moment, but she didn't really need to think hard about what she said next: "With your permission, I would like to put you in charge."

Rachel blinked. "In charge of what?"

"Everything medical," Anna said. "For years, Bronwen—that's Ieuan's wife—Mom, and I have been working with medieval doctors, some of whom are very good. But you have more knowledge in your little finger than all of us combined. We need you to coordinate research and treatment for the entire country—or rather, *countries:* Wales and England."

Rachel was very good at controlling her expressions, but Anna had learned something of her in the past five minutes and noted the tightening of the muscles around her lips before she relaxed them again. "You're not serious."

"I am completely serious," Anna said. "Rachel, there is nobody else."

Rachel looked away from Anna, taking in the order growing out of the chaos and carnage on the field. "How do you live like this—live *with* this?"

"Up until now, we've had no choice," Anna said. "But if there's one thing we've discovered—all of us who've traveled here from the modern world—it's that by staying here, we have a chance to make a difference in people's lives. I imagine that's why you became a doctor?"

She nodded. "Of course."

"Well ... you'll never have a better chance than this."

23

November 1291

David

Callum had sent a rider to let David know that his father was okay. Or if not okay, at least that he wasn't about to die. When Dad had told David he was too sore to ride with him to Harlech, David had been surprised but happy, as if his father were finally showing some common sense. After he'd ordered David to leave, however, David had begun to have second thoughts. His father still didn't always tell him the whole truth, as if David were a boy who needed protecting from it. This time Dad had probably just wanted David to go in his stead and would have said anything to make it happen.

Harlech Castle was situated on a cliff edge above the sea. In the modern world, the sea had moved far from the castle, but in this time, the water lapped at the bottom of the rock on which Harlech perched. This Harlech Castle was not the same one that Edward had ordered built in 1283 either, since in this world he'd never conquered Wales. Here, Dad had commissioned Harlech himself, and it was built in stone in a style similar to Rhuddlan. The castle was impenetrable from the west, with a defended stairway that plunged two hundred feet down to the water, and had a main gate that looked east. Its towers loomed over the landscape for only a short distance, though, because the ground increased in elevation as it went inland.

That was Harlech's main weakness and the reason for the massive gatehouse with three portcullises, as well as the tricky twisting entrance that prevented an enemy force from bringing a siege weapon to bear on the door. Even as a stone castle, it was also vulnerable to fire arrows launched from beyond its curtain wall that could burn the wooden structures within.

All of this David knew before he arrived at Harlech. The initial journey to Maentwrog had taken a few hours on horseback. The village was located at the ford of a river that became an estuary farther west. Therefore, they had to ride east from Beddgelert in order to go west to Harlech.

Gratifyingly, especially since this country had once belonged to Madog's father, a thousand men had gathered, mostly spearman and bowman from the surrounding countryside. A few herdsmen were less well-armed with axes and farming implements. Many fathers had brought their teenage sons. War had become rare here since King Edward had died, but that didn't mean the citizens wouldn't come when Dad called.

David had sent scouts ahead in a wide swath, needing to know what they were walking into before they walked into it. If it had been summer, he might have rested his men through the night, in order to take advantage of the sun rising behind them as they approached Harlech. But while the fog of the morning had burned off, clouds had moved in, and the temperature hovered around freezing. They were due for snow or very cold rain by tomorrow. Because the men they'd picked up at Maentwrog were fresh, David decided it was better to keep moving and march the nine miles to Harlech before the sun set.

From Maentwrog, they followed the coastal road west along the south side of the estuary and then headed southwest to Harlech along the cliff edge upon which Harlech perched. The sea frothed below them, another sign that a storm was coming, as if the dark clouds that squatted on the western horizon weren't warning enough. The sun—such as it was—was close to setting by the time they came to the edge of the plateau upon which they'd been traveling. There, they formed a line half a mile from the castle, looking down on it from four hundred feet above. Madog's pavilions lay below on the plain that had been cleared of trees.

Carew blew out a breath. "It isn't taken." Smoke curled into the air from inside the castle but David saw no flames. In fact, he didn't see much in the way of activity anywhere.

"They've hunkered down for the night," Math said. "The scouts' reports were accurate."

"I never believe them until I can see what they say with my own eyes," Carew said, reflecting a sentiment after David's own heart. "Whoever Madog has left in charge hasn't made an attempt to take the castle."

William rubbed his chin in mimicry of Math and said sagely, "Surely he knows that Madog is dead, his forces defeated, and that you are coming, my lord? Why is he not better prepared for our arrival?"

"We didn't encounter any scouts on our journey here," Justin said. "Maybe the leader down there doesn't know."

Carew barked a laugh. "If that's true, I can't decide if Madog was so confident in his overwhelming numbers and in his strategy that he didn't think he needed them, or if he was merely sloppy."

"The scouts could have seen our numbers and abandoned their companions rather than share their fate," Ieuan said.

While they spoke, a groundswell of murmurs came from the men. They'd known as much as David about what they might face, since he'd shared with them the scouts' reports, but no one had dared believe it.

"Unfurl the banners," David said.

Justin repeated the order, more loudly than David had given it, and his dragon banner rose above his head and caught the wind. The banners of the other lords who rode with him appeared a moment later. David put the binoculars to his eyes and focused on a group of men clustered near one of the tents. In the growing darkness, he'd nearly missed seeing them. They seemed to be conferring, and then a lone man broke away from the group and strode in David's direction. He followed a well-worn pathway that led straight up the hill to their position.

David focused the binoculars on his face. "Madog."

"Madog is dead," Ieuan said from beside David. "You killed him."

David handed Ieuan the binoculars, knowing he would recognize the man's face. "Not that Madog." It would have been easier to keep everyone straight if the Welsh didn't insist on choosing baby names from the same pool of ten. Of course, the English did the same with their Toms and Harrys. Those names were just easier for native English speakers to pronounce.

Ieuan looked through the binoculars for a few seconds without speaking, and then he dropped his hands to his chest. "Huh."

"Your orders, sir?" Justin said.

David could feel the unreleased tension behind him. The thousand men who'd marched from Maentwrog hadn't come all this way to stand around. Though that was exactly what David viewed as the best-case scenario, and what he'd made clear to them before they started. He glanced down the line. The bowmen were ready; some had arrows resting in their bows, but none of the bows had been drawn.

"Ieuan, you're with me." David dismounted to a tsk of disgust that Justin couldn't suppress. Justin hated it when David exposed himself to the enemy. The Kevlar vest underneath David's mail wouldn't help him if an archer aimed at his eye.

"Who is Madog?" Math said.

"You'll recognize him when he gets closer. He was the leader of our bowmen at the battle of Painscastle, back when I was sixteen," David said.

That didn't sit too well with anyone within earshot. David had liked Madog, the little he'd spoken with him, and he was, quite frankly, surprised to see him leading Madog ap Llywelyn's siege of Harlech.

As they'd been talking Madog had covered all but the last hundred yards to David's army. Ieuan and David walked the rest of the way to meet him.

Madog stopped and bowed a few paces before he reached David. "My lord."

"I would not have expected to find you here," David said.

Madog's eyes went to dragon banner on the bluff. "How many have you brought?"

"Over a thousand. What happened to your scouts?"

"I wouldn't know," he said. "I have two hundred bowmen. They could cause you damage."

"They could," David said. "But I have bowmen too, and I imagine that my man, Evan, who defends Harlech, has seen our banners."

"Every commander knows that he can't maintain a siege when the enemy comes behind him," Madog said.

David's shoulders relaxed slightly. Every commander did know that, and for Madog to state it boldly gave David hope that he was looking for a way out. "Until this moment, I would not have said that I was your enemy. Nor my father."

Madog stared down at his boots and didn't answer.

"How came you to fight for Madog ap Llywelyn?" David said.

"My father and his father before him served Rhys ap Maredudd," Madog said. "He called us to him, my brothers and me. They went, and I followed to protect them."

This had always been the way of it for the common man. He fought for his lord without question. The idea that a man's lord and his country were not the same thing was foreign to David.

But it was David's problem today—maybe his most important problem. Back at Rhuddlan, Bronwen had enumerated the barriers thrown up by the Church, Ireland, or David's own barons that would divert his quest to form a united and peaceful Britain. But it was Madog's heart and mind that David really needed to win—not for himself—not because he was Madog's lord, prince, or king—but for Wales, and ultimately, Britain. And if David had them, he had everything.

"It is hard to accuse a man of treason when he fights beside his brother," David said.

Madog lifted his head. David saw hope in his eyes—and he hoped that Madog saw understanding in David's.

"What of Lord Madog and the sons of Rhys?" Madog said.

"Madog is dead," David said. "We have not seen Rhys or Maredudd."

Madog nodded at this, accepting their disappearance, as he had his scouts', without comment and as one of the realities of war. "If I surrender to you, what of my men?"

"If they lay down their arms, they walk free," David said.

"Most serve because they always have," he said. "None of us have an argument with King Llywelyn."

When David didn't answer right away, Madog nodded, taking his silence as meaningful, though David had been thinking again about what it meant to be a patriot. "I will speak to the men. We surrender. You may do with us as you will." Madog bowed and turned away.

Unlike the other Madog, this Madog hadn't even asked about himself.

David returned to his men. "We have won." He kept on walking, past where Math and Justin waited for him, into the ranks of men who'd come when Dad had called.

The men bowed and gave way before him. As David approached each man, however, he raised him up, grasping the arm of whoever would take his (everyone) and thanking him for his offer of service. It may have been that the offer was to David personally or to his father, and not to Wales. David had heard his mother refer to such loyalty as the 'cult of personality'. She hadn't meant David to overhear her, because she'd been talking about him.

"What about Lord Rhys, my lord?" one man said, and David recognized him as one of the men he'd spoken to at the earlier encampment. He must have appropriated a horse for himself in order to finish what he'd started. "He won't be so easy to defeat."

"No, he won't," David said. "But we won't be fighting him—or anyone else—today." David had been about to keep walking, but then he had another thought. "You are Cadoc, yes?"

"Yes, my lord."

"Who represents your village at Brecon, Cadoc?" David was referring to the meeting of the Welsh Parliament, the most recent congregation of which had taken place during the summer.

Cadoc smiled and thumped his chest. "I do, my lord."

David nodded, not at all surprised, given how outspoken Cadoc was. "If my father were to call you to vote rather than to battle, would you come?"

"Every time, my lord."

"What if you were given the opportunity to elect your leader, as happened in Scotland two years ago? Would you take it?"

Cadoc looked taken aback. He lowered his voice. "The king—he is well isn't he?"

David hadn't expected that to be the result of his query. "He is. I ask this hypothetically."

Cadoc chewed on his lower lip. David had taken a chance in asking him, and he was really putting him on the spot. Cadoc was outspoken, but he was talking to the King of England, the Prince of Wales—and the man who under the old system would inherit the throne after his father. But David really did want an answer. He could feel the intense interest of the men around them.

"I would take it," he said finally. "Though it is our tradition to divide a kingdom among all of a man's sons."

"Wales needs a single ruler," a man beside Cadoc said. Men around him nodded. Despite tradition, they could see as well as David how keeping Wales undivided had benefitted all of them.

"That would mean choosing between Padrig and me," David said, knowing that today such a choice would be no contest, and Padrig would lose. "I know what I'm asking. And it's hardly a fair question so you don't have to answer. I do want you to think about it, however." David raised his voice. "I want you all to think about it. God willing, there will come a day when you will be given the chance to choose the one who leads you. If I have my way, that man will not be the one with the most land or wealth."

David bent his gaze on Cadoc again. "Or whom tradition says should lead. When that time comes, I expect you to vote for the one you believe most worthy."

"Yes, my lord," Cadoc said.

As David returned to his horse, Math leaned in to say, "You might as well ask them to fly to the moon. It would be as likely." David shook his head. "That's just it. The men of Avalon have visited the moon and lived to tell the tale. Nothing is impossible anymore."

24

November 1291

Callum

As the hour approached midnight, Callum had checked in with all the sentries, conferred with the scouts who'd returned, and sent out new ones. In perhaps the greatest triumph of the evening, he had even talked sense into Cadwallon. Under normal circumstances, the organization of the camp would have fallen to Llywelyn's young captain, but Callum had convinced him that delegating his responsibilities to Callum so he could focus exclusively on Llywelyn's well-being was in the king's best interests.

Even now, Cadwallon stood sentry outside Llywelyn's tent, glaring at anyone who passed by who might even *think* about disturbing his lord's rest. Callum would leave to Meg the prospect of convincing Cadwallon that even he had the right to sleep.

"How are we doing?" Callum clapped a hand on Samuel's shoulder. As Callum had asked, Samuel hadn't left Cassie's side since Callum had sent him to guard her. She'd spent the rest of the day overseeing the well-being of the passengers, most of whom had fallen asleep at last, exhausted and spent. They all understood—or at least could articulate—what faced them now, though Callum couldn't say that any had come to terms with it. That might be a long time coming.

For everyone.

"All is quiet, my lord," Samuel said.

Callum nodded, feeling the big man's eyes on him, but he didn't meet them right away. He and Samuel had developed a camaraderie in Scotland, even if Callum was a lord and Samuel his captain. The contours of their relationship would be different from now on, not only because they'd spent two years apart, but because Callum had spent those two years in Avalon. To know that, to know that Callum had returned in a double decker bus, was a big thing for Samuel to accept.

Callum took in a breath, dreading this conversation but knowing they needed to have it. "I know this is all very strange—"

But he stopped as Samuel waved a hand, dismissing Callum's words. "Do you remember the ambush on the road to Edinburgh?"

"How could I forget?" Callum said. "It was your warning that saved us all."

It looked like Samuel had been about to say something else, but he arrested his speech before the words reached his lips and said instead, "That's what you remember?"

"Was there something more important to remember about it?" Callum said. "I was hit on the head, so I admit I could have forgotten some of the more salient bits."

"That's—" Samuel laughed silently, his broad shoulders shaking. "What was important to remember is that because we were ambushed, you saved Scotland."

"Ach," Callum said. "We worked together."

Samuel shook his head. "That ambush put your feet upon a path that has led you to this day. Because I follow you, I have shared in that path, to my benefit. Fortune has shone upon me since I met you."

"I wouldn't have said being held prisoner and almost dying from it was a fortunate thing," Callum said.

"Ah, but because I followed you, I was never forgotten. You saved me, James Stewart, and the boy. And Scotland."

Callum was starting to feel uncomfortable. Samuel was sincere, and he was talking like Cobb. Callum certainly tried to do the right thing, pretty much all the time. It wasn't too often that anyone but his wife—or David—noticed. Usually, that was enough.

Callum cleared his throat and changed the subject. "I hear you've kept Shrewsbury for me in my absence."

"Yes, my lord," Samuel said. "All was well there, too, when I left."

"Samuel's being modest." Anna had snuck up on them, having made her way silently through the clusters of sleeping time travelers. Cassie had been reading from a notebook a few feet away, and Anna caught her by the arm and pulled her forward.

When they reached Callum and Samuel, Anna continued, "You're going to have the same problem David has, Callum: losing captains left and right because you can't help but promote them."

Callum reached out a hand to Cassie, who took it. "I am well aware of my good fortune."

"Where are Darren and Peter?" Anna said.

"They resisted sleeping, but I told them I needed them fresh," Callum said.

"And they obeyed," Anna said. "Of course they did." Then she smiled and Callum knew she didn't mean for the words to bite.

"Whether or not they'll actually sleep is a different matter," Callum said.

"Any news from David?" Cassie said.

"That's why I'm here, actually," Callum said. "A message from David arrived five minutes ago. Harlech is safe, with no loss of life."

"How did he manage that?" Cassie said.

"By being David, of course." Then Anna ran the back of a hand across her brow. "I'm sorry. I didn't mean that to come out the way it sounded. I'm just tired."

"We all are," Cassie said.

"You don't have to apologize. I know exactly what you mean," Callum said. "Going forward, David needs to keep being who he is if we want to turn this world into the one we dream of."

"*We*," Anna said. "I wish David were here to hear you say that."

"Does he still think he's in this alone?" Callum said.

"Not as much as he did," Anna said.

Callum nodded. "None of us are alone." He gestured to the modern people, most of whom, for the first time in their lives, were sleeping with only a blanket between them and the ground. "We need to make sure all of them know it too."

It was that issue that was bringing Callum to his next quest. Leaving Cassie with the promise that he would join her in sleep soon, Callum walked towards the bus. It remained where it had come to rest, standing sentry like Cadwallon but in the middle of the battlefield, some hundred yards from the closest fire circle. As Callum left the light behind, the bus loomed before him, a dark bulk against the darker hill behind it. Occasionally, the metal siding glinted, reflecting a flicker of light coming from the camp.

Callum's boots made crunching noises in the frozen grass as he walked to the back door (the front door was still stuck shut), and pushed through it. Coming up the stairs, he peered towards the front of the bus. He wondered if he'd have to check upstairs, but then Mark Jones's voice came to him out of the darkness. "I suppose you're looking for me."

Callum walked down the aisle to where Anna had been sitting moments before the bus had crashed through time to get here. Jones hunched in the seat opposite, his backpack at his feet. To Callum's knowledge, he hadn't actually left the bus yet.

"Don't worry. I'm not going to throw a wobbler."

Callum sat heavily in the seat facing him. "Sorry the day went so wrong."

"It wasn't your fault."

Callum just looked at him. It was his fault. Because of Callum, Jones had been on the bus.

Jones tipped his head back to indicate the camp, the lights of which Callum could see from where he sat. "They all right out there?"

"As well as can be expected. Thanks for getting them organized. There'll be more of that tomorrow and for days, if not months, to come."

"We are well and truly snookered." Jones raised a hand and then dropped it onto his thigh.

Callum didn't want to see his friend in such despair. "Why haven't you left the bus?"

"If I sit here, cold as it is, I can pretend for a few more minutes that none of this is happening. I'm sitting on an empty bus, waiting for the driver." Jones paused. "Oh, wait. He's dead."

Callum had been hearing this kind of talk for hours already. Somehow, he hadn't expected it from Jones.

Jones read his silence correctly. "You're disappointed in me. You think I'm a wanker for not getting on with it like Cobb and Jeffries."

"I didn't expect it from you, no. Which makes me think there's something more to this. Why don't you tell me what that is so we can get off this bus?" Callum tugged his cloak more tightly around himself. His muscles were stiffening from sitting in the cold.

"You're happy to be back. I could see it right way. Overjoyed in fact."

Callum nodded.

"Cassie too?"

"Yes."

Jones sighed and looked away. "So, here's my problem."

Callum braced himself, with no real idea of what was coming.

"I was thinking just now about my parents," Jones said. "To them, I died today."

"Yes," Callum said. There wasn't any point in sugarcoating it. "I imagine even if some people swear they saw the bus disappear, cooler heads will prevail and the story will be that the bus was pulverized by the explosion."

"MI-5 will know."

"They will know."

"I wasted my life," Jones said. "Twenty-seven years old, and I hadn't even lived yet. I spent it in a windowless office, playing with computers. Making a difference sometimes, sure. But how often? How many minutes of my life did I actually make a difference to anyone?"

Jones had made a difference to Callum, but somehow he sensed that wasn't the answer Jones was looking for.

"I haven't seen my parents since the summer," Jones went on. "I'd started dieting. I haven't eaten pizza in three weeks. Look—" Jones lifted his right arm in mimicry of a weight lifter and showed Callum his bicep. "I've been working out."

Callum had thought Jones looked a little thinner.

"I hadn't even lived yet and now I'm dead. And you know what the worst thing is? How many people really are going to miss me?"

Callum licked his lips and ventured a comment. "You made a difference for forty people today."

Jones laughed without humor. "Did I? I spent the whole time hating the fact that I had to talk to total strangers and sure they were mocking me behind my back. I want to be in my warm office, hacking into the Oregon DMV, eating chips and biscuits and pouring too much cream into my tea." He leaned forward. "Don't you understand? I don't want to be here!"

"But you are here."

"Too right I am."

Callum studied him for a second. Callum could see that Jones was frustrated. But so was he. "Are you going to sit on this damn bus and whinge at me for another half hour, or are you going to get off your duff and help?"

Jones gaped at him. "You haven't heard a single word I've said, have you?"

"I heard every word. I just don't care. I need you smart and sober, like you've always been. All these years, you've hidden behind that computer. Well, now you don't have one. Time to figure out what you do have." Callum stood and stalked down the aisle towards the door. When he reached it, he stopped and looked back. "Bring the backpack when you come. You have maps in there

David needs." He pushed through the door and set off across the frozen grass.

Tough love didn't always work. Jones had been sulking on the bus for six hours now. Callum decided to give him until morning, at which point hunger and a full bladder might force him from the bus. Callum would have preferred he'd come of his own accord.

And then he heard the crunching of feet behind him and turned to see Jones, backpack over his shoulder, hurrying towards him. Callum stopped and waited for him to catch up.

"My arse was frozen to the seat. If you hadn't showed up, in another minute I'd've come to you." Jones paused. "That was quite a speech. Did you save it for me or have you used it six times already tonight?"

Callum laughed. "The latter."

"I'm not going to be another bloke who needs saving. Bugger that. Tell me what to do and I'll do it. Like always."

25

March 1292

David

The barn-like building sat in the middle of a muddy clearing, adjacent to the educational mecca that Anna and Math had established on the outskirts of the village of Llangollen. The family dismounted in front of the double doors, built big enough to allow a fully-loaded farm cart admission. This was the first stop on the grand tour Anna had organized of her burgeoning domain, so David could see with his own eyes what had become of the bus.

Too bad the passengers weren't so easy to see to.

"We need to confer." Mom had been trying to get David to talk to her about them since he'd arrived at Dinas Bran the day before.

"After this," David said.

What Mom didn't know was that David was already well aware of what was going on with the passengers, even if he'd managed to skirt much in the way of responsibility towards them up until now, happy to leave their well-being to Mom, Anna, and Mark. At first David had thought to keep them together somewhere—at Caerphilly or even Cardiff—because what he wanted more than anything was access to their combined knowledge. They all had skills, hobbies, and expertise in areas David hadn't even begun to tap.

But it quickly became clear that the passengers didn't want to be corralled, and trying to contain their movements led to unrest. Over the last four months, more than half of them had found some kind of employment and were doing okay. Some were doing better than okay.

Like Callum's new lieutenants, Jeffries and Cobb. They'd found meaning in employment similar to what they'd been doing back in the old world—which even David had started to call 'Avalon' as a shorthand. They rode among Callum's *teulu*, and not only had their medieval English and Welsh improved to not-quite-atrocious, but they were learning—as Callum had—how to be medieval warriors.

Among the others, two families with young children had moved to Llangollen. The father of one family and the mother of another had been maintenance technicians at the University of Cardiff. Their spouses were a school teacher and an engineer. That fateful Saturday, the two families had traveled together into Cardiff for an excursion—which had clearly ended a bit differently than they'd planned. Along with the three medical personnel, all four had become teachers and sources of knowledge at the school. All of a sudden, everybody was excited about the future.

Others had come to grips with their circumstances too: a man and his two teenage sons had set up a carpentry business; two retired couples who'd been visiting Cardiff for the day had moved back to their own village and were living relatively comfortably on the beach (thanks to a stipend from Dad that all the passengers were being given); even George Hardin had found a kindred spirit in Tudur and was helping Dad run his country.

But that left a number of people doing less well. Several college students, two of them Americans spending their junior year abroad, were having a terrible time adjusting to the restrictions of the Middle Ages. Cassie and Bronwen were trying to work with them, but Mark was not the only one whose life had been lived at the computer. Others were outright malcontented: a couple in their fifties; a family with a rebellious teenage daughter; and three twenty-something men, one of whom was Mike, who'd caused trouble that first day on the bus. These eight spent their days moping about Mom's castle at Caerphilly, doing little but drinking to excess. Dad had proffered his very medieval solution to their angst, but Mom was hoping for something more reasonable from her son.

"Is that it, Ta?" Arthur had ridden from Dinas Bran in front of David, tightly gripping the pommel of the saddle. The words Arthur had spoken at Rhuddlan had been the beginning of a torrent that rarely ceased. David felt he should have seen it coming, since he'd never been a child who did things by half-measure either.

"My God, it is." David helped Arthur down from the horse, all the while staring at the bus, which took center stage in the middle of the barn. "I didn't think they were going to rebuild it."

The bus looked better than when David had last seen it. He'd debated whether or not to leave the bus where it was in the field at Aberglaslyn or move it somehow. Having mechanically minded people from the modern world available had made his decision for him. They had not only dismantled the bus, carted it all the way to Llangollen, and rebuilt it, but they'd done the same for David's aunt's minivan and Bronwen's little Honda. To see them lined up, lovingly restored and objects of research and scrutiny, made David's heart beat a little faster. This was his history and his future. And his son's.

Everything David had done and said these last four months had been bent on securing that future, initially in Wales and then in England, as the aftereffects of the rebellion were felt.

As David had predicted, Rhys ap Maredudd had pleaded the innocence of youth as an excuse for his sons' behavior—and denied his own guilt. But unlike past insurrections, Rhys had gone on bended knee to plead not before the king but before the Welsh Parliament. The members of the Parliament, however, had remained unmoved. Rhys had lost his lands and his life. Dad had called it justice. Mom had sighed and said that some men couldn't escape their fate. And Lili, ever practical, had declared it necessary.

David couldn't disagree with any of their assessments, but his vision for the future—of Avalon made real—was forcing him to narrow his focus and look even more closely at every decision he made. And while sometimes an ending seemed like fate or necessity, it was justice that had to be David's guide if he was to safely travel the treacherous road before him.

Arthur ran straight for the bus, pressing his small hands to the metal side as if it would give way if he pushed hard enough. But the doors were on the other side, and he wasn't getting very far with his efforts.

"Come with me." David tipped his head to indicate the direction he was going, and Arthur raced around the bus ahead of him.

All the children had come on this excursion. Bringing them, in fact, had been practically the whole point. The parents had decided it was time to show them—and tell them—as much of the truth about their origins as they could bear. They'd resolved to answer every question the children asked to the best of their ability, no matter how long it took or how outrageous the question.

By now, everyone else had dismounted too, even Dad—with all his former grace. He'd recovered from his injuries and, as always, looked younger than his years. Mom had commented just yesterday that her husband's workout regimen would put a twenty-year-old's to shame. But though David hadn't said as much to his father, they'd both been tempered by the experience at Aberglaslyn. As far as David was concerned, that had been his father's last battle.

Gwenllian held Elisa's hand, and the two girls followed David to the front door of the bus. It was the one that had become stuck during the crash but was now restored to its former glory.

One by one, the children scrambled inside.

Lili came up behind David and put her arms around his waist. He reached out an arm, and she ducked under it so he could pull her closer.

"Are they okay to do that?" she said, her eyes following the progress of the children down the aisle. Arthur and Cadell had climbed onto one of the seats halfway along. At first the two boys jumped up and down on it, but then they gave that up in favor of pressing their faces against the glass window.

David laughed to see it, thinking of the years he'd ridden a school bus and entertained himself in the same way. "Yeah." He kissed his wife's temple. "They really are."

The End

Acknowledgments

First and foremost, I'd like to thank my lovely readers for encouraging me to continue the *After Cilmeri* Series. I have always been passionate about these books, and it's wonderful to be able to share my stories with readers who love them too.

Thank you to my husband, without whose love and support I would never have tried to make a living as a writer. Thanks to my family who has been nothing but encouraging of my writing, despite the fact that I spend half my life in medieval Wales. And thank you to my beta readers: Darlene, Anna, Jolie, Melissa, Cassandra, Brynne, Gareth, Taran, Dan, and Venkata. I couldn't do this without you.

About the Author

With two historian parents, Sarah couldn't help but develop an interest in the past. She went on to get more than enough education herself (in anthropology) and began writing fiction when the stories in her head overflowed and demanded she let them out. While her ancestry is Welsh, she only visited Wales for the first time while in college. She has been in love with the country, language, and people ever since. She even convinced her husband to give all four of their children Welsh names.

She makes her home in Oregon.

www.sarahwoodbury.com

Printed in Great Britain
by Amazon.co.uk, Ltd.,
Marston Gate.